# THE CORPSE
# WORE TARTAN

**Books by Kaitlyn Dunnett**

KILT DEAD

SCONE COLD DEAD

A WEE CHRISTMAS HOMICIDE

THE CORPSE WORE TARTAN

Published by Kensington Publishing Corporation

# THE CORPSE
# WORE TARTAN

## KAITLYN DUNNETT

KENSINGTON BOOKS
www.kensingtonbooks.com

KENSINGTON BOOKS are published by

Kensington Publishing Corp.
119 West 40th Street
New York, NY 10018

All Kensington titles, imprints and distributed lines are available at special quantity discounts for bulk purchases for sales promotion, premiums, fund-raising, educational or institutional use.

Special book excerpts or customized printings can also be created to fit specific needs. For details, write or phone the office of the Kensington Special Sales Manager: Kensington Publishing Corp., 119 West 40th Street., New York, NY, 10018. Attn. Special Sales Department. Phone: 1-800-221-2647.

Library of Congress Card Catalog Number: 2010930792

ISBN-13: 978-0-7582-3879-5
ISBN-10: 0-7582-3879-7

First Hardcover Printing: November 2010

10  9  8  7  6  5  4  3  2  1

Printed in the United States of America

# THE CORPSE
# WORE TARTAN

# Chapter One

"Sure are a lot of kilts in town," Sadie LeBlanc said to her two companions.

Her housekeeping cart rolled silently ahead of her along the second-floor hallway of The Spruces. Six months earlier, the stately, historic hotel in rural Moosetookalook, Maine, had reopened its newly renovated doors to the public, providing employment for a good many of the tiny village's residents.

"Long as they got money to spend in them sporran things, I don't care how silly their clothes are." Rhonda Snipes pushed her own well-maintained cart over thick carpeting that still had a trace of new-rug smell to it. She was short and squat, with no bosom to speak of.

"Sporran? You mean that leather pouch that looks like a purse?" Sadie sniggered. In contrast to Rhonda, Sadie was a beanpole, one of those painfully thin women who always look as if they'd blow away in a good wind.

"It is a purse," Rhonda said. "Though why they'd want the thing banging against them at crotch level is beyond me."

Like Sadie, Rhonda had been hired to clean guest rooms and, on special occasions, to help out the small waitstaff. Neither job paid all that well, but sometimes there were tips. She rubbed the back of her neck as she headed for the service elevator. It was the end of the shift, but all three of them would be back in only a couple of hours to help serve drinks and canapés at the cocktail party that preceded the Burns Night Supper.

"Disgraceful, I call it." Dilys Marcotte's voice was rife with disapproval. "I hear some of them don't wear a blessed thing under their kilts. Take a peek and you'd see bare skin all the way up."

"Who told you such foolishness?" Sadie demanded. "Stands to reason it's too cold in January not to wear *something* underneath."

Two bright flags of color stained Dilys's plump cheeks. "Never you mind. I know what I know." She appeared to be a little older than the other two and was of middling stature.

The elevator doors slid open with a quiet whoosh and the three women hauled their housekeeping carts inside for the ride down to the basement. The carts would be stored there overnight and restocked with towels and other supplies in the morning.

Liss MacCrimmon, a tall, slender brunette in her late twenties, waited another minute to be certain the coast was clear before she stepped out from behind a potted palm. Her face wore a broad grin. She'd had to struggle not to laugh out loud during the conversation she'd just overheard.

Eavesdropping on members of the housekeeping staff had been accidental, but once she'd realized what they were talking about, she hadn't wanted to embarrass them by revealing her presence. After all, she was the one who'd asked the three local women to put in overtime that evening.

Dilys had it wrong, of course. Would she be disappointed, Liss wondered, to know that most men preserved their modesty by wearing cutoffs or swim trunks under their kilts? The more daring made do with regular under-wear. That modern Scotsmen wore nothing at all under their kilts was just another of those ridiculous things that "everyone knew" was true. In other words—nonsense.

Liss was confident she was right. Even though she'd only visited Scotland once, as a teenager with her parents, she was very familiar with the Scottish-American community. She'd grown up competing in Scottish dance competitions at Scottish Festivals and Highland Games. Then she'd performed for nearly eight years with a Scottish dance troupe, until her knee gave out and ended that career. Now she was half owner and sole employee of Moosetookalook Scottish Emporium, a small shop in the village that sold Scottish imports and other items with a Scottish theme. She was in the process of buying out her aunt, Margaret MacCrimmon Boyd, just as Aunt Margaret had bought out Liss's father when he retired and went to live in Arizona.

These days, the Emporium relied heavily on online and mail-order sales to stay in the black, but the brick-and-mortar store was in no danger of closing. Furthermore, Liss's aunt would continue to be her landlady even after she sold Liss her share of the business.

With a glance at her watch, Liss headed for the service stairs leading to the mezzanine. It was already four. She'd be late if she didn't hustle.

Ever since Christmas, Liss had spent almost as much time at the hotel as she had in the shop. Aunt Margaret had a new job—events coordinator at The Spruces. As such, she had a lot on her plate. Liss had agreed to help out by acting as a liaison to the Scottish Heritage Appreciation Society.

SHAS was a small group. Most of the members came from the Portland, Maine, area, with a few from as far away as Portsmouth, New Hampshire. All were proud of their Scottish roots. Because of that, they gathered every twenty-fifth of January to celebrate the birthday of Scottish poet Robert Burns. One quirk of the organization was that the Burns Night Supper was never held in the same location twice. The Sinclair House in Waycross Springs had been its venue the previous year. When The Spruces had been chosen as the next site, everyone had been thrilled. The booking was for two dozen of the hotel's most expensive rooms plus a private dining room. That was no big deal by city standards, but it was a lifesaver for a small-town business that was hanging on by a thread.

Three people waited for Liss in that dining room. Eunice MacMillan was a rawboned woman in her mid-fifties who stood only an inch or two shorter than Liss's five-foot-nine. She had sharp features and an intense gaze that Liss found disconcerting. During the weeks of preparation for the Burns Night Supper, Liss had spent considerable time with Eunice. She couldn't say she'd come to know the woman particularly well—just enough to dislike her.

Looking for all the world like a pair of bookends, Phil and Phineas MacMillan stood on either side of Eunice, who was Phil's wife. Liss could not tell one twin from the other. Their graying hair was styled exactly the same way and their features—square jaw, beak of a nose, and close-set dark brown eyes—were identical. So were their outfits. Although they were not yet in formal Scottish attire, they were wearing kilts in the MacMillan tartan, a pattern of bright yellow and orange.

"Ah, Ms. MacCrimmon, so good of you to join us," one bookend said. He'd been using his skean dhu—a small knife—to clean under his fingernails while he waited. Without looking, he put it away in a sheath tucked into the top of his right kilt hose.

"I swear," Eunice muttered, "one of these days you're

going to slice your leg open doing that. You should be sensible, like your brother, and let the blade go dull."

"No point in sharpening it," the brother in question chimed in. "I don't plan to shave with it."

"No, you use yours as a letter opener." He turned on Eunice. "For God's sake, woman, don't fuss at me. It's not as if I'm going to slip and cut my own throat with it."

"Har. Har," his brother said, imbuing the mock laugh with enough sarcasm to sink an ocean liner.

There was no need for any of them to expand on the reference, Liss thought. They all knew that famous bit of Scottish history. The story went that when the Scots had at last been soundly defeated by the English, all weapons had been forbidden to them. The only exception had been the skean dhu, which was declared to be "only big enough for a Scotsman to slit his own throat with"—an outcome to which the English apparently had not had any objections!

Liss forced herself to keep smiling until the three MacMillans finally lost interest in bickering among themselves and turned their collective attention to her.

"Well?" Eunice demanded.

Liss held up the clipboard she carried. "Everything seems to be running right on schedule, Ms. MacMillan. All the members of your group have checked in."

"This meeting was supposed to have started ten minutes ago," complained the twin who preferred a dull blade. He looked pointedly at his watch.

"Don't give the girl a hard time, Phineas," Eunice chided him. "She's doing the best she can."

*Damned with faint praise*, Liss thought, and kept smiling. Her facial muscles already ached.

Phineas was Phineas MacMillan, president of SHAS. He was scheduled to give the opening remarks and make the toast. Liss could see no way to distinguish him from his brother, except to keep an eye on both of them and remember that the one currently standing to Eunice's left was her husband, Phil. Even their voices—complete with undercurrents of disdain—sounded identical.

While Liss watched, Phineas examined every place setting and piece of stemware in the dining room. He seemed disappointed when he couldn't find anything to complain about. Then his eyes lit up. He pounced on the clip-on microphone lying beside the plate at the center of the head table.

"I can't use this fiddly little thing." Phineas held it up with two fingers. From the expression on his face, Liss would have thought it was a cockroach he'd caught crawling across the tablecloth. "I want a real microphone. Something with some heft. And an on/off switch."

In other words, Liss thought, a big honking phallic symbol that he could wave around as he spoke. He probably thought wearing a small mike attached to his collar wasn't macho enough.

Schooling her features to show only a calm, helpful façade, Liss promised to take care of the matter before the supper got under way.

"See that you do," Phineas said.

"Is there anything else I can do for you?" Liss asked. She hoped not. She had a full plate already.

"Eunice forgot to pack toothpaste," Phil said.

"We stock several brands in the gift shop just off the lobby," Liss told him.

For a moment, her smile was genuine. The gift shop also carried a number of items from Moosetookalook Scottish Emporium. With any luck, members of SHAS would be inclined to buy a few of them, or at least pick up one of Liss's catalogues.

"A first-rate hotel would supply the basics for free," Eunice said in a snippy voice.

Liss gritted her teeth, kept smiling, and did not give

voice to what was on her mind. "I can assure you that the gift shop's prices are reasonable," she said instead.

"Come along, kiddies," Phineas said, putting one hand on Eunice's elbow and the other on Phil's shoulder. "We've got a busy evening ahead of us."

When they'd gone, Liss switched the microphones herself. That small task took only a few minutes. It was 4:30 when she left the private dining room. She decided she had just enough time to pay a visit to the hotel kitchen and grab a bite to eat before the cocktail party. For that she was profoundly grateful. Dealing with the MacMillans had given her an appetite.

From the top of the stairs that led down from the mezzanine, Liss had a bird's-eye view of a scene of Victorian splendor. Polished wood floors were dotted with large plush rugs to create cozy seating areas, and these were further divided into small pockets of privacy by a series of pillars. At the far end of the lobby was a huge fireplace with a tile-lined hearth and an ornate marble mantel and huge mirror above. Nearer at hand, at the foot of the gently curving staircase, sat a check-in desk made of rich woods polished to a high gloss. Behind it, backed up against a wall of old-fashioned cubbyholes used to hold guest keys and messages, stood Mary Winchester.

Liss frowned. That wasn't right. And Mary's expression was a classic—wide eyes and dropped jaw. Following the direction of the other woman's gaze, Liss spotted two men wearing kilts and cable-knit sweaters. At first glance, they appeared to be playing a game of tag around the pillars.

Then Liss noticed the bagpipe. One of the men held it like a club. He was attempting to beat his companion over the head with it. The tableau gave new meaning to the bagpipe's designation—by those same English authorities who'd permitted Scots to keep their skean dhus—as an "instrument of war."

Liss hurried down the stairs. She flashed a reassuring smile at Mary as she passed the desk but didn't stop. The two men were both strangers to her, but one wore the Grant tartan and the other sported the colors of Clan Erskine. Members of SHAS—no doubt about that!

"This is a worthless piece of junk!" shouted Grant, the man wielding the bagpipe. He slammed it down on Erskine's left shoulder. A sick-sounding blat issued from the bag as a small pocket of air was expelled. "This bag is dried up." Whack! "The drones are cracked." Thunk! "I want my hundred dollars back."

Shielding his head with upraised arms, Erskine did not appear to be in any immediate danger of serious injury. He bobbed and weaved, kilt swirling with every movement, and he managed to keep a series of wingback chairs, sofas, and coffee tables between himself and his attacker.

"Let the buyer beware!" he hollered, and ducked when Grant lunged. From the shelter of a pillar, a distinct whine in his voice, he attempted to reason with the other man. "You looked it over before you paid me. What did you expect for a bargain price?"

"Better than I got!"

Liss caught Grant's sweater-clad forearm as he reared back to throw the bagpipe. "Settle down," she said in a firm voice. "There's no need for violence."

"Who the hell are you?" Grant demanded. His eyes narrowed in his flushed face, but the interruption had thrown him off his stride.

"I'm your liaison with the hotel." She looked him right in the eyes. The moment he lowered his arm, Liss grabbed hold of the bag and tugged the instrument out of his hands.

"Hey!"

"This is neither the time nor the place for violence. If

you *must* fight, take it outside." Maybe the cold January air would cool them off!

Erskine sidled up to her. "We didn't break anything."

"For which we are all grateful." She glanced at him, then away. Grant was the volatile one. She hefted the bagpipe, looking it over with an expert eye. "You're right," she told Grant. "This is worthless. But you should have spotted that for yourself before you bought it. Or asked someone knowledgeable to take a look at it."

Grant glowered at Erskine. "I thought he was my friend."

Out of the corner of her eye, Liss caught sight of Eunice and Phil MacMillan watching them from a spot near the elevators. They were, she supposed, on their way back to their suite after a toothpaste run. She hoped neither would try to "help."

Meanwhile, a stubborn look had come over Erskine's face. "I'm not giving the money back," he muttered. "He bought it as is, fair and square."

"I don't want it anymore." Grant sounded like a sulky child.

"Okay," Liss said. "Here's what we're going to do. I'm tossing this in the trash." She hefted the bagpipe. "You got a problem with that?"

The would-be piper gave a deep sigh. "No, ma'am."

Erskine smirked, but the expression vanished when Liss glared at him. She addressed Grant again. "There's a shop in Waycross Springs. Tandy's Music and Gifts."

"Yeah. Russ Tandy's place."

"If you want to buy a bagpipe, go there. He even gives lessons. As for you"—she gave Erskine a firm poke in his wool-clad chest—"if you have any conscience at all, you'll offer to chip in on the cost."

Shifting his weight from foot to foot like a bully caught acting up in the schoolyard, Erskine had the grace to look ashamed of himself. After a moment, he nodded. "I guess I could do that."

"Excellent." Carrying the bagpipe under her arm, Liss left them to work out the details. She returned to the check-in desk and gave Mary another reassuring smile.

The other woman sagged in relief. "I can't believe you did that, Liss. I froze. Absolutely froze. I didn't even have the presence of mind to pick up the phone and holler for help."

"Just as well you didn't. Those two are here with the Scottish Heritage Appreciation Society. As a group, they're annoying, but mostly harmless. Besides, they're my responsibility."

"That doesn't mean you have to risk your neck breaking up a fight." Mary's molasses-brown eyes still had a slightly glassy look.

"Sit down before you fall down," Liss ordered. "Are you okay?"

Mary was pregnant again, though she hardly showed. Like everyone else in the Ruskin family, Mary Ruskin Winchester worked long hours.

Joe Ruskin, Mary's father, had bought The Spruces after it had been closed for most of a decade. He'd poured money and time into restoring it to its former glory with the hope that reopening the hotel would bring prosperity to everyone in Moosetookalook. Six months in, he was struggling to make ends meet. Mary and her brothers, Sam and Dan, temporarily held positions everyone devoutly hoped would soon be filled by experienced—and well-paid—professionals.

Running one hand through her short, sandy-brown hair, Mary took a few deep breaths and forced herself to smile. "I'm fine. It was just a little disconcerting." She cast a wary look at the bagpipe Liss still held cradled against her chest. "What are you going to do with that thing?"

Liss passed it over. It was awkward to handle—a leather bag covered with tartan cloth with three wooden drones and a chanter hanging off it at odd angles—but it wasn't heavy. It would have taken a lucky blow from Grant—or one aimed with savage viciousness—to have done any real damage to Erskine. "You're going to toss it," she told Mary. "It's trash."

Gingerly, Mary set the instrument down behind the check-in desk. "I'll put it in the Dumpster in the basement on my way off duty."

The ding of the arriving elevator drew Liss's attention. Belatedly, she realized that Phil and Eunice were only now entering the cage to return to their third-floor suite. She knew the elevators weren't that slow. They must have chosen to remain in the lobby until the show was over.

Grant and Erskine, Liss was glad to see, seemed to have resolved their differences. Arm in arm, they were just leaving the lobby, heading in the direction of the hotel lounge.

Mary sent Liss a worried look. "I should probably tell Dad what happened. Or Dan."

"There's no need to bother them. I've handled it. The crisis is over. We're good."

"Well, if you're sure."

"I'm sure. When do you get to go home?"

"At five, and it's almost that now. Thank goodness! I can't wait to put my feet up."

The two women chatted for a few minutes. Or rather Mary chattered about her husband and her son Jason, a toddler. Then Liss, definitely hungry now, resumed her trek to the kitchen.

She could well understand Mary's inclination to turn her troubles over to one of the Ruskin men. Liss smiled to herself as she walked briskly along a narrow service corridor. She'd rely on one of them more often herself if she weren't so afraid that such dependence might be habit-forming.

Dan Ruskin, all six foot two of him, had become a fixture in Liss's life soon after she moved back to Moosetookalook. She wasn't quite sure where their relationship was headed, but she knew there was a special bond between them. Dan was easy to get along with and even easier to count on when there was trouble. He wasn't hard on the eyes, either. Years of working for Ruskin Construction had developed muscles in all the right places.

The sound of raised voices reached Liss's ears when she was still a hundred yards away from the entrance to the kitchen.

"Here we go again," she muttered, and broke into a run.

# Chapter Two

Liss burst through the swinging doors and skidded to a stop just inside the kitchen. Richardson Bruce, treasurer of SHAS, blocked the aisle between two work stations. He was squared off with the head chef at The Spruces, Angeline Cloutier.

Bruce, a dapper little man with a naturally ruddy complexion, was already dressed for the Burns Night Supper, wearing a Montrose doublet with his kilt in the red, green, yellow, and white Bruce tartan. The waist-length jacket had a stand-up collar and silver buttons and epaulettes. Beneath it Bruce wore a blindingly white shirt with a lacy jabot. The contrast made high color in his face look all the more glaring.

"The haggis is the centerpiece of the evening!" he shouted at the chef, ignoring the fact that she not only towered over him but was standing right next to a rack of sharp butcher knives. "It must be made according to the ancient recipe—chopped sheep's heart, liver, and lungs, mixed with oatmeal, onions, suet, and spices in a sheep's stomach casing."

"Listen, mister!" Angeline poked Bruce in the shoulder with one bony finger, leaving a smear of flour on the expensive black velvet. "You know and I know that ain't about to happen. The FDA had the good sense to keep sheep offal out of the food supply."

"Who'd know? Slaughter your own sheep and—"

"Give it a rest! You've got what—three hours till your banquet starts? Thing has to boil that long. You'll take what I've cooked for you and like it. Damned nuisance as it is, like making sausages from scratch."

Bruce's face abruptly drained of most of its color. "Tell me you didn't use pork!"

"Lamb, beef liver, oats, and suet. The casing isn't sheep's stomach, but you don't eat that anyway." Angeline's expression of disgust was eloquent. Then it was her turn to go pale. "Do you?"

Bruce ignored the question. "We asked for *real* haggis. That means it's made from a sheep. You can't get the right nutty texture otherwise. Or the savory flavor."

"You won't be able to tell the difference," Angeline promised. "Now get out of my kitchen so I can get going on the turnips and the potatoes."

"Neeps and tatties," Bruce corrected her. "And don't forget the cock-a-leekie soup to start and the tipsy laird for dessert."

"Yeah, yeah. Sherry trifle. I'm on it."

"But about the haggis—I don't think my people will be happy with—"

Deciding it was time to step in, Liss cleared her throat, interrupting Richardson Bruce's complaint. As soon as she had his attention, she took his arm, exerting enough pressure to start him moving toward the door. "I'm certain everything is under control, Mr. Bruce, but if you like I can go get some of the canned haggis we sell at Moosetookalook Scottish Emporium. It's made in the U.S. from Highland beef. Of course, there are only four servings in a can, but I could sell you a case of twenty-four for, say, two hundred fifty dollars?"

During her previous dealings with Richardson Bruce, all of them protracted negotiations concerning the cost of various items needed for the Burns Night Supper, Liss had learned he was the sort of man who'd squeeze every nickel till it screamed. Since he was almost a caricature of the penny-pinching Scot, she was not surprised when the mere mention of additional expenses made him back off.

"No. No, I'm certain . . . that is"—he swallowed convulsively—"I'll just run along and check on the whiskey." He inclined his head in farewell. "Ms. MacCrimmon. Ms. Cloutier." He pronounced the chef's surname in the Parisian way, no doubt trying to show off how worldly and well-traveled he was.

Shaking her head, Liss watched him go, then sent a wry smile in Angeline's direction.

"Clue-chee," she muttered, scowling fiercely. "It's pronounced 'Clue-chee.'" Angeline might have been trained in the best Cordon Bleu tradition, but her roots were solidly French-Canadian. Her birthplace was only fifty miles from Moosetookalook, in the small city of Lewiston, Maine. Angeline's usual pronunciation of that place name was "Loys-tun."

Dan Ruskin hesitated with his hand on the kitchen door. Liss hadn't seen him yet. She was too busy slicing cold ham for a sandwich.

When he'd heard Mary's account of Liss's run-in with the two guests in the lobby, his first reaction had been sheer panic. He'd come looking for Liss to make sure she was okay. Plainly, she was. A flare of temper had him clenching his fists. Liss MacCrimmon was too damn impatient for her own good. She had a tendency to rush in, to do everything herself, without waiting for backup. One of these days, she was going to get herself hurt. Since Dan was in love with her, that would just about kill him.

Deliberately, he forced himself to relax. He'd learned the hard way not to try to run Liss's life for her. Not if he wanted to be a part of it. And he did. A permanent part. He'd been working up to asking her to marry him for some time now.

Liss glanced up and saw him. Her blue-green eyes—they changed hue depending on what colors she was wearing—lit with pleasure. "Hey, Dan. Want a sandwich?"

"Love one." He crossed the busy kitchen to fetch up beside a small table tucked into a corner of the huge room.

Today, Liss's eyes were more blue than green, reflecting the bouquets of hand-painted forget-me-nots that decorated her scarf. She was wearing a simple wool pantsuit—very businesslike—but on her, even plain clothing looked great.

"I ran into Harvey MacHenry earlier," he said as he foraged in the cabinets for two tall glasses and a couple of plates.

Liss looked up sharply, visibly bracing herself for bad news. "What nit did he want to pick?"

Dan chuckled. "Relax. He was full of compliments for both you and The Spruces. Seems like a nice old guy." MacHenry was eighty if he was a day, but spry for all that.

"Well, that makes a change. I've never met such a contentious group of people in my life, and it isn't just that they're difficult for me to work with. They don't agree with each other about anything, either. Except that they want to hold this supper every January."

Dan set two places, then went to stand directly behind Liss. Lifting her long, dark hair out of the way, he began to massage her neck and shoulders. They were rock hard with tension.

"Rough day?"

"Getting better." She almost purred.

Dan kept kneading until Liss shook him off. He repressed a sigh. He enjoyed the feel of her under his hands and the light fragrance of her shampoo. She'd never been one for heavy perfumes.

"You can finish later." There was a promise in her eyes. "I still need to check a few things before the cocktail party starts."

While Liss put together the sandwiches, she gave Dan a brief recap of her encounters with the MacMillans, the two pipers, and Richardson Bruce. Then she slid in beside him on the long bench, her back to the hustle and bustle of the kitchen, and bit into her ham and cheese on rye.

For the next few minutes, they concentrated on food, ignoring the clatter of pots and pans behind them. Dan stole glances at his companion as they ate, wishing he could think of some way to get Liss to settle. She was all tensed up again, in spite of the massage. Then inspiration struck and he smiled to himself.

"What's so amusing?" Liss sounded suspicious.

"I just realized something." He gestured with his half-eaten sandwich, indicating the paneled wall they both faced. "I never told you about the hidden door we found."

Her eyes lit up. "Secret passage?"

He laughed. "Just a shortcut to the back stairs." He pointed out the three slight anomalies in the otherwise smooth paneling. "If you look closely you can see the hinges, there and there, and the indentation for the finger pull, there. The door opens toward us. On the other side, the seam where the door meets the rest of the wall is just about invisible."

"Is that the only hidden door? It's a big hotel."

"It's the only one I know of that leads right through a wall like that. Of course, it wouldn't surprise me if there were more. And there are a couple of closets under staircases that are pretty hard to spot." He grinned at her. "Heck, for all I know, there *could* be a secret passage or two." She'd get such a kick out of it if he found one that Dan resolved to check the original hotel blueprints when he had a chance. Maybe there was something. Or maybe he could build one just for Liss. That would be easy enough for him to do.

Liss smiled back at him, but her lighthearted mood didn't last. When she reached for the glass of milk Dan had poured for her, her elbow struck the clipboard she'd left lying on the edge of the table. It fell to the tile floor with a clatter, spilling papers everywhere.

For a moment, Liss just stared at the mess. Then she heaved a deep sigh. "This just isn't my day."

"At least you didn't spill the milk." At her look, he shrugged. "Gotta look on the bright side. Sit tight," he added when she started to rise. "I'll get this."

As he gathered up pages, he glanced at each one to be sure he was putting them back together in the right order. All of them had to do with the Burns Night Supper except the last. On a piece of yellow-lined paper, Liss had written one of her famous to-do lists.

"Full plate much?" He handed her the single sheet separate from the rest. Those, he reattached to the clipboard.

"There are not enough hours in the day," she agreed. "Sometimes I feel like I'm trying to juggle flaming batons. I need to be twins. Or better yet, triplets. Or maybe I could arrange to have myself cloned."

"At least you've already checked off the first item on your list." It read "deliver stock to gift shop at hotel."

"That was the easy one. The gift shop was already open and selling an assortment of merchandise from Moosetookalook Scottish Emporium, in addition to all the usual hotel gift shop items. I just had to bring over a few more goodies."

The idea was to tempt hotel guests to visit the original

store and all the rest of the shops in Moosetookalook. Their picturesque town square featured white clapboard Victorian houses, several of them with businesses on their lower floors—the Emporium, Stu's Ski Shop, Angie's Books, and Patsy's Coffee House. There were also two empty storefronts, the unfortunate situation that Dan knew accounted for item number two on Liss's list: "MSBA."

The Moosetookalook Small Business Association, of which Dan was currently president, desperately wanted to attract new retailers to the community. Liss had been appointed head of a committee to figure out how they were going to do that.

"Too bad you aren't ready to open your storefront yet," Liss said, her thoughts apparently running in the same direction as his.

Dan shrugged. "Sometimes I wonder if I ever will be."

One day, he hoped to turn the downstairs of his house into a showroom for the furniture and other household items he made. His dream was to do custom woodworking full-time. But even before the hotel reopened, he'd had to fight for every hour in his workshop. He'd managed to produce a few decorative boxes, now for sale in the hotel gift shop alongside Liss's Scottish-themed merchandise, but nothing much more complex than that.

Liss placed her hand over his in a gesture that both warmed and comforted. "It will happen. I have faith in you."

"And you'll manage to juggle all those flaming batons. At least the third item on your list is no biggie. How hard can it be to decide on a name for a kitten?" Liss had been adopted by a little black fur ball just before Christmas.

"You'd be surprised," she said with a laugh. "So far, nothing has seemed quite right. I have a list of possibilities a mile long and none of them really fit." Liss polished off her milk, then dabbed with her napkin at the white mustache it had left behind.

"Write all the names on slips of paper, put them in a hat, and pick one," Dan suggested.

"I don't think so. The only thing I'm certain of is that I can't keep calling her Nameless."

Dan was about to ask how Lumpkin—a large yellow cat who'd owned Liss for the last nineteen months—was adapting to the presence of another feline in the house, when his cell phone rang. It was Mary, calling from the front desk. Dan glanced at his watch and frowned. It was well after five. His sister had stayed late again.

Then he listened to what she was saying and his frown deepened.

"I'll take care of it," he promised. "Aren't you supposed to be on your way home?"

Only when Mary assured him that their father had just come out to take over the check-in desk did Dan disconnect.

"Problem?" Liss asked.

"I'm afraid so. Phil MacMillan just called down with a complaint. He says he's been robbed."

"That will teach me to think I had everything under control and get cocky," Liss muttered as they approached the MacMillans' third-floor suite. "To paraphrase Bobbie Burns, in whose honor this evening's celebrations are being held, things were bound to *gae aglee*."

"You aren't cocky. You're confident." Dan rapped lightly on the door. With his free hand, he gave Liss's forearm a reassuring squeeze.

The man had an amazing ability to calm her down, Liss thought. If he could bottle that, he'd make a fortune.

A scowling Eunice MacMillan opened the door. "I suppose you'd better come in." With ill grace, she moved aside so they could enter the sumptuously furnished "parlor" of the two-room suite.

The Spruces had once been a "grand hotel" in the Victorian sense, splendidly ornate and sinfully luxurious. Dan's father had embellished that old-fashioned charm by adding modern conveniences. A cherrywood armoire hid a television, and although the bath still contained a clawfoot tub, there was a shower stall, as well. The bed, which Liss could just glimpse through the open door to the inner room, was a huge four-poster.

Phil MacMillan sat at a reproduction of a mid-nineteenth-century ladies' desk, hunched over a laptop. He didn't look up, even though he must have heard Liss and Dan come into the room.

Eunice's voice had a sharp edge to it. "Phil! Mr. Ruskin and Ms. MacCrimmon are here. You're the one who insisted on sending for them. *You* talk to them."

Phil tapped a few more keys, then shut down whatever he was working on. The look he sent his wife was frosty enough to ruin an entire citrus crop. She ignored him, and Liss and Dan, to get herself a bottle of water from a mini-refrigerator disguised as an end table. Without asking if anyone else wanted something, she plunked herself down in an armchair, unscrewed the cap, and took a long swallow.

"What seems to be the problem, Mr. MacMillan?" Dan asked.

Phil MacMillan stood and faced Liss and Dan. Beneath beetled brows, his dark brown eyes sparked with temper. "We came back to the suite after our meeting with Ms. MacCrimmon to find that the place had been ransacked."

Incredulous, Liss gave the suite another once-over. She saw nothing beyond the disorder normal for a hotel room that was currently occupied.

Dan had made a visual survey of his own. "I beg your pardon?" His clipped tone was at odds with his polite wording.

"We cleaned up. Put things away."

"I did, you mean."

"Yes, dear. My wife tidied up. She's compulsive about things like that. In any case, after she had done so, I discovered I'd been robbed. Someone who works in your hotel, Mr. Ruskin, is a thief."

Liss was standing close enough to Dan to feel how rigid he went at the accusation. She admired his self-control as he somehow still managed to keep his voice neutral.

"Most people would have called the front desk at once if they thought someone had been in their room," he said.

"Well, we didn't." MacMillan made a dismissive gesture. "That doesn't change the fact that a valuable brooch is missing. It's solid silver and decorated with my clan crest. There are a couple of rubies in the design. It was in the bedroom on the dresser when we went downstairs to inspect the private dining room and gone when we came back."

"You're sure you didn't just misplace it?" Liss asked. "Perhaps you thought you unpacked it and—"

"I have a very clear recollection of placing it on top of the dresser. I planned to wear it tonight. Besides, as I just told you, the place had been searched. Obviously someone was looking for valuables."

"Was anything else taken?" Dan looked from MacMillan to his wife.

Eunice shook her head. "Just the brooch." She picked up a magazine and flipped noisily through the pages, affecting disinterest.

"I want the police called in." MacMillan, arms folded across his chest, was the picture of stubborn determination. "In the meantime, I expect you to keep all your staff on the premises so they can be searched." The stance, the jutting jaw, the steady gaze, all proclaimed that there was no point in trying to reason with him.

"Very well, Mr. MacMillan," Dan said. "I will phone the police station, but I want to make sure I fully understand the situation first." He turned again to Eunice. "Ms. MacMillan, do you recall seeing this brooch on the dresser when you left the room?"

She looked up, her thin lips curving into a slow, malicious smile. "No. I didn't notice it. And I told Phil not to make a fuss just because he can't find it."

"It's a valuable piece of jewelry." Phil glowered at his wife.

Unperturbed, she turned another page in her magazine. Liss couldn't see the cover, but it was one of the glossy ones devoted to fashion, self-improvement, and profiles of celebrities.

She glanced back at Phil MacMillan, then decided to take a look at the crime scene for herself. In the bedroom, she was careful not to touch anything, but she checked the top of the dresser and the floor around it, and even bent over to look beneath the furniture. She peeked into the bath, too, and noticed the small gift-shop bag on the counter by the sink. The toothpaste Phil and Eunice had picked up, she assumed.

By the time Liss returned to the living room of the suite, MacMillan was fuming at the delay. Liss could all but see steam rising as his temper came to a boil.

"I want the cops!" he bellowed. "What kind of place is this? Are you going to sit back and let your guests be robbed?"

"Certainly not, Mr. MacMillan. If you'll just wait here in your suite, I will send for the local police. It should only take ten or fifteen minutes for an officer to drive to the hotel."

When Dan closed the door very gently behind him, Liss knew he was repressing the urge to slam it.

"Great. Just great," he muttered as they headed for the elevator. "And what is a guy doing wearing a brooch anyway?"

"It's a big round pin," Liss said, "used to hold a plaid in place at the shoulder." She pronounced the word as "played," since she meant the garment, not the pattern. It was a long strip of tartan cloth that men wore with a kilt. It wrapped around the upper body and looked quite dashing.

But Dan was no longer listening. He'd detached his cell phone from his belt and was already punching in the number for the Moosetookalook Police Department.

# Chapter Three

The drive from downtown Moosetookalook to The Spruces took under ten minutes. Officer Sherri Willett, a petite blonde who prided herself on being tougher than she looked, gave the sky a considering glance as she stepped out of the police cruiser.

The sun set early at that time of year and, because of the weather, neither moon nor stars were visible. Away from floodlit areas, it was pitch dark.

Snow drifted down at a steady rate, rapidly adding a new coat of white to the recently plowed parking lot. The forecast had been for five or six inches, but she could feel the heaviness in the air. The whirling flakes, although light enough in themselves, continued to pile up thick and fast.

"And to think," she said to Pete Campbell as he got out of the passenger side of her vehicle, "a little more than a month ago we were praying for snow."

Pete shrugged. "Maine in winter. What can I say?"

He was built like a linebacker, solid and square. He stood eight inches taller than Sherri and outweighed her by a good eighty pounds. He was off duty and wearing civvies—jeans and a sweater under a ski parka—instead of the uniform that proclaimed him a Carrabassett County Deputy Sheriff.

Sherri smiled to herself. Even if he were working, Pete

would have no problem deferring to her in this investigation. After considerable debate during the last few weeks, some of it heated, they'd finally resolved the issue of her career in law enforcement. She wasn't going to quit, not even after she and Pete were married. And, as this was clearly a Moosetookalook matter, she was the one in charge. He'd give her no argument on that score. He'd accepted that she was fully qualified to do her job, in this case to investigate the disappearance of a piece of jewelry.

Pete squinted at the hotel while Sherri extracted a fingerprint kit and an audio recorder from the spacious trunk of the car. The far-from-new Crown Victoria had been acquired from the county when the sheriff's department upgraded.

The Spruces stood on the crest of a hill, looking down on the rest of Moosetookalook. It rose three stories high, painted brilliant white and roofed in red tile, but what had given it the nickname "the castle" with the locals were the four-story octagonal towers at each corner and the five-story central tower with the cupola on top.

By the time Sherri was ready to go inside, Pete's dark hair had acquired a cap of snowflakes. He brushed them off with one gloved hand as they headed for the service entrance. Dan Ruskin had requested that Sherri keep things low-key. That wasn't a problem. Coming in with sirens blaring and blue lights flashing was hardly her style.

Dan was waiting for them, Liss MacCrimmon at his side, in the utilitarian conference room next to Joe Ruskin's equally plain office. Unlike the public areas of the hotel, all of which were very posh, this room was extremely plain. The walls were painted a soft green. The carpet was of the indoor-outdoor variety. The only furnishings were a long wooden table, a dozen folding chairs, and a side table that held the coffeepot, creamer, and packets of sweetener.

"You already know a little about the Scottish Heritage Appreciation Society," Dan began.

"I should. I've been listening to Liss bitch about them for weeks." Sherri had recognized the name MacMillan right off and knew that her friend thought Eunice Mac-Millan was obnoxious.

"Well, let me bring you up to speed." And Dan launched into an explanation of why he'd called the police.

"Clan crest brooch," Sherri murmured when he'd finished. She was familiar with that sort of jewelry, having once worked part-time in Moosetookalook Scottish Emporium, and knew she'd need a much more detailed description. Half the men at the Burns Night Supper probably owned similar pieces.

"There's something a little peculiar about all this," Dan said.

"A couple of things," Liss chimed in.

"Any normal person who discovered someone had been in their room would grab the phone and complain first thing," Dan said. "Instead, Eunice tidied up. She put everything back where it belonged and they weren't going to say a word about it . . . until MacMillan discovered the theft."

"And both MacMillans are champion complainers," Liss said. "There's another thing, too. It's probably nothing. Just odd."

Sherri looked at her expectantly. Often the smallest detail, if it sounded a wrong note, could be important, and Sherri knew that Liss had good instincts for such things.

"Phil MacMillan claimed he left the brooch out on top of the dresser because he was going to wear it this evening," Liss explained, "but a Burns Night Supper calls for more formal attire. The men will all be wearing jackets of some sort—everything from tweed to tails. Some folks do wear plaids on top of jackets, but I wouldn't expect someone like Phil MacMillan to. To tell you the truth, I'd be surprised to see a single plaid tonight on anyone but the bagpiper."

"So, no need for a brooch on the shoulder," Sherri summarized. "Good catch. Okay. Time to go talk to the victim. No." She held up a hand to stop Dan and Liss from coming with her. "This is police business, okay? I don't want you two involved any further."

Dan's scowl told her he wasn't happy to be taken out of the loop. Liss just looked disappointed. Sherri sympathized, but their presence wasn't necessary and it might interfere with getting answers.

"I want you to do something else for me," she told them. "I'll need lists of the staff and of the hotel guests. If Mr. MacMillan is determined to make a fuss about this, then I'll have to follow through, talk to everyone, find out where they were when the brooch went missing. You could also help me set up the interviews with the staff."

"None of Dad's employees are thieves," Dan objected.

"If the brooch was just lying out in the open—"

"Once the MacMillans checked in, no one on the hotel staff had any reason to enter their suite."

"Just get me those lists, okay?" Anxious to begin her investigation, Sherri headed for the door. "I'll be back after I talk to the victims."

"Sherri," Liss began, "I could—"

"Make lists," Sherri repeated, and closed the conference room door firmly behind her.

Pete was chuckling as they crossed the lobby, heading for the elevators.

"What?"

"When did Liss MacCrimmon ever *not* make lists?"

"Good point." Sherri jabbed the button to call the elevator and sighed. "She wants to help."

She knew Liss well. They'd gone all through school together and reconnected upon Liss's return to Maine. Liss
MacCrimmon did not like unanswered questions. And
when explanations failed to present themselves quickly
enough, she didn't wait for other people to provide them.
More than once, her impatience had led her into serious
trouble.

"Just keep telling her no," Pete advised. "Tell her it's a
conflict of interest for her to be involved."

"Easy for you to say."

They exited the elevator on the third floor and walked
down the quiet hallway to the MacMillan suite. Sherri
took a deep breath and squared her shoulders before she
knocked.

The first thing she noticed was that the MacMillans had
obviously changed their clothes. Liss had told her what
Phil MacMillan had been wearing earlier. Now he and his
wife were clearly dressed for the Burns Night Supper.

Phil's outfit consisted of all the normal Scottish apparel
on the bottom—ghillie brogues with leather soles that
laced up over the ankle, hose with flashes, kilt, fur sporran
with a chrome cantle and three fur tassels. But on top he
wore a Prince Charlie jacket and vest in Tartan green with
a tuxedo shirt and bow tie. The jacket was a nice one,
Sherri thought. The cutaway-style front had rampant lion
buttons and braided epaulettes . . . and no place at all for
him to pin on a brooch.

He demanded to see identification, especially from Pete.
After Sherri complied, she took Phil's statement while Pete
dusted the top of the dresser and the doorknobs for fingerprints. After she'd heard what Phil MacMillan had to say,
she informed both MacMillans that she'd need to take
their fingerprints for purposes of elimination.

"Is that really necessary?" Eunice looked annoyed.

"I'm afraid so."

While Pete did the honors, Sherri took the couple through their story one more time. It didn't hold together any better on repetition.

"I just want to make sure I have all the details straight," she said, flipping to the first page of her spiral-bound notepad. She had the recorder going, but backing up with written notes was always a good idea. Even the most advanced technological devices had glitches, and the equipment provided to Moosetookalook police officers was hardly top of the line. "You arrived at The Spruces around three. Is that correct?"

"That's right." The curt answer came from Eunice. She didn't look at Sherri. She was too busy wiping smudges off her beautifully manicured fingers, taking great care not to get any of the ink on her floor-length, off-white gown. Since, by tradition, women did not wear kilts, she showed her clan colors by draping a tartan sash over her right shoulder.

"We checked in, came up here and unpacked, and then went to make sure all the arrangements were in order." Phil sounded every bit as irritable as his wife.

"You had a meeting scheduled with Ms. MacCrimmon?"

"Yes. At four." Eunice rose from the sofa and picked up the small evening bag on the coffee table. Sherri ignored the hint that it was almost time for the SHAS cocktail party.

"We went down to the private dining room on the mezzanine at a little before four." Phil also stood and fussily made adjustments to his kilt.

"You met your brother there?"

"No. He was already with us. We met here and went down together."

Sherri slanted a sharp look his way. "You didn't mention that before."

"Didn't I?" Phil shrugged. "I don't see that it matters. *Phineas* didn't steal my brooch. Anyway, we went down to the dining room and waited there until Ms. MacCrimmon arrived. She was late."

"And after you three left the dining room? What then?"

"We came back here," Eunice answered. "We told you all this before."

And what else had they left out? Sherri barely managed to keep the skepticism out of her voice. "Yes, you have, Ms. MacMillan. But it bears repeating. Now, when you entered the suite, did you notice immediately that some-one had been here?"

"Of course we did!" Phil's nostrils flared in irritation. "The furniture cushions were askew. And the drawers were all pulled out of the desk."

"And in the bedroom, the closet door stood open when I know I closed it, and the pillows from the bed had been scattered all over the floor." Eunice gestured toward the other room and froze, her hand in midair, when she caught sight of Pete. He was down on his hands and knees, his head stuck under the bed. As they watched, he withdrew, having found nothing there.

"What did you think had happened?" Sherri asked.

Phil shrugged again and let his wife answer.

"We had no idea," Eunice said, just as she had the last time she'd told her story. "Then Phil said it must be some damned fool's idea of a practical joke. Some members of SHAS have a rather low sense of humor. It wasn't until I was done straightening up that Phil noticed the brooch was missing."

Sherri already had the names of the group's resident co-medians. There was always a chance that one of them had invaded the suite and taken the brooch as a joke, but Sherri didn't see where the humor would be in such a prank. She also doubted that another guest would have been able to get hold of a key to the suite.

She studied her written description of the missing piece of jewelry. It wouldn't mean much to someone who hadn't seen the real thing. Without much hope, she posed a new question. "I don't suppose you have a picture of the brooch?"

"Certainly," Phil said. To Sherri's surprise, he went directly to the laptop sitting on the desk and called up a file. "We had all our good jewelry photographed for insurance purposes."

That would make her job easier, Sherri thought, but at the same time she felt uneasy. Something wasn't right here. Why would a thief steal a brooch and leave a computer? Since the jewelry was bound to be missed, why not take everything else that was easily portable, too? She glanced at Eunice. By rights that pearl choker should also have gone in the swag bag.

"There," Phil said.

A photograph filled the screen. The MacMillan clan crest was impressive—two strong hands brandishing a double-handed sword inside a circle emblazoned with the motto *Miseris Succurrere Disco.*

"Translation?" Sherri's Latin was nonexistant.

"I learn to help the unfortunate," Eunice answered, her tone snide. "So approp—"

"The sword has a jewel-encrusted handle," MacMillan interrupted. "Rubies. And as I've already told you, the brooch itself is solid silver."

Sherri reached into the breast pocket of her uniform and pulled out a flash drive. It only took a moment to plug into the laptop and copy the .jpg file.

"If you're finished with us, Officer Willett," Phil said, snotty as ever, "we have a cocktail party to go to."

Sherri took her time answering. "I believe I have all I

need," she said when she'd let the silence stretch as taut as she dared. "But I'd appreciate it if you didn't mention the missing brooch to anyone."

Phil frowned, but agreed. Eunice looked as if she'd also like to object, but remained silent. Then Phil opened the door and gave Sherri and Pete a pointed look.

Sherri waited until she and Pete were once more in the elevator and on their way down to the lobby before she looked at her fiancé and rolled her eyes. "What a piece of work."

"Which one?"

"Either. Both. Oh, well. That's neither here nor there, I suppose. There's been a report of a burglary, which does make a nice change from the usual traffic tickets, O.U.I.s, and domestic disputes. I'll have to talk to everyone on the staff, even Liss and Dan. Hey, maybe I'll get lucky and someone will confess."

"That would be nice," Pete said.

"I don't hold out much hope, and we can hardly search the entire hotel for that brooch, even if the Ruskins are willing. The place is just too big. Worse, if one of the housekeeping staff did walk off with it, it will already have left the premises."

"Housekeeping staff would have a legitimate reason to leave fingerprints in the suite, too," Pete remarked.

"Did you get any clear ones?"

"A few, but Eunice MacMillan did a great job of smearing most of them when she picked up after the intruder."

"That's what I figured. Nothing like a contaminated crime scene."

Sherri's next stop was Joe Ruskin's office, where she plugged her flashdrive into his computer. It took only a moment to compose an e-mail and send the .jpg file out as an attachment, alerting both police and the appropriate civilian Web site that the brooch was stolen property. That done, she printed a copy of the picture for her own reference. She hadn't decided yet if she'd show it around. Sometimes keeping the details quiet produced better results and she could inform the people she questioned that something was missing without saying exactly what it was.

By the time they returned to the conference room, the lists Sherri had asked for were waiting for her on the long table. Less than a minute later, Dan appeared in the doorway.

"I hate to ask favors, but if you could talk to the staff members who are working the cocktail party last, it would be a big help."

"Not a problem."

"That includes the housekeeping staff—Sadie LeBlanc, Rhonda Snipes, and Dilys Marcotte. They clocked out around four and should be coming back anytime now to earn some overtime as cocktail waitresses."

Sherri put a small check mark beside each name. "Anyone else leave after four?"

"Fran Pertwee works in the gift shop. She took off just after you got here. So did my sister and brother. And Margaret Boyd went home at five."

"None of them are likely suspects," Sherri said. Besides, she knew where to find them if she needed to. Moosetookalook was a *very* small town. The Ruskins, like the MacCrimmons, the Willetts, and the Campbells, had lived in the village for generations. Margaret, Liss's widowed aunt, was currently dating Sherri's divorced father. As for Fran Pertwee, she lived right next door to Pete's mother.

"You may as well start your interrogations with me," Dan offered, and took a seat.

Pete closed the door, turned on the recorder, and accepted the notebook Sherri passed to him. It helped to have someone else taking notes. Relieved of the task of writing everything down herself, Sherri could concentrate on watching the reaction to her questions.

She didn't suspect Dan Ruskin of anything, of course. This interview would be purely routine. And before it began, she had a personal question to ask. She clicked the recorder off again.

"Where's Liss?"

Dan grinned at the wariness in Sherri's voice. "Don't worry. She promised to stay out of trouble. She's in the gift shop. She's going to keep it open until after the cocktail party gets going."

The space that had been turned into the hotel gift shop had been a card room in the old days, the province of men with cigars and a yen to gamble. The only trace of that left was in a small fireplace, these days used for display rather than heat, and the wainscoting Dan had lovingly restored on three of the four walls. The fourth was mostly taken up with windows, but Liss could see nothing beyond the glass except falling snow. A pity, she thought. The usual view was a delightful vista composed of the hotel's back lawn and the evergreen woods beyond.

"Any customers since Fran left?" Liss asked as she turned away from the glass.

Tricia Lynd, a twenty-two-year-old college student enrolled in a program to train budding hotel managers, worked at The Spruces as an intern. She was their "Jill of all trades," moving from one job to another as needed, sometimes filling several posts in the same shift. She'd been working as a waitress in the hotel lounge earlier that afternoon and in a few minutes would be heading for the mezzanine to set up a cash bar for the cocktail party. Her white blouse and black slacks served as a uniform for all three jobs. The combination looked good on her, Liss thought, feeling a tiny stab of envy. Tricia had been blessed with an athletic body and a luxuriant mane of blue-black hair. Heads turned whenever she walked by.

"Sorry," Tricia answered. "Not a soul. And nobody in the hour before that, Fran said, except for one couple who bought a tube of toothpaste and complained that it was overpriced."

Ordinarily, the shop's hours were eight to five. Joe Ruskin couldn't afford more than one full-time employee. On this occasion, however, since it was merchandise on consignment from Moosetookalook Scottish Emporium that Liss hoped would sell to stray members of SHAS, she had made arrangements to keep the gift shop open two hours later than usual and agreed to work behind the counter herself from six to seven.

"Was the bar busy?" she asked Tricia.

"You mean the lounge?" The younger woman chuckled and Liss smiled back at her.

Joe Ruskin was insistent that they not call that area of the hotel a bar. It lowered the tone of the place, he said. By whatever name, it had a liquor license. Liss imagined at least some of the SHAS members had gravitated there to kill time before the cocktail party started. In fact, Grant and Erskine had been headed that way when she'd last seen them. Curious as to whether their truce had lasted, she described them to Tricia.

"Oh, sure. I remember them. They joined a couple of other men who were already there. All four of them were still in the lounge, having another round of beer, when I left to come here." She made a face.

"What?"

"Nothing. Just . . . well, the first two guys had a real juvenile sense of humor. And one of them hit on me." Her moué of distaste spoke volumes.

"You don't have to put up with harassment, Tricia."

"He didn't go *that* far over the line."

Liss waited.

"He gave me a little pinch on the bottom and wanted to know if I knew what Scotsmen wore under their kilts. I told him I couldn't care less. It was no big deal. Really."

Liss wasn't so sure about that, but she let it go. Tricia was the only one who could decide where the "line" was.

After Tricia left the shop, Liss wandered the aisles, stopping here and there to straighten an item on a shelf or table but really just killing time. One display contained all the small personal items guests were prone to forget—everything from those tiny, possibly overpriced tubes of toothpaste to single-dose packets of aspirin. Next to it were two racks of postcards of local views, some specially printed to say GREETINGS FROM MOOSETOOKALOOK, MAINE. The shop had newspapers available, too, but the rest of the stock consisted of consignment items from Moose-tookalook shops.

Angie's Books had supplied a revolving paperback rack featuring bestselling titles. Wall shelves held some of the small, decorative boxes Dan Ruskin made. And Liss's permanent contribution to the shop's stock consisted of a display of tartan scarves, thistle pins, beret tams in colors that ranged from maroon to fawn, and several six-inch-high figurines of men in Highland dress. A strategically placed card holder held some of her business cards, which gave the phone number, Web site, and e-mail address of Moosetookalook Scottish Emporium on the front and directions from the hotel to the store on the back.

In honor of the Burns Night Supper, Liss had added a rack of kilts and a display of clan crest items—ties, pins, mugs, and the like. She'd also brought in a selection of imported Scottish delicacies—shortbread, oatcakes, and several varieties of teas. She had a feeling she'd be carting all of it back to town in the morning. Customers seemed to be in short supply.

When her wandering brought her to a locked glass-front case, Liss paused to study its contents. The center-piece of a selection of jewelry made by a local artisan was a gorgeous tourmaline ring. Liss had been drawn to it every time she came into the gift shop. She held out her right hand, imagining how that ring would look on her finger. Too bad it was priced so far beyond what she could justify paying to buy it for herself.

"I told you they'd still be open," a loud feminine voice announced.

Startled, Liss swung around to face the door. Her smile was automatic but genuine, especially when she realized that a total of four potential customers had just walked into the shop. That they were members of SHAS, or their wives, was immediately apparent. They all wore tartan sashes. One woman had on a floor-length gown, two wore cocktail dresses, and the fourth was dressed in a hostess skirt in the Royal Stewart tartan and a dressy blouse.

Before coming to the gift shop, Liss had changed from her pantsuit into a similar outfit, except that the Mac-Crimmon "tartan" was a solid light blue. This color, supposedly, had been worn by ancient bards. Members of the MacCrimmon family had been celebrated as pipers as far back as the fifteenth century.

"Oh, look at this, Elspeth," one of the women exclaimed. "Isn't this little figurine adorable? I ought to get that for Hank." She was a plump little person with bright eyes that for some reason reminded Liss of the as-yet-unnamed black kitten waiting for her at home.

"He won't appreciate it, Glenora," said her friend, plucking the tiny piper from her fingers and sneering at it before she returned it to the display. "And he won't appreciate you spending his money on knickknacks."

Glenora sulked, but she did not argue. It was one of the

other two women, a tall redhead, who spoke. "At least you still *have* money to spend. Not like poor Eunice."

"What have you heard, Maeve?" It was Elspeth who asked, an avid look on her long, narrow face.

"Stock market," Maeve said succinctly. Then she nodded toward the fourth woman. "Lara knows."

"Just gossip!" Lara, a thin, nervous type, was quick to deny any firsthand knowledge.

She looked, Liss decided, as if she was afraid someone might sue her for spreading false rumors. Come to think of it, Phil probably was the type who would take her to court.

"Can I help you ladies with anything?" Liss asked.

"Is this the best you can do on the price for this MacRae tartan tie?" Maeve asked, surprising her. Liss had pegged all four women as browsers who would handle the merchandise, leave it in disarray, and end up buying nothing.

Feeling considerably more cheerful, Liss let Maeve haggle her down to ten percent less than the price on the tag.

# Chapter Four

Sherri took Dan Ruskin through the story he'd already told her, how he'd been summoned to the suite by a report of a missing brooch. Then she asked him the same questions she'd asked the MacMillans, the same questions she'd be asking everyone, especially those who had access to a passkey.

"Where were you between three forty-five and four forty-five?"

Dan had a solid alibi. He'd been with his father in Joe's office.

"Okay. You're off the hook. Or you will be as soon as I talk to Joe."

"I checked on the last time the suite the MacMillans are in was occupied," Dan said as he stood. "It was a week ago. The only thing anyone had to do in there today was dust and vacuum. Rhonda Snipes took care of that this morning."

So Rhonda's fingerprints *should* be there. Sherri nodded. "Thanks, Dan. Send your father in next, will you?"

After Joe, Sherri moved on to the hotel employees. The interviews went quickly. No one admitted to being on the third floor while Eunice and Phil MacMillan were out of their suite. Most of them had been with other people at the relevent time.

Angeline Cloutier was the last of the kitchen staff to come in. She was no help in the matter of the missing brooch, but she gave Sherri an earful on the subject of haggis and a guy named Richardson Bruce. Sherri wondered if he was related to Eddie Bruce, who drove the Moosetookalook town snowplow.

As soon as Angeline left, Sherri poured herself a fresh cup of coffee. Until the servers were free at the end of the cocktail party, they could do nothing more. Just as well, she decided. She could use a break.

"If MacMillan wasn't going to wear the brooch," she mused aloud, "why was it on the dresser? And why did he lie about planning to wear it when he talked to Dan and Liss?"

"*Was* it there?" Pete tipped his chair back against the wall and closed his eyes. "If I owned something that valuable, I wouldn't just leave it lying around." Pete was a veteran of the Highland Games, having competed in several athletic events, and no stranger to kilts, plaids, and clan crest brooches.

"It's possible he's trying to pull some kind of insurance scam. Hide the jewelry. Claim it was stolen. Collect the cash. Except that the brooch isn't worth all *that* much. I mean, not hundreds of thousands of dollars or anything."

"Just enough to justify calling the police. Then again, the MacMillans seem to be the sort of people who enjoy disrupting other people's lives."

"And yet they didn't complain right away. They were prepared to . . . what? Cover up the fact that someone was in their suite?" It was all very strange. There was something *off* about the whole thing. It just didn't *feel* right. She wondered what MacMillan's financial situation was. Sometimes even a couple of hundred dollars could make a difference. No, Sherri decided, she could not discount the possibility of fraud.

As she sipped coffee, she played with the end of her ponytail. Her hair was long enough that she could scrape it back from her face, fasten it with a scrunchie, and forget about it. These days, she preferred to keep things simple. Those things she could control, at least.

Pete cleared his throat. His eyes were open again, but just barely. "What about the practical joke angle?" he asked.

"I'll be talking to the two men MacMillan mentioned, but opening drawers and throwing bed pillows around sounds more like someone was searching the place. Which doesn't make sense, either. I mean, the brooch was already right out in the open." Sherri sipped coffee and thought some more.

"Maybe taking the brooch was an afterthought," Pete suggested.

"But if the intruder stole something else, wouldn't MacMillan have reported that item missing along with the brooch?"

"Not if the thief didn't find what he was looking for."

"And that would be what?"

"Your guess is as good as mine." Pete waited a beat. "Maybe the MacMillans are spies. Or maybe international drug smugglers."

"Oh, please!"

Pete didn't contribute any further ludicrous suggestions. He closed both eyes again and looked for all the world as if he were about to drift off into sleep. A smile tugged at Sherri's mouth. She was pretty sure his super-casual attitude was all an act. Her fiancé was trying very hard to let her run the show, putting himself just as far into the background as someone his size could go. When this was over, he was going to get a big kiss for that. And then some.

Sherri glanced at her watch. "The cocktail party should be over pretty soon. Once the supper starts, we can interview the housekeeping staff."

"You don't really think one of them is responsible, do you?"

"No, but I'm hoping one of them might have noticed something suspicious."

The housekeeping staff consisted of Sadie LeBlanc, Rhonda Snipes, and Dilys Marcotte. Sherri knew Sadie fairly well. The older woman was friends with Sherri's mother. As for Rhonda, she had worked part-time in the school cafeteria when Sherri was a teenager. But the third housekeeper's name was not familiar.

"Is Dilys Marcotte local?" she asked Pete.

"Dilys is Rhonda's cousin," he said. "She rents a room from her. She's not from around here, but I'm pretty sure she's not from out of state, either."

"I don't think I've met her."

"You've probably seen her around. Late forties or early fifties. Plump going on stout. Bottle blonde."

That description would fit a lot of local women, Sherri thought. But Pete was right. Moosetookalook was a place where folks got to know each other, even if it was only to nod to in the grocery store or at the post office. Sherri would undoubtedly recognize Dilys once she got a good look at her.

On cue, she heard the sound of footsteps in the hallway. Pete pushed off from the wall, letting his chair settle back on all four legs. Sherri set aside her coffee cup and strode toward the door.

It was time to interview the next suspect.

Liss picked up a copy of the program for the evening as she slipped into the private dining room. Noisy conversations flowed as Tricia filled glasses with whiskey in preparation for the toast. Everyone was already seated except for Russ Tandy, the piper, who was still waiting in the wings.

Liss looked forward to hearing him play. She didn't know Russ well, but she had dated his brother, Gordon, on and off during the past year. Russ owned a music and gift shop in Waycross Springs, an hour or so away from Moosetookalook by car along winding country roads. That gave her a fair amount in common with Russ as business-people. In addition, he had done Liss a favor during the holiday season just past. She hoped she'd have a chance to thank him again, and to chat with him and his wife later in the evening.

Trying to remain inconspicuous, Liss edged toward the back of the private dining room. Everything looked to be in order, but she had a feeling she should keep her fingers crossed.

At the head table sat the three MacMillans, Richardson Bruce, and Harvey MacHenry. The seating arrangement looked a little odd, since Eunice was the only woman. Liss wondered if Bruce and MacHenry were unattached or if their significant others simply didn't share their enthusiasm for things Scottish in general and Robert Burns in particular. Curious, she scanned the lower tables. Gentlemen far outnumbered the ladies there, too. She counted only six females in the room besides Eunice and herself. Four of them were the women who'd just visited the hotel gift shop.

Liss's attention shifted back to the head table as Phineas MacMillan rose to deliver the opening address. He fussed with the Braemar sleeves of his Prince Charlie jacket and tweaked his braided epaulettes before he reached for the microphone. His outfit was once again identical to that worn by his twin, except for a slight difference in their black bow ties. The one Phil wore was made of some flat black fabric while Phineas's shone and was probably satin.

Liss moved deeper into the shadows. In the momentary silence, she could hear the wind rattling the windows behind her. Frowning, she parted the heavy drapes, pulled closed to conserve heat, and peered out into the darkness.

The storm had steadily increased in intensity during the last couple of hours. Swirling snow still obscured the view, but it was obvious this was more than a moderate snowfall. So much for that morning's weather forecast!

Since the snow showed no sign of stopping any time soon, Liss was glad that all the members of SHAS planned to stay the night at The Spruces. She hated to think of anyone driving farther than downtown Moosetookalook in that mess.

She didn't much relish the prospect of even that short trip. Although it took barely five minutes to get home in good weather, the way was narrow and winding and could quickly turn treacherous on a stormy night.

What sounded like a snarl distracted Liss from the white world beyond the window. The sound had come from a man at the table nearest her. He sat with fists clenched, glowering at Phineas MacMillan. Liss was almost certain she heard him grinding his teeth.

What on earth had Phineas MacMillan said to get such a reaction? Liss hadn't been listening to his address and hadn't a clue, but a closer inspection of the people seated at the head table told her that Harvey MacHenry was also visibly upset. His chair was two places down from the speaker. He had risen half out of it and was leaning forward, twisted around so that he could glare directly into MacMillan's face.

"Oh, relax, Harvey," Phineas said with a laugh. "I'm done with you."

"Bastard," MacHenry muttered as he slumped back into his seat.

Liss grew alarmed as one of the old man's hands went to his heart. His face had an unhealthy pallor. She heard the tooth grinder curse under his breath as MacHenry fished a small case out of his pocket and extracted a pill. When he dry-swallowed it, the man in the audience relaxed a little.

He must be MacHenry's son, Liss decided, studying the younger man's face. There was a distinct family resemblance. They both had noses that were large and slightly bulbous.

"Of course we know how some people get ahead," Phineas continued, leering at the crowd. "Pretty young girls are always a commodity, especially if they can smile and play the bagpipe at the same time."

Although he named no names, he looked straight at Russ Tandy's wife. She was a tall, willowy brunette, her face given distinction by almond-shaped eyes. She wore the MacDougall tartan in a sash, which meant that was probably her family's clan, and she looked as if she wanted to jump out of her chair and throttle Phineas MacMillan.

Russ, Liss recalled, had a daughter, Amanda, from his first marriage. Like her father, she played the bagpipe. Mandy was away at graduate school now, but when she'd been younger she'd entered the Miss Special Smile pageant. Russ's brother, Gordon, had told Liss that, though without any details.

The innuendo in MacMillan's comment struck Liss as particularly nasty, but before anyone could do more than glare at him, Phineas had moved on to his next snide remark. This one was aimed at Richardson Bruce. "It only makes sense that Rich Bruce would try to supervise the preparation of the haggis," Phineas said. "After all, he's had a lot of experience cooking the books."

Bruce's normally ruddy complexion went even darker. No one in the audience laughed, but one or two looked thoughtful. Liss didn't give much for Bruce's chances of serving another term as SHAS treasurer.

Since when, she wondered, had the Burns Night Supper turned into a Friars' Club Roast? Phineas's welcoming remarks had already gone well beyond what was acceptable. Liss had never cared much for sarcastic opening mono- logues, and stand-up comics who relied on insult humor rarely amused her. From the expressions on the faces in the audience, which ranged from mild disapproval and confu- sion to shock and anger, Phineas MacMillan was making himself very unpopular.

The speech concluded with two more digs at fellow members of SHAS. One was a clear reference to a nose job that had not been entirely successful. The other twitted Lara Brown—one of the gift shop ladies—for spreading unfounded rumors. Phineas was a fine one to talk, Liss thought.

"That's it, kiddies," Phineas concluded. "Harvey will now say grace." He gestured for Harvey MacHenry to take the microphone. "And who among us needs forgive- ness more?"

Harvey MacHenry's face was still pale and his hand trembled slightly as he jerked the microphone away from Phineas.

The grumbling from the crowd began to make Liss ner- vous. She hoped MacMillan was through hurling insults.

Athough it required a visible effort, Harvey MacHenry got control of himself. His delivery of the Selkirk Grace was flawless and his voice was strong and steady when he followed the prayer with a shouted command: "Stand to receive the haggis!"

Liss couldn't help but smile at the wording. Ritual was all at a Burns Night Supper. As the company began to clap slowly and in rhythm, Russ Tandy marched in playing his bagpipe. Indoors, in the relatively confined space, the sound was deafening. Liss resisted the urge to put her hands over her ears, but only just. Ordinarily, she enjoyed the skirling of the pipes, but this was a little loud, even for a fan of the instrument.

Following close on Russ's heels came Angeline Cloutier. She carried the haggis on a silver platter. Somehow she managed to look dignified, despite the apron and hair net. Liss wondered how the members of SHAS had persuaded the prickly chef to participate in the ceremony. A nice tip, no doubt. To judge by the pained expression on Angeline's face, she couldn't wait to escape back to her kitchen.

Once the haggis had been placed before Phineas MacMillan for carving, Liss made her way to the exit. No one had come to blows over Phineas's remarks, but if rude comments and snide innuendo were a normal part of SHAS ritual, she didn't want to stick around for the toasts.

She left the dining room just as Phineas MacMillan began to recite Robert Burns's poem, "To a Haggis." He'd slice the casing open with a sharp knife when he reached the line "an' cut you up wi' ready sleight." Then everyone would applaud and toast the haggis with whiskey.

After dinner there would be more speeches. "The Immortal Memory" was the standard tribute to Robert Burns. According to the program, Richardson Bruce would give that. Next would come the "Toast to the Lasses" followed by a response on behalf of the women who were present. Liss had been under the impression that these toasts were meant to amuse. She doubted they'd be particularly light-hearted that evening. The first was to be delivered by Phil MacMillan, with the response coming from his wife.

Songs and poems, all written by Robert Burns, would conclude the festivities. These could continue for some time, depending upon how many people felt compelled— or inspired by the whiskey—to sing or recite. Eventually they'd all stand, link hands, sing "Auld Lang Syne," and toddle off to bed.

It was going to be a long night.

Liss made her way to the hotel offices. On one side of a narrow hallway were her aunt's office and the conference room. On the other were Joe Ruskin's medium-sized office, a room with a copier and other office equipment and supplies, and a small restroom. Rhonda and Sadie were cooling their heels in Joe's office. Dilys, Liss assumed, was currently being interviewed in the conference room.

"Fine heck of a note," Sadie complained, catching sight of Liss. "Here we had to come all the way back to the hotel in bad weather to work that foolish cocktail party and now they tell us we can't go home."

"The weather's only going to get worse," Rhonda predicted. "I've got a husband to think about. And two of my boys. I don't like leaving them on their own."

"Now, Rhonda," Liss said in a soothing voice. "You went home and fixed them supper. Surely they can manage without you for a few hours."

Rhonda worried the cuff on her long-sleeved white blouse. "I guess. But they won't like it. They don't like me working up here at night, either."

Liss didn't know much about the Snipes family, but from the careworn look on Rhonda's face, she was willing to bet that the menfolk weren't inclined to help out around the house. Rhonda probably cleaned up after and waited on strangers all day and then went home and did the same thing there for her nearest and dearest.

Sadie was even more antsy than her friend. She occupied one of the two visitor chairs in front of Joe's desk, ankles neatly crossed. But one leg kept twitching restlessly and her fingers drummed in an irregular rhythm on the opposite knee.

"Have you two already talked to Officer Willett?" Liss asked.

"I have," Rhonda said. "But none of us can leave till we've all been questioned. We're carpooling. Well, Dilys and I would have anyway. Dilys rents a room from me."

"They're cousins," Sadie explained.

"Second cousins once removed." Rhonda corrected her.

"I've got family at home that needs seeing to, just like Rhonda does," Sadie added. "I tried to tell Sherri that, but did she listen? I've half a mind to give Ida Willett a call and tell her she needs to have a long talk with that girl."

Oh, that would go over well, Liss thought. "Why don't I check on how things are going?" she suggested, and beat a hasty retreat.

A few quick steps down the narrow hallway brought Liss to the closed door of the conference room. Tentatively, she knocked, then stuck her head inside. When Sherri, who was questioning Dilys Marcotte, didn't immediately tell her to leave, Liss took that for permission to enter. She slid into one of the chairs set up along the wall and tried not to call attention to herself.

"Let's go over it one more time," Sherri said to Dilys.

"Why?" The older woman's face wore a sulky expression.

Dilys was pushing fifty, Liss thought, and had light blond hair with telltale dark roots. She carried enough extra pounds to put a strain on the seams of the black slacks she wore as a uniform.

"Because sometimes," Sherri said patiently, "on the third or fourth repetition, the person telling the story remembers a new detail. Now, did you ever go up to the third floor at any time during the day today?"

"I've already told you!" Defiance replaced the sullen expression in Dilys's faded blue eyes. "I was nowhere near that suite, and you can't prove anything different."

"You didn't go in to dust this morning?"

"I dusted and vacuumed a lot of rooms. That's my job. But not on the third floor. The third floor is Rhonda's."

"Where were you just before the end of your shift?"

"Cleaning the top floor of the center tower. That's a luxury suite, but nobody's booked in there tonight, so I left it till last."

Reasonable, Liss thought, but hard to verify. And Dilys would have had to pass through the third floor both going and coming.

"Then what?" Sherri asked.

"I met up with Rhonda and Sadie. We put our stuff away, clocked out, and went home to supper. Had to be back here before six-thirty, so we didn't waste any time. Rhonda's a stickler for the whole family sitting down to eat together. She had the meal on the table right at five. That's when her husband expects to eat. Rhonda's got two grown sons living with her. Bounced right back on the apron strings," Dilys added in a disgruntled voice. "Too shiftless to go out and find a place of their own to live. A couple of lazy louts, if you ask me."

Dilys had been quick enough to provide that information, Liss thought, and wondered what the Snipes boys had done to offend her.

"Did you see anyone on your way down from the tower suite?" Sherri asked. "Either a guest or another hotel employee?"

"I already told you. No. Can I go now? This storm is getting pretty bad. Can't you hear the way that wind is howling?"

Liss frowned. The weather *was* awful. Foul enough, she supposed, to account for the nervousness of all three members of the hotel's housekeeping staff. Their uncooperative attitudes probably had less to do with the missing brooch than it did with resentment at being questioned by the police when they were already anxious about getting home.

"We're done," Sherri said. She waited until the door

closed behind Dilys before turning to Liss. "How long till the supper finishes up?"

"It will be a while yet."

Sherri stood and stretched. "Talking to hotel employees has yielded nothing. Zip. Nada. If MacMillan wants his brooch back, then his friends are going to have to cough up alibis. I suppose I'll have to talk to them all." She consulted the list lying on the table. "That's thirty-two people at the supper. Plus the hotel has another eight guests who aren't with SHAS."

Liss gave a low whistle. "You'll be here all night. Do you always go to this much trouble for a single piece of jewelry?"

Sherri laughed. "I can't answer that. This is the first time it's come up. But the MacMillans strike me as the type to make a stink if they think their complaints aren't being taken seriously. I figure I'd better dot all my i's and cross all my t's."

Pete, who had been standing by the window, let the drapes fall closed with a soft whoosh. "Getting bad out there, all right."

"Then we'd best have Sadie in." Sherri grimaced.

"You want me to stay for moral support?" Liss asked when Pete left the room to fetch the third housekeeper. "Or to run interference?"

"I shouldn't have let you stay just now, during the interview with Dilys." Sherri sent her an apologetic look. "Not exactly by the book."

"Police business and none of mine?"

"Pretty much, yeah."

Liss tried to give in graciously, but it hadn't been that long ago that Sherri had welcomed her help in solving a case. Liss couldn't help feeling a tiny flare of resentment at being left out of the investigation.

She turned in the doorway to look back at her friend. It was only fair to warn her. "Sherri? Be careful with Sadie."

"Why?" Sherri's eyes narrowed and a wary expression came over her features.

Liss grinned. "Because she's already threatening to tell your mother on you."

# Chapter Five

Sadie LeBlanc, Ida Willett's bosom buddy, stomped into the room two seconds after Liss departed, preceded by the overpowering smell of the musky perfume she always wore and followed by Pete Campbell. Under the florescent lights in the conference room, Sadie's face appeared more deeply lined than Sherri remembered. The shriveled skin had a grayish cast, but it was blotchy, too. Sadie looked at least ten years older than she was. Sherri wondered if she was ill. She was certainly skinny enough to qualify as emaciated.

Sadie took a seat at the conference table with ill grace and eyed Sherri's empty coffee cup. "You could at least offer me something hot to drink."

"Would you like a cup of coffee, Ms. LeBlanc? Or tea?"

"Do you have decaf?"

"No." Sherri had never seen the point, and apparently whoever stocked the conference room agreed with her.

"Pity." Sadie studied her fingernails, one of which was ragged. "Ida tried to raise you right," she muttered, not quite under her breath. "I told her it was hopeless. Disrespectful little thing. All those pretty yellow curls, but underneath? Hard as nails."

Sherri tried not to let any reaction show. She *had* been a difficult child and a rebellious teenager and Sadie had been right there at Ida Willett's side to witness the shouting matches and the inevitable running away from home. Sherri had dropped out of high school during her senior year and hit the road. She didn't like to remember those lost years. She'd come back to Moosetookalook determined to start over. Well, she'd had to, hadn't she? For her little boy's sake.

Adam was nearly seven now and the light of Sherri's life. And soon, once she and Pete were married, Sherri and her son would no longer have to share a trailer with her irascible mother. Ida loved her grandson and was good with him, but she'd never quite forgiven Sherri for taking off on her own.

"I'm sorry you had to wait so long, Ms. LeBlanc," Sherri said, "but there's been a theft and it's my job to question everyone in the hotel."

"Are you accusing me of stealing something?" A dangerous glint came into Sadie's beady little eyes.

"I'm asking for your help in discovering the identity of the thief." Sherri tried not to sound defensive but she wasn't sure she succeeded. She did feel certain that Sadie wasn't the one she was looking for. The older woman might be hard on the nerves, but she was as honest as the day was long.

Sadie's sniff was full of disdain, but her expression brightened. No doubt she was hoping to hear some juicy detail no one else knew, something she could share with all her friends at the first opportunity. "I suppose it's my duty to help the police," she said. "What do you want to know?"

"Were you on the third floor at all today?" Sherri asked.

With obvious disappointment, Sadie admitted that she had not been. "My guest rooms are on the second floor, and we all worked on the function rooms off the mezzanine, but the third floor is Rhonda's."

"Okay. Thank you."

"That's it?" Outrage laced Sadie's voice. "Do you mean to tell me that I stuck around all this time and that's the only thing you wanted to ask me?" In high dudgeon, she left the table and stomped to the door. She stopped to look back over her shoulder as she grabbed the knob. "I always said you were an inconsiderate brat, Sherri Willett, and I've seen nothing here tonight to make me change my opinion."

Sadie slammed the door behind her.

Sherri, who had remained seated, slowly lowered her forehead to the conference table. Then she banged it on the hard wooden surface. Twice.

"Stop that," Pete said. "Don't let that old witch get to you."

"Easy for you to say." Lifting her head, Sherri reached for the list of guests and sighed. Liss had been right. It was going to be a long night.

At the check-in desk, Dan studied the display on the screen in front of him. The Spruces had plenty of available rooms. He'd just finished, somewhat arbitrarily, assigning a fair number of them to the members of the hotel staff who were still on the premises. His father, meanwhile, was making the rounds of kitchen and lounge to let everyone know they were welcome—make that encouraged—to spend the night at The Spruces rather than try to drive home in the storm currently raging outside.

Armed with three key cards, Dan headed for his father's office to issue the invitation to stay overnight to the housekeeping staff. He hoped they hadn't already left. What had begun as just a heavy snowfall was now predicted to turn into a full-scale blizzard. The Ruskins didn't want anyone in their employ trying to navigate narrow, twisting roads in whiteout conditions.

The sound of raised voices reassured him as he turned into the narrow corridor that led to the offices and the conference room.

"Fine heck of a note!" That was Sadie's raspy voice. "Some guy gets robbed and the first thing they do is suspect us. Of all the—"

Rhonda cut in. "It happened on my floor. That—"

"Doesn't make it your problem," Sadie snapped, cutting her off.

"Whose room was it, anyway?" Rhonda asked. "Sherri didn't mention a name."

"Who cares?" Dilys sounded peeved. "It's nobody we know."

"Excuse me, ladies," Dan interrupted.

All three turned to stare at him. Sadie looked irritated. Rhonda appeared apprehensive. And Dilys's expression struck Dan as three parts defiance and one part chagrin, probably because he'd caught them gossiping about the theft.

"It's beastly weather out there. I realize the center of town isn't all that far away, but it wouldn't take much to go sliding off the road and into a tree in these conditions. On behalf of the management, I'd like to offer you each a room for the night." He held up three folders containing key cards. "Breakfast in the morning is also included."

"Free?" Rhonda asked.

"Free. No strings."

Rhonda looked at the other two.

Sadie shrugged. "Your call. You're the one driving."

Dilys glanced uneasily at the windows, just as the wind made them rattle. "Better safe than sorry, Rhonda. You can go if you like, but I'm staying put." She took one of the key cards from Dan, glanced at the room number written on the folder, and scurried away, as if she was afraid he'd renege on the invitation.

Still Rhonda hesitated. "My husband and my boys expected me home hours ago."

"Call them," Dan suggested. "I'm sure they won't want you to take any unnecessary risks."

"Well . . ."

"Oh, for heaven's sake," Sadie snapped, grabbing the second key card. "Grow a backbone, Rhonda." Then she, too, disappeared.

Dan set the last little folder on his father's desk and addressed the remaining housekeeper in a gentle, coaxing voice. "You need to think of your own welfare sometimes, Rhonda. If you like, you can use this phone."

"Thank you," she whispered.

He left her alone in the office and went back to the front desk, busying himself with odds and ends that needed doing until Pete turned up some time later.

"You want the middle tower suite for you and Sherri?" Dan asked his friend.

"I don't think she plans to sleep."

"There are other things you could do besides sleep," Dan said with a wink. "And there's a king-size four-poster up there."

"Tempting," Pete admitted, "but my girl is in full cop mode. No point in wasting the luxury."

"Maybe I'll give the tower suite to Liss, then," Dan said. "She might appreciate it after the day she's had." He keyed the appropriate information into the computer.

"So," Pete said, "when are you going to stop procrastinating and propose to her?"

"As soon as I'm sure she'll accept."

"How soon is Gordon Tandy due back?"

"In a couple of months." Trust Pete to go right to the heart of the matter. Dan's rival for Liss's affections was currently out of state. A state trooper by profession, Tandy had been sent for special training to some police academy out west. Dan didn't know the details. He didn't want to remind Liss of Gordon Tandy by asking.

"Better get a move on, chum. Time's a wasting. Speaking of time, shouldn't the supper be breaking up pretty soon? Sherri wants to talk to all of them."

Dan glanced at his watch. He'd lost track of time and was surprised to see that it was nearly ten. "They booked that private dining room until midnight. Still, it wouldn't hurt to let them know not to call it a night until they've seen Sherri. I—"

The lights went out.

"Damn."

After a moment, they flickered and came back on again.

"Better check the phone," Pete said.

Dan lifted the receiver and heard nothing but dead air. "Landlines are out."

"Not too surprising, I guess."

"At least we've still got cell phones."

"Don't count on it." Sherri entered the lobby, police band radio in hand. "My portable isn't working." She returned it to its holster on her utility belt. "The tower must be down."

Dan checked his cell phone. "No service. Just how bad is this storm supposed to get?"

As if in answer, the lights flickered again.

"Well, hell," he muttered.

An outage wasn't totally unexpected, but neither was it something to take lightly. Like everyone else who'd lived in that part of Maine for a long time, Dan still had vivid memories of the ice storm of '98. That one had knocked out power for the best part of a week. He still had the T-shirt that commemorated it.

If the hotel lost power, backup generators would kick in. They'd provide enough juice to pump water in from the well and run the refrigerators and freezers in the kitchen.

Fortunately the stoves and ovens ran on gas. The generators would keep lights and heat going, too, but not at full capacity. Faced with the possibility that they might lose electricity for days rather than just hours, especially if the winter storm turned really wild and wooly, the Ruskins had prudently stockpiled emergency supplies. To conserve energy, they had plenty of battery-powered lanterns for light and they could stoke up the fireplaces in the public rooms to augment the heat.

"We'd best grab a few flashlights and head for the private dining room," Dan said, suiting action to words. There were three in a drawer behind the counter. "If the power does go out, we may have to do without electric lights for a while. There will be less panic if our guests are prepared. I'd like to get everyone down here to the lobby. Once we gather them all in one place, I can brief them on safety measures and hand out lanterns."

"*And* tell them I'm waiting to talk to them," Sherri said, taking one of the flashlights and trailing after Dan toward the stairway to the mezzanine.

"Tell me where you keep the lanterns," Pete said, armed with the third flashlight, "and I'll start bringing them up."

"I'll show you," said Joe Ruskin, coming up behind Pete. He dumped a large cardboard box full of them on top of the check-in desk.

"Better take the stairs," Dan called after them as his father and Pete headed back the way Joe had come. The storage room was in the basement, and it wouldn't help matters any if the two of them ended up trapped between floors in the freight elevator.

"Can you leave the check-in desk unattended?" Sherri asked when they reached the mezzanine.

"If the power goes out, calls from guest rooms won't get through anyway. And, trust me, this is one night when no one is likely to wander in off the street to ask for a room."

They slipped quietly into the private dining room, not that anyone would have noticed them if they'd thumped and clattered. The members of SHAS were all on their feet, singing at the top of their lungs.

Liss intercepted Dan and Sherri before they'd gone more than a few steps inside the door. "The supper is just wrapping up," she mouthed.

The singers belted out last few words of "Auld Lang Syne" and abruptly fell silent. People started gathering up their possessions, preparatory to leaving the room. Anxious to make his announcements before they could scatter, Dan headed for the microphone. Liss and Sherri were right behind him.

"Ladies and gentleman," he said, "if you could just stay put for a moment?"

He heard grumbling, but everyone obediently stopped moving.

"Thank you." He drew breath to ask them all to adjourn to the lobby, but before he could say another word, the room plunged into darkness.

A woman gasped. A man cursed. Someone bumped into the table and let out a colorful oath. For a moment, confusion reigned, but everyone present lived in Maine or New Hampshire. They were not exactly strangers to power outages.

The emergency lights flickered to life. The word EXIT lit up over the doors and a few dim bulbs shed pale illumination from strategic spots along the walls. Dan turned on his flashlight and shone it up at his own face. The microphone was dead, but he had a good loud voice when he needed it.

"Sorry about this, folks," he bellowed. "If you could all just hold on another minute?"

He waited for them to settle again.

"Well, we've got a beaut of a storm tonight," he said, opting for a folksy tone he hoped would soothe rattled nerves. "Just about everything is on the blink—electricity, phones, computers. And I'm not even going to try to guess how long we'll have to do without. But, as you can see, we do have emergency lights and we have plenty of flash-lights. We also have battery-powered lanterns. Enough for everyone. What I'd like each of you to do right now is go down to the lobby—use the stairs, please—and collect the illumination of your choice. Even if the power comes back on in short order, you'll probably want to keep another light source handy tonight, in case of further outages."

"Will the johns work with the power out?" someone called from the back of the room.

Dan waited for the laughter to die down. "You'll be glad to know that the hotel's generator will indeed keep the plumbing going."

Applause greeted this announcement.

"We do ask that you don't take any long, hot showers or baths until power is restored. As for heat, we will have to keep the thermostats turned low—around sixty de-grees—and the fireplaces some of you have in your rooms are not approved for use by the fire marshall, so please don't try to use them. However, we already have a fire lit in the hearth in the lobby and there are fireplaces in most of the public rooms. We have a plentiful supply of wood to keep all of those going, and the stoves in the kitchen run on gas, so providing you with hot meals will not be a problem."

Someone tugged on Dan's sleeve. He looked down to see Sherri Willett standing beside him. For a moment, he'd forgotten about that stolen brooch. He cleared his throat.

"There is one other thing. This is Officer Willett of the Moosetookalook Police Department. She needs to speak briefly with each of you before you turn in for the night. I'll let her explain, and then we can all head down to the lobby together."

He stepped back and hoped for the best. So far, everyone was being pretty understanding about the loss of utilities, but Dan had a feeling that their tolerance was about to be put to the test. It was one thing to be asked to do without a few creature comforts, especially when an act of nature was responsible for the situation and everyone else was in the same boat. It was quite another to have a uniformed police officer imply that you might be a thief, even when everyone else was a suspect, too.

Sherri set up an interview space in the lobby near the sweeping staircase that led to the mezzanine. She'd decided to limit her questions to asking when each guest had checked in, where they'd been between 3:45 and 4:45, and—for those with rooms nearby—if they'd seen anyone suspicious near the MacMillans' suite. She was pretty sure this line of questioning would not turn up the missing brooch, but she had no better idea how to proceed. At least Phil MacMillan wouldn't be able to complain that she wasn't doing anything.

It was slow going, even with only those few questions. The replies were so similar that before long the members of SHAS, and their tartans, became little more than a blur.

At least everyone seemed to be in a cooperative mood. It helped that the Ruskins had set up a free buffet table and opened a couple of portable cash bars. The first round of drinks had been on the house. There had been cheering when Joe announced that breakfast the next morning would also be free.

"Next up is one of the practical jokers Phil MacMillan fingered," Pete whispered as yet another man in a kilt approached. "Eric Buchanan. I've met him before, at one of the Highland Games."

Sherri took Buchanan through the same questions as everyone else. He claimed he'd been in the lounge during the relevant hour. Sherri had no reason to doubt him, but she took the precaution of talking to Tricia Lynd next.

"Oh, yeah," the hotel's only intern agreed. "He was there the whole time. Him and his friend." She pointed out a man with buck teeth and cauliflower ears. "His buddy there pinched my butt, so I definitely remember him!"

Sherri had a sneaking suspicion that the pincher would turn out to be the second practical joker MacMillan had named, but several loud blats, the sound of a bagpipe tuning up, made asking her next question a challenge. "Who else was in the lounge?" she shouted.

Russ Tandy was one of the SHAS members Sherri had already interviewed. The noise he was making prevented her from hearing Tricia's answer. He chose that moment to launch into an impromptu bagpipe concert. It was suddenly impossible to think, let alone continue the interview.

Holding up one finger as a signal for Tricia to wait, Sherri semaphored her arms until Liss MacCrimmon looked her way. Then Sherri pointed to Russ and mimed zipping her lips. If there was a signal for "make the piper shut up," she didn't know it, but Liss got the message. By then, Russ was well into a spirited rendition of "Scotland the Brave." Liss waited patiently until he finished the piece, then caught his arm and whispered in his ear. A moment later, she led him away, bagpipe in hand.

As silence descended, Sherri breathed a sigh of relief.

"About those two men, Tricia—how long had they been in the lounge?"

"Awhile. They came in right after we opened at three."

"Did either one go out and come back in again?"

Tricia shook her head. "I'd have noticed. Until two more guys in kilts came in, they were our only customers."

"Huh," Sherri said. That seemed to rule them out as suspects. When she'd confirmed the name of the bottom-pinching practical joker was Norbert Johnson—the second name MacMillan had mentioned—Sherri decided to talk to him next. He had an alibi, all right, but she indulged herself by leaving him with the impression that if he didn't behave himself in the future he was going to find himself charged with sexual harassment.

"Dumbass," she muttered as she watched Johnson scurry back to the bar. But he was an innocent dumbass. She turned to Pete. "Who's next?"

"Hank and Glenora Huggons." Pete gestured for a middle-aged couple to come forward, but before they could reach the table where Sherri and Pete sat, a tall man in an orange and yellow kilt shoved rudely in front of them.

"Run along, kiddies," he told the couple. "I'm talking to the officer next."

Sherri frowned. Even in the dim lighting, she recognized Phil MacMillan's beak of a nose and square jaw. "Have you remembered something else, Mr. MacMillan?"

"You haven't talked to me yet. I'm *Phineas* MacMillan and I'm tired of waiting around."

Sherri felt herself grow warm with embarrassment. She'd known Phil had a brother, but she hadn't realized the two were identical twins. Still, that being the case, it was entirely natural that she might mistake Phineas for Phil. He didn't have to be so rude and contemptuous about it.

She gestured to one of the chairs they'd set up on the opposite side of the table. "Please sit down, Mr. MacMillan."

MacMillan took his time getting settled. He adjusted his kilt and sporran, tugged on the bottom of his jacket, and made sure his bow tie was straight. When he was satisfied with his appearance, he cleared his throat. "I hope this won't take too long. It's a bit nippy sitting this far from the fireplace."

"Perhaps you should change out of the kilt," Sherri suggested in saccharine tones.

"I may do that. Or perhaps I'll just turn in for the night. I was under the impression that I was not permitted to leave the lobby to do either until after I'd answered your questions. Shall we get on with it?"

"Certainly. I understand you were with your brother when his brooch went missing."

"Ah, so that's what this is about? That absurdly overpriced clan crest brooch?"

Sherri nodded. She had asked Phil and Eunice not to mention the theft, but she was a little surprised Phil hadn't confided in his own brother.

Phineas looked thoughtful. "Am I to assume it disappeared while Phil and Eunice and I were inspecting the private dining room with Ms. MacCrimmon?"

"That's right." Who was asking the questions here, anyway? Sherri supposed it didn't matter. Phineas MacMillan had a solid alibi for the time of the theft. He'd been with Phil, Eunice, and Liss. Still, she needed to confirm his movements. "I understand you met your brother and his wife in their suite?"

Phineas nodded. "Yes. We went down to meet Ms. MacCrimmon together. I was back in my room in under an hour."

"Did you see anyone else on the third floor?"

"Not that I recall. If that's all . . . ?" He stood, fussily smoothing the pleats in his kilt as he did so.

"Thank you for your help," Sherri said, as she had to everyone she'd questioned.

Phineas started to walk away, then turned back, a malicious glint in his eyes. "You have considered, I suppose, that the brooch may not be missing at all?"

With that remark, Phineas sauntered off toward the blazing hearth. Sherri darted an astonished look at Pete. "Did he just suggest that his own brother might—?"

"He sure did. What a prince of a guy!"

"Well, it isn't as if we didn't think of that possibility ourselves," Sherri said, "but that's just nasty."

Phineas MacMillan was a sour note in what had otherwise been a surprisingly harmonious group. Sherri took a moment to study the crowd in the lobby. The fireplace and lanterns cast eerie shadows, but the overall atmosphere was convivial. Almost all the guests were still up, even those Sherri had already questioned and dismissed. They seemed to be enjoying the hospitality The Spruces offered—warmth, free food, and access to alcohol. One portable bar was manned by Simon, the bartender from the hotel lounge, and the second by Dan Ruskin.

Best of all, Russ Tandy and his bagpipe had not returned to serenade them.

# Chapter Six

---

"You've done a good job with this." Russ Tandy's gesture encompassed the whole of the hotel gift shop. He held a powerful battery-operated lantern high so that it shed its light over counters and tables, racks and displays, all of which he'd already examined more closely.

"Thanks, Russ," Liss said. "I appreciate having your opinion."

As a distraction, requesting Russ's input had worked well. He'd abandoned his efforts to serenade the crowd and trailed after Liss into the wing that housed, among other things, the gift shop, a game room, and a library. With any luck, Sherri would be able to finish taking statements before anyone else decided that the party would not be complete without bagpipe music.

"Hello?" called a female voice unfamiliar to Liss.

"We're in here, hon," Russ answered.

A moment later, Russ's wife entered the shop. She went immediately to her husband's side. She was tall, but her head only came up to his shoulder. At a guess, he stood around six foot four, a little taller than his brother, Gordon, who only topped six feet by an inch or two. Russ had already filled Liss in on what Gordon was up to. He knew little more than she did. Gordon Tandy was not much of a letter writer, nor did he bother with phone calls home.

"Hello," Liss said. "Victoria, isn't it?"

"It is, but I go by Tory." She held out a smooth, beautifully manicured hand and shook Liss's with a firm, no-nonsense grip. "Nice to meet you at last."

"I was just showing your husband around the gift shop and trying to decide about opening it in the morning. If this snow keeps up, our regular clerk will have a hard time getting to work tomorrow." One more thing to add to her to-do list, Liss thought—fill in for Fran. She heaved a silent sigh at the thought of dragging herself out of bed by seven. She'd been looking forward to a night spent in the lap of luxury—the fabled tower suite at The Spruces—but it was likely to be a very short night.

Tory made approving sounds as she moved from a rack of hand-knit mittens and scarves to Liss's display of Scottish paraphernalia. Tandy's Music and Gifts carried a few of the little figurines of Highlanders, but only the ones who held tiny bagpipes. Still, Liss was glad Russ's business was located far enough away from Moosetookalook to keep them out of direct competition with each other.

As Liss watched the other woman wander, she wished that she'd brought a few more items to the hotel from the main branch of the Emporium. Some of those nice warm imported sweaters would have been nice. The temperature in the gift shop had been turned down when it closed for the night. Liss hadn't felt the cold at first, but now she had to wrap her arms around herself and stamp her feet to keep the shivering at bay.

"Oh!" Tory exclaimed, catching sight of the display of jewelry. "What a gorgeous ring!"

"The stone is a tourmaline," Liss told her. *Please don't buy it*, she added silently.

Standing side by side, they peered at it through the glass, angling their flashlights for a better look. They jumped in unison when the door creaked open behind them.

A snarl that could only have come from Russ Tandy had Liss whirling around, dreading what she'd find. Her fears were justified.

"Get out of here, MacMillan," Russ said in a voice so cold it sent shivers down Liss's spine. "You've already done enough damage."

"It's a free country, Tandy. I'm just exploring the hotel."

Russ had set his lantern down on one of the tables. He stood in shadow, but Liss could tell from the set of his shoulders that he had both hands clenched into fists at his sides. When he took a threatening step toward the new arrival, she made a grab for him, catching one of his arms while Tory latched onto the other.

MacMillan's response was to unsheath the skean dhu tucked into the top of his hose. The small knife glinted in the light of a second lantern, the one MacMillan carried in his free hand.

"As a defensive weapon, that's pretty pathetic," Russ taunted him.

"One of these can still do a lot of damage at close quarters," MacMillan replied, baring his teeth so that they, too, gleamed in the lantern light.

Liss tried desperately to remember which twin it was who kept his skean dhu razor sharp. Was it Phineas? Or Phil? A dull blade wouldn't do nearly as much damage. She hoped.

"He's not worth an assault charge!" Tory's agitated whisper sounded loud in the tense silence that followed MacMillan's threat.

Liss didn't trouble to lower her voice. Suddenly impatient with their childish behavior, she snapped at the two men. "Grow up! Both of you. And put that sticker away before you cut yourself."

*What is it with these SHAS people?* First one idiot tried to beat his friend over the head with a bagpipe. Now these morons appeared ready to fight a duel because MacMillan had insulted Russ's daughter during his speech.

"He owes me an apology," Russ muttered, even as MacMillan obeyed Liss's order and sheathed the skean dhu. "And he owes Mandy one."

MacMillan snickered. "You're the one who named the kid Mandy Tandy, Russ. She should be used to fielding snide remarks."

Russ lunged, very nearly breaking free of his wife's grip. Liss did lose her hold on him. She staggered back a few steps, off balance, as he slipped out of her grasp.

Holding on to her own temper by a thread, Liss abandoned her attempt to control Russ and advanced on MacMillan. He, wisely, was already retreating. Still chuckling to himself, he backed out into the wide corridor that connected the gift shop to the lobby. She paused in the doorway. There was just enough light for her to see the dumbfounded look on his face when he found his way blocked by yet another dimly lit figure in a kilt.

Before MacMillan could escape, the newcomer seized him by the lapels. Then he slammed him back against the opposite wall. Liss hoped that ominous cracking sound wasn't breaking bone.

She rushed out of the shop after them as the fisticuffs continued, moving erratically down the hall. Both men cursed loudly as they scuffled, but she did not hear any blows land.

"You'd better help her, Russ," Tory said from the shop doorway.

"Not a chance," Russ said. "I'm perfectly happy to let Will MacHenry beat Phineas to a pulp. I'd rather bash his head in myself, but this is the next best thing."

Behind her, Liss heard Tory make an exasperated sound and then the patter of light footsteps as the other woman left her husband to come to Liss's aid herself.

"Tory, get back here!" Russ shouted. "Damn. All right. Stand down. I'm coming."

The fight, such as it was, continued to move away from the lobby and toward the music room the hotel used for small, intimate gatherings. The two men appeared to be evenly matched and, so far, neither had inflicted any serious damage on the other. MacHenry was younger, but MacMillan was in better shape, and Liss was grateful he'd sheathed the skean dhu.

Russ Tandy stalked the combatants, watching for his chance. The moment there was an opening, he came up behind Will MacHenry and wrapped his arms around him. Holding MacHenry in a bear hug, Russ hauled him away from the object of his fury.

MacMillan made no attempt to follow. He sagged against the wall, trying to catch his breath. As soon as he had wind enough to speak, however, his words came out as a bellow.

"I'm Phil, you imbeciles!" he shouted at them. "Not Phineas!"

Even in the poorly lit hallway, Liss could see the color leach out of Will MacHenry's face. Russ gave a start of surprise. Tory just looked embarrassed.

Will blew out a ragged breath. "Christ, Phil. I'm sorry. I thought—"

"I know what you thought! Go beat on my brother and leave me alone!"

The moment Russ freed him, Will MacHenry beat a hasty retreat in the direction of the lobby, stopping only long enough to collect the flashlight he'd dropped when he first accosted the man he'd thought was Phineas.

Narrowing her eyes, Liss stared hard at MacMillan. "Are you really Phil, or did you just say that to get off the hook?"

MacMillan made a production of straightening his bow tie and his jacket. "I outgrew trading places with my twin when we were both in high school."

Liss wasn't sure she believed him. She was surprised Will MacHenry had. Then again, all three men had probably had quite a bit to drink, what with the whiskey at the supper and Lord knew what else from the cash bar.

"I wouldn't put it past Phineas to lie to us," Russ said.

Neither would Liss. "How could we tell?" she mused, ignoring MacMillan's glower. "How could anyone?"

"I would hope Eunice would know the difference," Russ muttered.

Liss made the mistake of catching Tory's eyes. The glint of wry amusement she saw there echoed her own reaction. Obviously, they'd both seen too many movies on the Lifetime and Oxygen networks. In real life, it simply could not be that easy to fool people.

Taking a closer look at the MacMillan twin in the hallway, she noticed a single detail that decided the issue. "He's Phil," she said.

"You sound awfully sure," Tory said.

"I am. It's the bow tie."

Both Russ and Tory squinted at the accessory in question. "It's black," Russ said.

"This one is brocade," Liss clarified. "Phineas's tie is satin."

Phil's bark of laughter broke the tension. "You've got a good eye, Ms. MacCrimmon." He turned to Russ, hesitated for a moment, then shrugged. "I suppose I do owe you an apology for that Mandy Tandy crack, although I spoke nothing but the truth. And it's also true that my brother was out of line earlier this evening, but I can't apologize for him." He spread his hands wide. "I can't be blamed for anything Phineas says or does, now can I?"

When Russ said nothing, Tory smacked her husband on the arm. "Tell Phil that you accept his apology and apologize to him for wanting to brain him."

"When hell freezes over," Russ muttered. "For my money, he's almost as bad as his twin."

Phil laughed again. It was not a good-natured sound. Liss felt a sudden chill that had nothing to do with the temperature.

"Never mind," Phil said, sounding almost cheerful. "I'll just be on my way."

"Your way where?" Liss asked. "You're headed in the wrong direction if you mean to return to your suite, and the lobby is the only place on this level that's warm right now."

"Oh, I was just exploring a bit," Phil said. "Stretching my legs before I turn in. What *is* down this way?"

Liss collected her wits and answered politely, reminding herself that, obnoxious or not, he was still a paying guest. She indicated the door to her right. "Library. Game room opposite. There's a billiard table in there, plus a couple of arcade games. Of course, those won't work with no power. You've already gone past the gift shop and the business center. Up ahead is the music room. There's a grand piano in there. When the hallway hangs a right, the lounge is straight ahead, but that's closed now. The bartender moved his operation to the lobby when the lights went out."

"Ah, I see. And there's an indoor pool somewhere, is there not?"

Liss nodded. "The lounge overlooks the pool from above. The entrance to both the health center and the pool is down one flight." Because of the slope of the land, the basement was below ground level at the front of the hotel

but almost fully above ground at the back. The view from
the health club and from poolside windows was of an ex-
panse of lawn and the woods beyond.

"I don't suppose the pool is open." Phil sounded wist-
ful. "I wouldn't mind a swim before I went to bed."

"You can take one if you want, but there are no lights
and there's no power to heat the water. And no one is on
duty to help you if you get a cramp." Not that the Ruskins
had a lifeguard anyway. The staff working in the lounge
were instructed to keep an eye on what was going on
below, but they weren't in a position to effect a quick rescue if someone got into trouble. For that reason, the pool
was clearly posted to tell guests that they swam at their
own risk.

Phil considered for a long moment. His gaze came to
rest briefly on Russ Tandy. Then he shook his head. "No, I
think not, but I will just take a peek at the facility to sat-
isfy my curiosity. Good night, all."

They watched him in silence until he rounded the bend
in the corridor and disappeared from view. Then Russ
flung an arm around Tory's shoulders and steered her toward the lobby. "I think I need another drink and some
music, in that order. Did either of you see where I left my
bagpipe?"

Sherri was nearly done with her interviews. She'd already questioned almost everyone who'd attended the
Burns Night Supper. A few had been the worse for the
amount of whiskey they'd consumed, but they'd all been
pretty cooperative.

She'd also talked to the five hotel guests who had been
in the lounge when the power went out. Simon and Tricia
had herded them into the lobby as soon as it became obvious that the outage was going to last awhile. Then Simon
had gone upstairs to talk to the remaining guests and to

the hotel staffers who'd already retreated to their rooms and tell them that their presence was required downstairs. The guests had all been skiers who had turned in early because they planned to head for the slopes at the crack of dawn.

Good luck with that, she thought. She'd kept her best guess about likely road conditions to herself.

Next up was an elderly gentleman who identified himself as Harvey MacHenry. "I saw you arrange for Russ Tandy to be taken away earlier, Officer," he said with a mischievous sparkle in his faded blue eyes. "Don't you enjoy the skirling of the pipes?"

"In moderation, Mr. MacHenry," she told him. "In moderation."

He chuckled. "Well, then, we'll have to arrange for a little concert later on. In the meantime, what can I do for you?"

"I understand your room is on the third floor. Did you see anyone in the hall between three forty-five and four forty-five this afternoon?"

MacHenry was in his eighties, but he was as sharp-witted as someone half his age. "Where on the third floor?" he asked. "This lovely old hotel is quite large, you know."

"Let's say near the suite Phil and Eunice MacMillan are occupying."

"Ah. Busy place. First the two of them came in, bringing half their wardrobe with them if I had to judge by the number of suitcases they dragged down the hallway. Then Phineas banged on their door and they let him in. All three of them came out again a few minutes later. I saw them getting into the elevator as I came out of my room. I took the stairs. Good exercise, you know."

Sherri leaned toward him, ever hopeful. "Did you see anyone else? Another guest? One of the housekeeping staff with a cart?"

"Sorry, no." Then his deeply lined face creased even further. "Or maybe I did. Just a shadow, you understand. Someone behind a door that wasn't quite closed." He thought for a moment, then shook his head. His voice conveyed genuine regret. "I'm sorry. It was just an impression. I didn't actually *see* anyone."

"Was it a door near the stairwell?"

"I'm sorry, I don't recall."

"Were you gone from your room very long?"

"Not long, no. I went downstairs to take another look at the restoration work they've done in the lobby. Then I inspected the music room and the game room and the library. Oh, and I spoke with the Ruskin boy. Dan, is it? And then I realized that I'd better get going if I expected to have time for a nice long soak before I dressed for the supper. I figured my boy would be out of the tub by the time I got back upstairs."

"Your boy?"

"My son. Will. We're sharing a room."

Sherri had interviewed Will MacHenry early on. He *had* said that he'd been taking a bath at around four that afternoon. As alibis went, it wasn't a great one, but she had no reason to disbelieve it.

"Anyway," Harvey continued. "I went back to our room and took my bath and I was . . . well, not to put too fine a point on it, I was amusing myself by watching through the peephole to see who else from our group might walk by. My late wife used to insist that we never be the first to arrive at any event, so I wanted to let a few of the others go down to the dining room before Will and I did. I saw Dan Ruskin and that charming Liss MacCrimmon heading toward the MacMillans' suite. They looked rather concerned about something. And when they came back a short time later, they looked even more unhappy. It wasn't too much later before I saw you and Deputy

Campbell repeat the same process. And then Phil and Eunice left the room, sour-faced and steaming." MacHenry looked extremely pleased that he'd been able to provide so much information.

"Well, that's certainly a thorough account," Sherri said. Too bad he'd been in the hotel lobby at the most crucial time. If he'd been looking through his peephole then, he'd probably have caught sight of the thief.

"Anything else I can tell you?" MacHenry asked.

Sherri hesitated. "I suppose you know the MacMillans pretty well?"

"I've been acquainted with them for years. We're founding members of SHAS, you know. The MacMillan twins, Richardson Bruce, and my late wife and I."

"So you've seen this brooch before?" Sherri reached for a manila folder and retrieved the printout she'd made from the .jpg file she'd downloaded from Phil MacMillan's laptop. She slid the page closer to the lantern so that Harvey could get a good look at it.

"Gaudy thing, isn't it?" Harvey chuckled. "Phil sets great store by that, especially since he found it before Phineas did and there was only one to be had."

"Valuable?"

"Reasonably. I don't pretend to know what things like that are worth. I prefer less pretentious decorations myself." His kilt, Sherri noted, was one of those anyone could wear—the Black Watch tartan. His jacket was of plain black wool. It had silver buttons and gauntlet cuffs but no epaulettes or other furbelows. His sporran was black leather with leather tassels and looked as if he'd owned it for a good many years.

"Well, thank you, Mr. MacHenry," Sherri said, dismissing him. "You've—"

"You know, I suppose, that Phil MacMillan is having . . . financial difficulties?"

Sherri exchanged a look with Pete. "Go on."

"As a rule, I don't tell tales out of school, but it's hardly a secret that Phil made some bad investments. That's what I've heard, anyway."

"I see." She smiled encouragingly. "What kind of investments?"

"I don't have many details." His thin lips set in a prim, disapproving line. "And, as I say, I'm not inclined to spread stories. Idle gossip can be harmful, you know."

Sherri waited.

"He lost a bundle on the stock market. And I understand that the MacMillans now have their house on the market." He lowered his voice. "Can't meet the mortgage payments."

The MacMillans and a lot of other people, Sherri thought. "Well, again, thank you for your insights, Mr. MacHenry."

This time he accepted the dismissal. It took him two tries to get out of the chair, but once he was on his feet he was as spry as a man twenty years his junior. Moving at a good clip, he headed back to what had long since turned into the Maine equivalent of a "hurricane party."

At just past two in the morning, Dan Ruskin shut down the portable bar he'd been operating. It looked as if the crowd was finally thinning out. More than half of the guests had retired for the night. Those who were still in the lobby, however, seemed reluctant to leave the warmth of the hearth for their chilly bedrooms.

Bed sounded pretty darned good to Dan, especially if he could convince Liss to let him share hers. At the least, he hoped for a little quality time with her, snuggling together by the hearth. The fireplace in the tower suite was one of those approved for use. It wouldn't take any time at all to get a cheerful blaze going.

"Too late to get another drink?"

Jerked out of a very pleasant daydream by Russ Tandy's slightly slurred voice, Dan took in the other man's bleary eyes and unsteady hands and decided that Russ had consumed more than enough alcohol for one evening. Good thing he wasn't planning to drive home to Waycross Springs tonight.

"Sorry, Russ. We're closed."

When Russ had returned to the lobby after his tour of the gift shop, Sherri had still been interviewing guests. Liss had persuaded him not to resume his impromptu concert. Instead, aside from a couple of trips to the john, Russ had spent the entire time since then slouched in the chair closest to Dan's station and knocking back one Scotch after another.

" 'S okay," he said now, but in lieu of another glass of whiskey, he reached for his bagpipe.

Before Dan could think of a way to stop him, a horrible screeching filled the air. This time no one intervened. Sherri had talked to everyone she wanted to and no longer required quiet. In fact, she and Pete looked as if they were actually enjoying the racket.

Whether the piper was drunk or sober, the pipes well or badly played, Dan found the resulting noise both mind-numbing and deafening. It made him think of cats fighting. Or maybe just one big cat being strangled. He fled into the office area, but that didn't provide enough distance. Not by half. He wished he'd thought to soundproof the conference room.

Desperate to find a refuge, he backtracked. At first he thought he might cut through the dining room to the kitchen, maybe make himself a snack while he was at it. He changed his mind when he passed the door to the basement. It would be even quieter down there. And there was food in the staff break room.

Just closing the stairwell door behind him muffled the sound of the bagpipe. Dan breathed a little easier, but his sense of relief was short-lived. Before he was halfway down the steps, he heard something that was even more distressing than the screeches produced by Russ Tandy's playing.

The high, eerie, keening, but clearly human cry came from the basement. Fearing that someone was hurt, Dan rushed headlong down the remaining stairs. Two steps beyond the door at the bottom, a running figure barreled into him. It nearly knocked him off his feet and his flashlight did go flying.

Dan grabbed on to the other person for support. His hands clenched hard on bony arms. In the glow of the exit signs and of the nearest of the small emergency lights spaced at intervals along the corridor, he belatedly recognized Sadie LeBlanc.

Tears streamed down her gaunt, deeply lined face. Deep, hacking coughs racked her body, alternating with that odd, high-pitched wailing. Beneath his hands, Dan could feel the shudders running through the housekeeper's skinny frame. She'd been traumatized by something. Or someone.

Shifting Sadie so that he could retrieve the flashlight, which had gone out but had not been broken, Dan switched it back on. Then, keeping an eye peeled for potential assailants, he half dragged, half carried the distraught woman to the room the hotel staff used for their breaks. He eased her into one of two overstuffed armchairs and snagged a bottle of water from the refrigerator. Kneeling in front of Sadie, he unscrewed the top and extended the bottle. Her hand shook so badly that the water slopped as she lifted the bottle to her mouth.

"What's wrong, Sadie? What happened to you?" He

saw no blood, no tears in her clothing, but that didn't mean she hadn't been attacked.

She swallowed several big gulps of the water, then choked. Dan pounded her on the back, growing more worried by the minute. Clearly something had terrified the woman, but what?

"Sadie! You're safe now. Everything's okay. But you have to tell me what it is that upset you."

The horrible hacking cough had stopped, but she was weeping even harder than before. She fumbled in the pocket of her plain black slacks for a tissue and noisily blew her nose. Her face scrunched up, as if she might go on crying forever, but after another minute or two of gulping and sniffling, she managed a few words.

"He's dead," she croaked. "There's a dead guy in the number two storage room."

# Chapter Seven

Reluctantly, Dan left Sadie alone in the break room. He had no choice. He had to verify her story.

Storage room #2 was the one where the lanterns and flashlights had been stockpiled. Whoever had been the last one out hadn't locked the door behind himself. The knob turned easily. Right inside, lying facedown in the narrow aisle between two rows of shelving, as if he'd come through the door only to fall flat on his face, was a man in a kilt. Blood had pooled beneath him. A lot of blood.

Careful where he put his feet, Dan stepped close enough to squat down, lift the man's wrist, and feel for a pulse. No spark of life remained. Dan hadn't expected to find any. Not with that much blood.

Cautiously, he backed out of the storage room. As he closed and locked the door behind him, he felt a curious sense of detachment. The reality of the death—and a violent death, at that—had not yet sunk in.

Without saying a word, Dan collected Sadie from the break room and escorted her upstairs. She'd stopped crying but now wore a dazed look on her face. She went with him without protest, allowing him to steer her as far as the arched entrance to the lobby. There he stopped and scanned what remained of the crowd for Sherri Willett. It didn't take long to spot her. She was sitting on a couch with Pete, laughing at something her fiancé had just said. Dan tried to catch her eye, but she wasn't looking his way. No one was except the hotel's intern, Tricia. Something in his expression must have given away his state of mind. Tricia reached his side a moment later.

"Boss? Something wrong?"

It took more effort than he'd expected to give her a coherent answer. *Snap out of it,* he ordered himself. There were things he needed to do. At the moment, he couldn't think exactly what they were, but he knew that they were important.

With excruciating slowness, his mind began to function again. He remembered that his father had already turned in for the night. That meant the responsibility for reporting what had happened fell to him. So did looking after the poor woman who'd made that grisly discovery. He forced himself to speak.

"Tricia, take Sadie to the conference room and keep her company until Sherri can come talk to her."

He saw questions in Tricia's eyes, but the look on his face apparently convinced her that it was not the time to ask them. She grasped Sadie firmly by the elbow and led the older woman away. Dan watched them go and then pulled himself together and made a beeline for Sherri and Pete.

This was so not good.

With one hand shielding her mouth and nose, Sherri Willett bent toward the body. The battery-powered lantern she held in the other hand provided the only light and made everything look surreal.

She wished this were a hallucination, but she'd already confirmed what Dan had told her, and what Sadie LeBlanc had told him. This man had no pulse. He was definitely dead. More than that, he had been murdered.

Sherri now had to do what Dan hadn't. She swallowed convulsively, then bent closer. She saw the cause of death all too clearly. The victim's throat had been cut.

The murder weapon lay nearby. A skean dhu. Sherri could make out a clan crest on the handle, but the angle was wrong and the lighting too poor to allow her to identify it. She glanced at the top of the victim's kilt hose and spotted an empty sheath. Apparently, he'd been killed with his own knife.

Spots appeared before Sherri's eyes. Suddenly the smell of blood was too much for her. She started to gag.

Hands clamped down on her shoulders, hauling her out of the storage room and into the corridor. She made no objection when Pete closed the door on the horror within. Neither did she protest when he wrapped his arms around her and held her tight. Her stomach roiled, then settled, but shudders continued to rack her body.

They stood that way, clinging to each other, for several more minutes, until Sherri finally managed to stop shaking. She'd seen death before, even murder, but not like that. Even with the solid wooden door separating her from the body, the sharp tang of all that blood stayed with her. She wondered if she'd ever be able to forget that smell.

"I'm okay," she said at last, easing out of Pete's embrace. She had to be. "I've got work to do," she added in a voice that was slightly steadier. "First off, we need to contact the state police and . . ."

The words trailed off as she realized she wouldn't be able to follow standard procedure on this one. The same howling winds that had knocked out power and phone service had damaged the towers that relayed signals for cell phones and police radios. Until work crews braved the storm to make repairs, she was cut off. On her own. She, Officer Sherri Willett of the Moosetookalook Police Department, was solely responsible for securing and preserving the crime scene and for handling the initial stages of the investigation. If she screwed up . . .

Well, she wouldn't. True, she couldn't complete the first two steps—calling the state police and the attorney general—but she would go by the book for everything else.

She just wished she had a copy of "the book" with her.

Sherri glanced at the storage room door. Had she touched anything? She didn't think so. Still, she should have put on gloves *before* she went in. Why hadn't she thought of that sooner? Had she gotten the victim's blood on her hands? She stared at them, but didn't see any stains. That didn't mean they weren't there. Lantern light didn't provide the best illumination in the world.

"Okay. Okay, I can do this," she said, more to herself than to Pete. "The scene has already been contaminated. Sadie. Dan." She swallowed bile. "Me."

"Couldn't be helped," Pete said. "Obvious as it seemed that he was dead, you had to confirm that there was nothing you could do to save the victim's life."

She leaned against the wall, trying to organize her scrambled thoughts. "Oh, God, Pete! This is a bad dream. The state police will have my head—and my job—if I screw this up."

He couldn't deny it. Expression somber, he nodded. "Pretty much the worst-case scenario possible from their point of view," he agreed. "And a no-win situation for us."

"Me."

"Us. You're in charge, Sherri, but I'm here to help."

She pressed both hands to her temples. If only she could wrap her mind around what she had to do. The problem was that there was no good way to handle the body and the crime scene. Both ought to be left just as they were, but who knew how long it would be before a proper detective and his team of technicians could get there?

"Could you ID the body?" Pete asked.

Sherri groaned. She'd seen the sides of the victim's throat from the back. That had been enough to make her forget all about taking a look at his face. "I'll have to go back in. Lift his head." *Look at the full horror of a slash that most likely cuts straight across the front of the neck.*

She took a deep breath. She could do this. She *had* to do this.

"What can I do to help?" Pete asked.

"I need you to go out to the cruiser for a box of disposable gloves, the roll of yellow crime-scene tape, and the department's digital camera. You'll find all that stuff in the trunk."

"You'll be okay?" His dark eyes bored into her, as if he needed more reassurance than her verbal answer could provide.

Sherri didn't bother to lie. "I'll have to be. Go. Please. Oh, and bring chalk and a tape measure, too."

Before she touched the body again, they'd take pictures and measurements. Even do a chalk outline, old-fashioned as that was. She'd disturb the scene as little as possible, but even a small change could be detrimental in a homicide investigation.

Once Sherri was alone, she eyed the storage room door with distaste. She did not want to go back in there. She *could* just cover the door with the yellow tape that read POLICE LINE DO NOT CROSS, and leave everything as it was until the state police turned up. But then they'd have to wait until someone was reported missing to discover who had been killed. She wasn't sure that was wise.

She had to stop dithering. She was a law enforcement professional. It was time she started acting like one. But when the stairwell door suddenly burst open, she shrieked like a heroine in a bad horror movie and jumped about a

foot. Hand over her heart, she turned to see Liss Mac-
Crimmon running toward her.

Dan was hard on her heels. "Stay away from the storage
room," he called after her. "I've seen what's in there, and
you don't need to!"

Liss ignored him. She caught Sherri by the shoulders
and peered worriedly into her face. "Are you all right?
Pete said that seeing the body really shook you."

"I'm fine. But Dan's right. You shouldn't be here. Pete
and I will handle this."

"Who is it?" Liss asked, casting wary eyes toward the
closed supply room door.

"I don't know yet."

"He was wearing a kilt," Dan said.

"So, one of the Burns Night Supper people. Sherri, did
you recognize the tartan?"

That *would* narrow it down, Sherri realized. She *really*
hadn't been thinking straight. Apparently, she still wasn't.
She *knew* that pattern. She'd seen it earlier. But she'd seen
a lot of different tartans since she'd arrived at the hotel.
The ID wouldn't come to her. "A lot of yellow," she told
Liss, "and a kind of orangey red."

Liss's voice was faint and shook a little. "That's the
MacMillan tartan."

As soon as her friend said the name, Sherri knew who
the victim was. Or at least she was able to narrow the
identification down to two possibilities. The dead man
was either Phil MacMillan, the guy whose brooch had
been stolen, or his identical twin, Phineas.

"There . . . there might be ID in his sporran," Liss suggested. "Or a room key."

"That would be good," Sherri said, "but I can't touch
anything till Pete gets back with gloves." And she wasn't
sure she should do so even then. Now that she'd been

spared looking at the victim's face, she wasn't anxious to go back inside for any reason.

Liss stared at the closed door, her face creased with worry.

"Liss? Do you know something that might help with the identification?"

"They wore different bow ties."

Sherri grimaced. "Probably not going to help," she muttered.

"Why not?" Liss asked.

"Covered with blood," Sherri answered before she thought. "Oh, damn. Forget I said that."

"His throat was cut," Dan said, tightening his grip on Liss's shoulder.

"Suicide?"

Sherri stared at her. "Why would you think that?"

"Sorry. I just . . . well, you know the old story about the skean dhu being just big enough for a Scot to slit his own"— she broke off at the expression on Sherri's face—"What? It *was* a skean dhu?"

Sherri nodded. "His own, by the look of it."

Liss buried her face in Dan's shoulder. Her voice was muffled. "That's horrible."

No one said anything else until Pete returned. A coating of ice crystals clung to his head and shoulders.

"Storm's still bad," he reported, handing over the items Sherri had asked for. He'd also collected the fingerprint kit and audio recorder they'd used earlier in the evening. "I tried the radio in the cruiser and got nothing but static. Visibility's a bit better. Just good enough to tell me that no one's going to be getting in here to help us out any time soon. We won't be leaving, either. At least one of those big spruces—the ones that give the hotel its name—came down right across the driveway."

"Damn," Dan swore. "That's going to be a bitch to cut up and haul away."

"By the time the wind finally dies down, trees and fallen limbs are likely to be blocking a good many roads," Pete said. "There will be more downed power lines, too."

Sherri blew out a breath. The upshot was that she was going to be the one in charge of this investigation for some time to come. She had a slew of doubts about her ability to avoid mistakes—the kind that got a case thrown out of court—but she'd just have to do the best she could.

"Someone," she said, "needs to find out which of the MacMillan twins is still alive."

The tremor in Liss's voice was still there, but she didn't hesitate. "I guess that would be me."

Liss gave herself a stern lecture as she and Dan headed back upstairs. By the time they reached the first floor, she felt a little steadier. She shouldn't complain, she thought. Compared to what Sherri had to do, hers was the easy job.

"I should let Dad know what's going on." Dan glanced at his watch. "Maybe not. I guess the bad news can wait until he's had a few more hours of sleep."

Liss put a sympathetic hand over his. "I'm sorry. I know all this will mean negative publicity for the hotel."

"And to think I was worried about a story on the missing brooch hitting the news."

"It's a funny coincidence that the same family, maybe the same person, should be involved in both a theft and a murder."

"You don't hear me laughing," Dan said.

"Funny peculiar, not funny ha-ha." She gave him a half-hearted thump on the arm with her fist. "So, Phineas MacMillan's room first?"

"All right. If he's not there, we'll go to Phil's suite."

Whichever twin they found alive would have to be told that his brother was dead. The prospect made Liss squirm.

So did the thought that there might be a murderer loose in the hotel. Difficult as that possibility was to accept, the alternative was even more difficult to believe. Liss did not really think that either MacMillan twin was the sort to kill himself.

The victim had had his throat slashed with a skean dhu. A shiver raced through her. She was suddenly very glad she had not been the one who'd discovered the body.

They reached the second floor, where Phineas had a room, and started down the carpeted corridor.

"What was Sadie doing in the basement in the middle of the night?" Liss asked.

"I have no idea," Dan said. "And right now, I don't care." He stopped in front of a door and knocked. When repeated attempts to rouse someone had no effect, he pulled out a passkey and was about to open the door himself when it suddenly swung inward.

"Mr. MacMillan!" Liss yelped.

Until that moment, she hadn't realized that she'd been assuming it was Phineas who'd been killed. After all, Phineas was the one who'd managed to offend at least a half dozen members of SHAS earlier in the evening.

But it was unmistakably Phineas MacMillan, wrapped in a paisley bathrobe and sporting a bad case of bed head, who was standing in the doorway and frowning at her. "Who did you expect?" he demanded in a testy voice.

"May we come in for a moment?" Dan asked. "I'm afraid we have some bad news."

The room was as beautifully furnished as all the others at The Spruces, and Phineas MacMillan had kept it almost as neat as it had been when he'd checked in. True, the bedding was rumpled, but there were no clothes strewn about

and his toiletries were arranged with almost military preci-
sion on the bathroom counter. The only touch that made
the place look lived-in was the James Patterson novel on
the bedside table next to the lamp and clock radio, and
even that was neatly aligned with the edge of the night-
stand.

"Well? What is so important you had to wake me up at
this ungodly hour of the morning?"

"I'm sorry to tell you this, sir," Dan said, "but your
brother is dead."

"Impossible!" He dismissed the idea out of hand.
"There must be some mistake."

"I don't believe so, Mr. MacMillan."

"We thought it might be you," Liss blurted out. She felt
heat creep into her cheeks at the ill-considered revelation,
but there was no taking back her hasty words. And there
was no way around telling Phineas the rest of it. "I'm
sorry, Mr. MacMillan, but Phil was found in a storage
room in the basement of the hotel a short time ago."

"Nonsense. There's a simple way to settle this once and
for all. Come along, kiddies. We'll go up to Phil and Eunice's suite and you can see for yourself that there's nothing wrong with my brother. He's my twin, for God's sake.
Don't you think I'd know if something had happened to
him?"

They didn't argue. Phineas was in denial. He'd have to
have proof of what they'd told him. Liss dreaded having
to give Eunice the bad news, but at least Phineas would be
there to comfort his sister-in-law.

The three of them trooped up another flight of stairs
and knocked at the door bearing the number 312. It took
some time for Eunice to answer. Like Phineas, she showed
signs of having been asleep. She was bundled into one of
the thick, white terrycloth bathrobes the hotel provided to

guests who booked suites. As her gaze went from Dan to Liss to Phineas, her lips pursed in annoyance.

"Where's Phil?" Phineas asked before she could speak. His voice sounded odd, as if he'd finally begun to believe Dan and Liss.

"He hasn't come up yet." Eunice's eyes remained trained on Liss's face as she spoke. They narrowed abruptly at whatever reaction she glimpsed there.

"There's been an . . . accident," Dan said.

Eunice gave an exasperated huff. "Don't beat around the bush with me. What happened?"

"We knew it was either your husband or his brother," Liss said. "We couldn't tell which one until we . . ." She gestured helplessly at Phineas.

"Since I'm here," Phineas said in a subdued voice, "that leaves Phil."

"Why didn't you just *ask*—oh!" Eunice took a step backward before she caught herself. "I see. You mean he's badly hurt. Unconscious?" She blanched as Liss struggled to find the right words. "Dead?" Eunice whispered.

"I'm sorry," Dan said. "Yes."

Leaving the door open, Eunice retreated into the suite lit only by the lantern she'd placed on the coffee table. Another illuminated the bedroom.

"I'll dress. I won't be a moment." She slammed the inner door behind her.

Phineas took a seat in the shadows, saying nothing. Not wishing to intrude, neither Liss nor Dan tried to talk to him, but Liss could not help but entertain a few cynical thoughts about the new-made widow. Where were the hysterics? Where were the tears?

In an effort to be charitable, she considered that perhaps Eunice was in shock. After all, she couldn't know what the other woman was going through, alone in the bedroom. But when Liss glanced at Dan, she knew one thing for certain—if she'd just heard that he was dead, she'd be a lot more shaken up by that news than Eunice MacMillan appeared to be.

Sherri ticked off items on a mental list. Photographs. Measurements. Chalk outline. They had not dusted for fingerprints. Those would still be there when the state police took over.

"Go back out," she told Pete, "and guard the door. I'm just going to take one last look around."

The room was cold. No heat. That was good when you wanted to preserve a body. Freezing would be even better. Belatedly, Sherri wondered if there was a window she could open. She should have asked Dan.

She shone the bright beam of her flashlight between the shelves forming the last aisle to the right of the door. No one had been down that way recently. There was a coating of dust on the cement floor. And at the far end she could see a cellar window that opened inward. It had been insulated with a block of pink Styrofoam, but that should be easy enough to pull out. There would be piled-up snow on the other side, blocking the opening, but that was good, too. She could lower the temperature in the storage room significantly without creating another means of entrance.

Her footprints in the dust were clearly visible. There would be no confusion about when or how they'd gotten there. She'd explain her reasoning to the state police. She was sure they'd understand the need to keep the room as cold as possible. This would preserve the integrity of the crime scene without compromising it in any way.

Or so she hoped. Too late now. She was at the window. If she was wrong, she'd already screwed up royally. It took only a few minutes to open the window and remove the insulation. The snow, as she'd expected, made a satisfactory barrier.

"Okay," she whispered, talking to herself. "Now get out."

But she took one last look around prior to returning to the hallway, locking the door, and plastering it with yellow crime-scene tape. Once that was done, this room would stay sealed until the state crime lab team arrived.

Sherri had no desire to go close to the body again. The cause of death was obvious. Even without seeing the full extent of that gaping wound in the throat, she suspected she'd have nightmares about it for years to come. A shudder ran through her that had nothing to do with the chill in the air.

She shone her flashlight into the dark corner at the other end of the room, then turned the beam into the aisle between the dusty one and the one into which the body had fallen. There were footprints in the center aisle. Lots of them. And empty spaces on the shelves where the lanterns and flashlights had been stored.

How on earth had MacMillan had ended up here? For that matter, what had Sadie been doing opening the door to the storage room? And why did it have to be Sadie LeBlanc, of all people, who had found the body? Sherri did not look forward to questioning her. She hadn't handled their earlier session well, and back then—had it only been a matter of hours ago?—she'd only been investigating a robbery.

It was tougher than she'd thought, being in charge, especially when she had to deal with someone who remembered her as a sixteen-year-old troublemaker and treated her as if nothing had changed in over a decade.

The beam of Sherri's flashlight swept over the half-empty shelves as she turned to go back the way she'd come. She froze, startled, when it reflected off an object on a top shelf. Slowly, she played the light over a carton of furniture polish. There it was again. Only an inch or so of cellophane-wrapped package stuck out, but that was enough. Sherri smiled for the first time since Dan had come to her with the news that there was a dead man in the basement storage room.

At least one of her questions now had an answer.

# Chapter Eight

---

Eunice MacMillan, dressed in jeans and a sweater, emerged from the bedroom looking composed. "I want to see my husband," she announced.

Liss exchanged a look with Dan. That would not be a good idea, but she did not know how to dissuade Eunice without giving her all the gory details. Liss was sure Eunice would be better off not knowing them.

"She's right," Phineas chimed in. "How else can we be sure you have the right man?"

"MacMillan tartan," Liss said succinctly, hoping that would suffice.

It didn't.

"I insist on seeing the body," Eunice said.

Liss gave up. Sherri would have to convince the MacMillans. She didn't envy her friend the task.

They emerged from the stairwell and entered the basement a short time later, just as Sherri finished attaching two crossed strips of yellow tape to the storage room door. Eunice gave the less-than-plush corridor a contemptuous look.

"I told you this was a mistake," Eunice said. "Why on earth would Phil be down here?"

"Phil?" Sherri echoed, her gaze shifting to Phineas, who was still in his bathrobe.

"Let's get on with this, kiddies. Eunice is right. I'm sure this is all a mistake."

Sherri glanced at the storeroom door. "I'm sorry, but this is a crime scene. I can't let you go in."

"Crime scene?" Phineas repeated, incredulous. "What do you mean, crime scene?" He turned to glare at Dan. "You just said he was dead."

"Mr. MacMillan appears to have been murdered," Sherri said.

"Impossible," Eunice insisted. "And how do we know it's Phil you've got in there?" But her face worked, as if she might be starting to doubt her earlier certainty.

"Ms. MacMillan," Sherri said, "is the man with you your husband or your brother-in-law?"

"This is Phineas, of course. Do you think I can't tell the difference? But—"

"And when is the last time you saw your husband?"

"Phil was . . . I'm not sure . . . I . . . I don't know." Her voice hitched and she swayed. She had to brace one hand against the wall for support. Then, without warning, she whirled, screeched, and flung herself at Phineas.

Liss watched in amazement as Eunice landed solidly against her brother-in-law, knocking most of the wind out of him.

"Ooof!" he exclaimed. "What the hell?"

"He's dead, Phineas!" Eunice wailed. "Phil's dead! And not just dead—he was murdered!" One fist struck the center of his paisley-covered chest with a solid blow. "It's all your fault, damn you, Phineas MacMillan. All those innuendoes in your speech. You ticked somebody off but good, and that somebody killed my Phil. The killer thought he was you!"

"You're crazy, woman!" Phineas shouted back.

Liss wasn't so sure about that.

Eunice continued to pummel her brother-in-law until

Sherri stepped in and hauled her away from him. Once she had a good grip on Eunice, she caught Pete's eye. "Take Mr. MacMillan to Joe's office, will you please? I'll talk to him in a little bit. Come along," she said to Eunice. "It would help if I could ask you a few questions. Just a few minutes of your time is all I'll need."

"What?" Her outburst over, Eunice stared at Sherri with a dazed look on her face.

"Questions," Sherri repeated. "To help us find out who did this terrible thing."

"Oh, yes. Of course." She let Sherri lead her into the nearby staff break room.

Liss followed, as did Dan.

Sherri settled Eunice in a chair and took the one facing her. "When did you last see your husband, Ms. MacMillan?" she asked again.

"I don't remember. It must have been shortly after everyone congregated in the lobby. You didn't need statements from us, so when I was ready to go up to bed I looked around for him. When I didn't see him anywhere, I assumed he'd already retired." She frowned, creating deep wrinkles in her forehead.

"But he wasn't in the suite when you got there?" Sherri prompted her.

"No. No, he wasn't. I didn't think much of it at first. Sometimes, when he can't sleep, he takes long walks. He said something earlier about exploring the hotel, so I guess I assumed that's what he was doing." She gave a choked laugh. "Lots of room to wander in this old monstrosity. I never thought . . . he'd never have expected—"

She broke off and buried her face in her hands.

Liss had been trying to stay in the background, but now she went to the refrigerator and took out a bottle of water. She offered it to the bereaved woman. Eunice waved it away, but not before Liss got close enough to see that her eyes were still dry. In fact, she looked more angry than grief stricken.

"Ms. Mac—"

"Whoever did this made a mistake." Eunice's voice took on a sharper edge. "He . . . or she surely meant to kill Phineas. They're twins, you know. Identical."

"But why would anyone want to kill Phineas MacMillan?" Sherri asked.

"Because of the speech," Eunice said impatiently, and looked to Liss for support. "You heard it. I saw you there. Phineas's speech was chock full of insults and innuendos. He upset quite a number of people."

"Anyone in particular?" Sherri asked. She was taking notes now, Liss saw, scribbling frantically on a small spiral notebook she'd fished out of the breast pocket of her uniform.

"Lots of people." Eunice's words came out in a broken whisper, but Liss still saw no sign of tears, nor was there any loud, heart-wrenching sobbing.

While it was true that some people simply didn't cry, Liss found it odd that Eunice MacMillan showed so little grief. Was it possible that she wasn't entirely unhappy to find herself a widow? If that was the case, she really should try to coax out a few crocodile tears. Didn't she know that the wife was always the number one suspect when a husband was murdered?

Liss glanced at Sherri. Her friend was watching Eunice with professional detachment coupled with a fair amount of suspicion. "I need names, Ms. MacMillan," she said. "Who were the individuals Phineas insulted at the Burns Night Supper?"

"I can't remember anyone in particular. I didn't pay much attention." Eunice made a vague gesture. "I just know that he upset people."

After ten more frustrating minutes spent trying to get

useful answers out of Eunice, Sherri gave up and asked Dan to escort Eunice back to her suite.

"We need to work out a time line," Liss said as soon as the door closed behind them. She'd already found another, larger notepad and a pencil in one of the drawers next to the stove.

"We?"

"Can't you deputize us or something? Dan and I can help interview people. You and Pete will be overwhelmed if you have to do it all yourselves."

"Pete has training. You don't." Sherri held up a hand to stop the protests she knew were coming. "Besides, this isn't my case."

"You have to do the initial interviews, don't you?"

"Liss, I realize that you read a lot of mystery novels, but that isn't real life and you aren't a cop. I really shouldn't have let you stay in the room while I was talking to Eunice just now. Not if I'm going to go by the book. And I am. I *have* to, or I risk blowing the case."

"It isn't that I want to meddle in police business, especially murder," Liss insisted, leaning against the counter, "but I'm responsible for keeping everything running smoothly for the Burns Night Supper, and the murder has to be connected to that. So I'm already involved. I have an obligation to help straighten things out." She sent Sherri a pointed look. "*And* I know the names of most of the people Phineas MacMillan insulted during his speech."

Sherri gestured at the pad of paper Liss held. "Write them down, then, along with everything you remember him saying. Then you're done."

"What about Phineas MacMillan?" Liss asked as she scribbled. "If Eunice is right and the killer finds out that he killed the wrong twin, won't he go after the right one?"

"That's all I'd need," Sherri muttered. "Two murders for the price of one."

A few minutes later, Liss handed the tablet to Sherri. She'd written six names: Russ Tandy, Victoria Tandy, Lara Brown, Richardson Bruce, Harvey MacHenry, and Will MacHenry. After each was a brief summary of why he or she had been angered by Phineas's remarks. She'd also made a note that someone who'd had a nose job had been another of Phineas's targets.

"There's something else, too."

Liss hesitated, knowing full well the trouble she was about to cause, but Phil had been murdered. Viciously murdered. She had to tell Sherri what she knew.

"Go on."

"Will MacHenry and Phil MacMillan got into a scuffle outside the gift shop. And Russ Tandy—God! I really hate tattling like this! Russ said he'd like to bash Phineas's head in. Because, you see, both he and Will thought Phil was Phineas."

"Are you sure it *was* Phil?"

Liss nodded. "Yes. Because of the bow tie."

Sherri looked blank.

"Phineas wore satin," she remined her friend. "Phil wore—"

"Okay. I remember now. You told me that earlier." Sherri sighed and rested her head against the back of the chair. "My brain has turned to mush."

"And this surprises you?" Liss asked. "Anyone with any sense went to bed hours ago."

Sherri glanced at her watch and grimaced. "No rest for the wicked, but you should call it a night. As much as I appreciate your offer to help, there's nothing more you can do."

"And you've still got to talk to Phineas," Liss said, her voice full of sympathy.

"And Sadie," Sherri reminded her, but there was something in her tone that made Liss think her friend was not dreading that second interview quite as much as she had been.

Dan Ruskin hid a yawn behind his hand. Now that Eunice MacMillan had been safely tucked away in her suite, he was more than ready to pack it in. Guessing that by now Sherri would have moved on to interviewing either Phineas or Sadie, Dan left the stairwell on the first-floor level.

A glance through the glass panel in the door to his father's office told him he'd been right. The thickness of the wood muffled the voices inside, but he could see that Phineas was agitated. Sherri stood with her butt propped against the side of the desk, her arms folded across her chest, but the man she was questioning didn't seem to be able to stay still. He paced as he talked, waving his arms about.

Dan didn't care much for Phineas MacMillan, but he did sympathize with the other man's loss. Dan knew how upset he'd be if it had been his brother Sam, who'd been murdered, and twins were supposed to have a closer bond than regular siblings.

Pete Campbell was also in Joe's office, leaning against the far wall. Dan caught his eye and a moment later Pete joined him in the hallway. "Problem, Dan?"

"When isn't there one, but at least there are no new bodies."

"Wiseass."

"There's an unused meat locker off the kitchen. I was thinking we could put the corpse in there."

They'd have to replace the small walk-in freezer afterward. Dan couldn't imagine that any health inspector worth his title would allow them to store food in it again, no matter how well they cleaned and disinfected it. That meant more expense for the hotel, but it couldn't be helped.

He was both surprised and relieved when Pete shook his head. "Body stays put. But I'm wondering if we need to post a guard on the storage room. How many people have keys?"

"Any master key will open it, so me, Dad, the house-keeping staff." He shrugged. "Quite a few."

Pete grimaced. "Guess I know where I'll be spending the night."

Dan sympathized, but didn't offer to take his place. "Did Liss turn in?" he asked.

"I think so. Sherri wouldn't let her help with the inter-views."

"Thank God!"

Pete chuckled. "You should probably go up and check on her, though. Tower suite, wasn't it?"

"Yeah," Dan said. "Tower suite. And that's the best idea I've heard all night."

Sadie LeBlanc sat hunched in her chair, a resentful look on her face. There was a distinct whine in her voice when she spoke. "You've got no call to threaten me, Sherri Wil-lett."

"I'm not threatening you, Sadie. I just want you to con-firm why you went into the storage room."

"I'm not talking." They sat opposite each other at the conference table. Sadie concentrated on picking at the label on a bottle of Poland Spring water.

Sherri sighed and wondered if she'd have been better off leaving her interviews until after the sun came up. She hadn't gotten anywhere with Phineas MacMillan, either. He'd been uncooperative from the get-go, only reluctantly telling her that he'd gone to bed right after she'd "interro-gated" him about the missing brooch. Once Pete left the room to talk to Dan, Phineas had apparently decided that Sherri was accusing him of his brother's murder. Prickly as the proverbial porcupine, he'd refused to answer any more questions. A few minutes later, he'd announced that he was going back to bed and stormed out of Joe's office.

By the time Sherri turned her attention to Sadie LeBlanc, she'd already been worn to a frazzle. That Sadie was giving her a hard time pushed her past her limit.

"Okay, Sadie," Sherri said, "if you won't tell me, then I'll tell you. There is a pack of cigarettes hidden on a high shelf in that storage room where you found the body. I think you stashed it there. That's why you went down to the basement and into that storage room. You were planning to sneak a smoke."

"You can't prove that." Sadie sounded defiant, but she couldn't meet Sherri's eyes.

"No? Have you looked at your own face in a mirror lately? You show all of the classic signs of a person with a long-term tobacco addiction. You look older than you are. Smoking has ruined your complexion. Your face is deeply lined, Sadie. Anyone can see that much. And I know for a fact that you were a chain smoker when I was a little kid. I don't think you ever stopped."

Sadie didn't move, but the very stiffness of her posture told Sherri she'd hit a nerve. Sherri bit her lip. Her words had been blunt to the point of cruelty. She told herself she'd had to say them to get through to this obstinate woman, but her conscience called her a liar.

Sherri told it to shut up. She had a job to do.

"Back then," she continued, "both of my parents smoked, too. After my mother quit, she wouldn't let anyone else in the house with a cigarette, so I haven't seen you light up recently. But if you didn't kick the habit, then you'd find a way to get your fix, wouldn't you, Sadie? Even if it meant risking your job to do it."

Sadie's continued silence provoked Sherri into pushing harder.

"State law mandates smoke-free workplaces, Sadie. Employees aren't allowed to light up anywhere on the premises, indoors or out. Is that why you always wear such heavy perfume? To cover up the smell of smoke that clings to your clothes and hair?"

Sadie crossed her arms across her bony chest and glared. "I'm not admitting a thing."

Sherri resisted the urge to growl. "I'm willing to ignore the fact that you broke the no smoking rule. Once. But only if you stop being difficult and tell me exactly what you saw tonight."

New wrinkles appeared in Sadie's forehead. She knew she didn't have a leg to stand on if Sherri reported her. She'd lose her job and any chance of a good reference. She huffed out an exasperated breath. "I didn't see anything except a dead body."

"When you went to retrieve your . . . property?"

"Yes! All right, yes. I hid a pack of cigarettes in the storage room and I went in to get them."

Finally! She'd broken through. Sherri wondered why she didn't feel better about her success. Probably because she'd lived down to Sadie's expectations. She'd badgered and insulted a woman who'd just been through a traumatic experience. She'd treated Sadie as if she were a criminal, instead of a potential witness.

Well, it was too late for a do-over now. The best she could do was adopt a conciliatory tone. "Just a few more questions and you can get some rest, okay?" Sherri didn't wait for a reply. "Did you hear anything on your way down to the basement? Voices? Footsteps?"

Sadie shook her head.

"How about smells? Perfume? Aftershave?"

"I wasn't paying attention." Sadie still sounded aggrieved.

"But you must have been keeping an eye out. You wouldn't have wanted to get caught."

"There was nobody around except the dead guy."

Sherri repressed a sigh. "Okay, then. I'm sorry to put you through this, but I need to know how far into the room you went, if you touched anything, how—"

"Are you nuts? The second I saw the blood I was out of there. I didn't touch anything but the door handle."

"Did you have a flashlight or a lantern?"

"Flashlight. Damned near dropped it when the beam picked out a guy's legs. I thought at first that I'd interrupted a couple going at it. Then I realized that he wasn't moving." She sent Sherri a sickly smile. "You wouldn't believe how bad I need a cigarette right now. I don't suppose you could go get that pack for me?"

Reluctantly sympathetic, Sherri shook her head. "And please don't try to get it yourself. That's a crime scene now. Sealed off until the state cops get here."

"Body still in there?"

"As a matter of fact, it is." Sherri was pretty sure that would discourage Sadie from attempting to retrieve her cigarettes. "Okay, Sadie. We're done here. The state police will want to talk to you, of course. And if you think of anything else, please let me know right away." She stood. "Thank you for your cooperation." There wasn't even a hint of sarcasm in those last five words.

Sadie made a production out of gathering up her purse and opening it to fish out her key card. She regarded it and Sherri with the same disgruntled expression. "You'd think," she said as she made her way to the conference room door, "it being the hotel's fault that I'm stranded here overnight and all, that they could have given me a room with a decent view."

Liss rubbed at her eyes, wishing she weren't so exhausted. The long climb to the aerie had just about finished her off, but the tower suite deserved to be appreciated. Carrying her flashlight and a bag from the gift shop that contained the oversize T-shirt she intended to sleep in, she made her way through the living room and into the bedroom with its big, four-poster bed, its huge bank of windows, and its ornate fireplace.

She shivered. It was even colder there than it had been downstairs, but she couldn't resist going to the windows and looking out at the night. On her way by, she grabbed the hand-knitted afghan neatly folded across the foot of the bed and wrapped it around her shoulders.

She couldn't see much except the few fat, wet flakes of snow that stuck to the glass. Liss frowned. If the temperature warmed up another degree or two, those would turn to sleet, and that would cause even bigger problems. When ice accumulated on tree limbs, they broke off under the weight. That would be all they'd need! Driving into Moosetookalook, close as it was, would be impossible if that happened. They could be stuck there for days before road crews managed to clear away that kind of debris.

Her thoughts went to the two cats waiting for her at home. She told herself they'd be fine. She'd left them plenty of food and water, knowing it would be a late night. And surely Aunt Margaret would check on them. Liss's aunt had gone home at five, so she'd missed the worst of the weather. And she lived right above Moosetookalook Scottish Emporium. She'd be able to check on Lumpkin and the kitten as soon as the storm let up. After all, it was only a matter of a few steps from Margaret's back door to the entrance to Liss's kitchen.

She turned away from the window, meaning to crawl into bed and catch what sleep she could. Her eyes were already at half mast, but they popped open again when the beam of her flashlight revealed that she was not alone. A figure loomed in the doorway, blocking off the only escape route. Liss swallowed hard and whispered, "Who's there?"

"It's just me," Dan said. "I didn't mean to spook you."

Liss sagged in relief. She'd thought, earlier, when Dan had told her that she'd be sleeping in the tower, that he intended to share the suite with her. She'd been looking forward to spending some time alone with him. They saw each other all the time, but there were almost always other people around. But then Sadie had found the body. Homicide and romance might mix well in romantic suspense novels, but Liss had a feeling that in real life it was harder to combine them.

"I thought you might like a fire," Dan said.

Without waiting for her response, he entered the bedroom and headed for the stone fireplace. When Liss directed her light that way, she saw that there was already wood and kindling laid in the hearth, ready to be lit. Dan knelt down, match in hand, and held the flame to the crumpled newspaper that made up the bottom layer. A moment later, it caught.

"I thought fires weren't allowed in the rooms," Liss said, coming up beside him to stare down at the winking flames.

"This is one of the exceptions, although we still have to be careful." He set the fire screen in place to keep sparks off the hearth rug.

When he stepped back, it seemed the most natural thing in the world to move into his arms. He kissed her lightly on the forehead and tugged her toward a love seat already positioned to view the romantic glow of the fire.

"I had this planned for a lot earlier in the evening," he whispered.

She toyed with the buttons on his shirt. He'd had a rough night, and things wouldn't be much better in the morning. Even without Phil MacMillan's murder, Dan had to have a lot on his mind. Opening the hotel had been a gamble from the first. The Ruskins needed every paying guest they could find to cover the operating costs. When the power went out, Joe Ruskin had offered free food as a way of making up for the lack of amenities. That alone probably broke the budget. If some of the guests demanded their money back, Joe would be in even worse financial trouble.

She nestled closer, finally beginning to feel warm again as the fire crackled in the hearth. Dan kissed her forehead.

"Man, am I glad I'm not a cop," he murmured.

"Why?"

"Pete. He's stuck sitting on a hard chair in the basement hallway for the rest of the night. Guard duty. I guess I'll have to spell him tomorrow, though. Or find someone else to. Maybe Simon, if I offer him enough overtime."

"Wait a sec. Are you telling me that Sherri and Pete think someone might try to get into the storage room? Why would anyone want to go in there?"

"An excess of curiosity?" he suggested.

When Liss felt Dan's lips curve into a smile, she just knew he was thinking of her. "I've got no interest in viewing dead bodies. Let me just say—eeew!"

"No plans to play Nancy Drew on this one?"

Liss hesitated, then opted for honesty. "I did offer to help Sherri conduct interviews, but she turned me down flat. I think she's afraid I'll mess up the chain of evidence or something."

She glanced up to meet his cool, steady gaze. That expression said more than words could express. He didn't want her involved in the investigation any more than Sherri did.

"I just want to give her a hand." Liss knew she sounded defensive, but she couldn't help it. She *felt* defensive. "She can't do everything herself. Besides, this could be another case where I have special knowledge that may be useful to the police. Don't forget, most of the hotel's guests are members of the Scottish Heritage Appreciation Society, and I've been working with them since just after Christmas."

"I haven't forgotten anything." Dan tightened his hold on her and rested his cheek against the side of her head. She couldn't see his face, but she could hear the exasperation in his voice. "I remember what it's like to be afraid for you, Liss."

She lacked the energy to pull away from him, but she did muster up enough to object to his misgivings. "I'm not planning to do anything *dangerous*."

"And we already know how often *plans* can go wrong. A man had his throat slit tonight, Liss. I don't want you to be next. Look, I understand why you feel you should get involved. I do. Hell, I've got a vested interest in solving this crime myself, for the sake of Dad's hotel. But Sherri knows what she's doing. She has to be the one who calls the shots because she's the one who knows what we have to do to make sure that whoever did this gets convicted."

"But if there's a way we *can* help, we should. Right?"

Liss didn't know why she was being so stubborn about it, but she was relieved when Dan nodded. She felt the movement as a soft up-and-down brush of his cheek against her hair. Then he turned her in his arms. She was unsurprised to find their lips in perfect alignment for a kiss.

She wasn't being fair to Dan, Liss thought as she melted against him. Clearly, he needed to be distracted from his worries. She didn't particularly want to spend what was left of the night talking about murder, either.

"What am I going to do with you, Liss MacCrimmon?" Dan whispered when they came up for air.

Liss smiled. "I hope that's a rhetorical question."

# Chapter Nine

Liss woke up slowly, aware that she was lying on a sinfully soft mattress, snugly wrapped in something lightweight but warm. What did they call those feather-filled coverlets? Duvets? And instead of one of the comfy flannel nightgowns she tended to wear on cold winter nights, she appeared to have on a T-shirt with some sort of appliqué on the front.

Still groggy, she kept her eyes closed and tried to remember where she was. Not at home, that much was certain. If she were home, she'd have two cats in bed with her, hogging the space. And if it was after dawn, as her internal clock insisted it was, both felines would be clamoring for attention . . . and food.

A scent tickled her nose. Coffee. Liss's lips curved into a contented smile. But there was something else in the air, another smell that puzzled her. It didn't belong in a bedroom. Well, neither did coffee. Not ordinarily. But this second one was even more out of place. It was . . . smoke!

Abruptly, she sat up in bed. Her eyes popped open and she gave a little cry of alarm. Then the events of the previous night and early morning came back to her in a rush. Phil MacMillan had been murdered. A storm had trapped everyone at The Spruces. And she was in a gigantic four-poster bed in the swankiest suite the hotel had to offer, the one on the top floor of the central tower.

Directly opposite her was a stone fireplace. A cheery blaze burned in the hearth, heating not only the bedroom but also a kettle of water. Dan Ruskin rose from the chair he'd pulled close to the warmth.

"Morning, sleepyhead. Coffee?"

He gestured toward a small side table and the French press—almost full—cups, and coffee supplies it held. There was also a covered dish containing some kind of food. Liss's mouth watered.

"Yes, please."

Dan brought her a mug of coffee and a doughnut on a plate and sat gingerly on the side of the bed with one in each hand. He looked bemused when, instead of taking them from him, Liss seized his face between her hands and kissed him smack on the lips.

"You're pretty chipper on only three hours of sleep," he said.

"Quality time. But hold the breakfast, okay?"

Tossing back the covers on the other side of the bed so that she could climb out, she hopped down, instantly glad that the fire had already warmed the floorboards under her bare feet. The T-shirt she'd commandeered from the gift shop was oversized, so that the sleeves reached her elbows and the hem hit her at midthigh, but it wasn't designed for late January wear. She hastily collected her clothes—the pantsuit she'd worn during the day yesterday—and hurried into the bathroom to dress.

When she came out, Dan had opened the drapes and was standing at the window. She joined him there, taking the mug of coffee he'd been holding for her. She anticipated a spectacular view, but sunrise had brought little improvement in the weather. The snow had let up, but the wind had not. Icy flakes blew sideways past the glass, obscuring the landscape.

"Brrrr," Liss said, and took her first reviving hit of caffeine.

"I woke up at dawn and went down to take a look around. Dad was out there ahead of me. We walked out to inspect the tree that's blocking the driveway. It's worse than I anticipated. More than one of our big spruces came down in the storm. They're going to have to be cut up and cleared away before anyone can get out of the parking lot."

"Oh, Dan. I'm so sorry." It was more than just the inconvenience that saddened her. Those trees had given the hotel its name. They'd been standing for well over a century.

"Dad wants to take a crew out with chain saws as soon as we can work safely, but when that will be is anybody's guess." He sounded discouraged. "It's not even worth starting up the snowplow yet. Not with this gale still blowing."

Wild weather, Liss thought. And unpredictable. Suddenly, she lost her appetite.

"It will all work out," she said aloud, but she didn't entirely believe her own words.

"How?" Dan asked. "The power and phones haven't come back on. We've lost those trees. And we've got a dead guy on the premises."

"I take it you told Joe about the murder?"

"Yeah. He put up a good front, but he was thrown by the news. He's thinking it might be the final straw. I'm thinking he could be right. Who's going to want to stay in a hotel where there's been a murder?"

"The sooner the case is solved, the better for everyone," Liss said in bracing tones. She hastily finished the rest of the coffee in her mug. "Let's go down and see how Sherri's doing. Maybe she's changed her mind about wanting help."

Ten minutes later, Liss and Dan located Sherri in the hotel restaurant, which was not yet open, although it would be soon. Angeline and her staff were almost through setting up a breakfast buffet.

Sherri's appearance shocked Liss. While a few hours in bed had left Liss refreshed and raring to go, it was obvious that Sherri had not slept well, if at all. Her smile looked forced when she gestured for Liss and Dan to join her.

She'd chosen a table in the far corner of the restaurant. It was set off a bit from the others, but it was still close enough to benefit from the heat of the fire in the fireplace.

The restaurant, in an earlier incarnation of The Spruces, had been the main dining room. Shaped like a boot, it took up one end of the hotel's first floor, extending into both the front section and the east wing, where the kitchen was located. The ceiling rose two stories, just like the ceiling in the lobby, and ornate windows lined the outside walls.

Liss couldn't help but notice the audio recorder and notebook Sherri had next to her. "Are you going to interview everyone again?"

"Only a select few, but I do want to get Dan's statement, since he was the second person on the scene. It won't take long."

"No problem," Dan said, settling into a chair.

Five minutes later, Sherri's finger hovered over the STOP button on the recorder. "And you're sure you didn't touch anything else in the storage room?" she asked.

"Pretty sure," Dan said. "Trust me, I had no desire to stick around."

Sherri depressed the button. "Okay, then. Thanks.

What do you say we get some breakfast and talk about something else for a half hour or so?"

Dan was all for Sherri's suggestion. So was Pete, who had just joined them after being relieved of guard duty by Simon the bartender. Joe had arrived, too. He opened the door to let in the first of the hungry guests and some of the equally hungry staff.

"You're really not going to investigate?" Liss asked. "Or even speculate about suspects?"

"I won't ignore relevant information, but there's not a lot I can do. I can't even make a good guess at when he was killed, so there's no point in trying to pin down alibis."

"I bet we can figure it out. We know when Phil visited the gift shop and when he was found. And we certainly know who the prime suspects are."

"Food, Liss," Dan said, gesturing toward the breakfast buffet.

Her stomach growled. Loudly. "I guess I could do with bacon and eggs and another cup of coffee," she admitted.

Twenty minutes later, replete, she drained her cup and took a look at the people around her. There were no kilts in evidence, making it hard to distinguish between SHAS members and skiers.

In theory, aside from herself, Sherri, Pete, Dan, and Joe, no one but Sadie, Eunice, and Phineas knew anything about Phil's murder. And the killer. Oh, and Simon, since he was guarding the body. But she took note of the surreptitious glances slanted their way and heard a few nervous titters. It was obvious that someone had been talking, or at least hinting, at dire happenings during the night.

"Are you going to make an announcement?" she asked Sherri.

"No. It's better to keep things under wraps if we can."

"That horse may already have escaped from the barn," Liss warned her.

Right on cue, Will MacHenry sidled up to their table. He toyed nervously with the hem of his sweatshirt. "Has there been another robbery?" he asked.

"No," Sherri said.

"But something has happened," Will persisted.

Sherri hesitated, still trying to downplay the situation. "An unattended death," she admitted.

Liss didn't understand why was she being so cautious. The truth was bound to come out. Too many people already knew what had happened to Phil. Losing patience, and very curious to see Will's reaction when he heard the news, Liss spoke up. "Mr. MacMillan is dead, Will."

"Dead!"

Conversations stopped. People turned to look at them in consternation.

Will lowered his voice, but the damage was done. "But . . . but I just saw—" He broke off to look frantically around the restaurant. His gaze fell on a man sitting alone and he pointed. "Phineas is right over there. He—good Lord! You don't mean that Phil—?" Will swallowed convulsively. "He didn't die of natural causes, did he? You'd have said if he had."

"Mr. MacHenry," Sherri began.

"He was murdered, wasn't he?" Will's voice rose in pitch. Everyone in the restaurant heard him clearly.

"Shit," Sherri said under her breath.

Looking resigned, she tapped a fork against the side of a glass until everyone quieted down.

"Sorry," Liss mouthed at her.

"No, you're not."

"What's going on?" someone shouted.

Sherri took a deep breath. "I just want to set the record straight. There is no reason for any of you to be con-

cerned, but there has been an unattended death in the
hotel. Under the law, that means there has to be an investigation. Some of you may be asked a few questions by a
state police detective."

"Is this going to hold us up even longer?" a man demanded.

"I already have all your names and addresses. There
should be no problem about leaving the hotel. However,
as you already know, the storm has knocked out power
and all communications. Your cars are buried under the
snow and there are trees down, making it impossible at
present for any of us to leave."

Several loud groans greeted this announcement, although Liss was sure that all those present had already figured out that they weren't going anywhere today. The
skiers were frustrated by not being able to get to the
slopes. SHAS members groused that they had families and
jobs to get back to, but Liss didn't put much stock in that
last complaint. Very few businesses stayed open when the
weather was this bad.

"I don't see why I can't leave," Sadie LeBlanc complained, loud enough for everyone to hear. "I can walk
home as soon as the wind dies down." She flounced off toward the entrance to the restaurant.

"Good old Sadie," Liss murmured.

"The one person the state police will undoubtedly want
to talk to." Shaking her head, Sherri scraped back her
chair and stood. "I guess I'd better tell her she needs to
stick around. *That* will go over like a lead balloon!"

Sherri caught up with Sadie in the vestibule just outside
the restaurant. The encounter was just as acrimonious as
she'd anticipated. Sadie stormed away in a huff after
Sherri informed her that she was not to even think of leaving the hotel without checking with Sherri first.

"I'm sorry," Sherri called after her, "but none of us has any choice in the matter. Your cooperation is much appreciated," she added, sotto voce, as Sadie disappeared into the lobby.

A timid voice spoke at Sherri's elbow. "Can I talk to you, Officer Willett?"

Sherri gave a start, surprised to find Dilys Marcotte standing right next to her. She wondered if Dilys had overheard her go-round with Sadie. Probably. Dilys seemed to have a talent not only for moving silently but also for blending into the background.

"Do you know something about the, er, unattended death, Dilys?"

"It was a murder, wasn't it? That's what Sadie's been hinting."

Sherri tried not to grind her teeth in frustration. So much for keeping this whole thing under wraps to prevent a panic.

"Sadie said the dead guy was wearing a kilt. I just wondered who—"

"His name was Phil MacMillan," Sherri said, keeping her voice low even though no one else was in the vestibule at the moment. "Did you know him?"

Dilys looked startled.

Sherri's eyes narrowed. "*Did* you know him?"

"No! No, of course not. It's just that . . . well, once you put a name to a dead man, he isn't just a body anymore." Dilys frowned. "This is all very upsetting. I've got delicate sensibilities, you know. I don't want to stay where there's been a murder. And I've got an alibi. I went to bed just after midnight and slept like a log until morning. So, is it okay if I go home now? It isn't far. I can walk."

"Not in this weather."

Sherri sympathized with Dilys's desire to leave the hotel. Sherri wanted nothing more herself than to go home to her son. As things stood, she couldn't even talk to him on the phone to assure him that Mommy was all right.

"Just sit tight, Dilys. Okay? Besides, aren't you scheduled to work today?"

Dilys dithered a moment longer, mumbling something about her shift having started at seven. "Guess I'd better get cracking," she said, and scurried away so fast that, since she wasn't looking where she was going, she nearly ran smack into Phineas MacMillan, who was on his way out of the restaurant. Dilys took note of the irritable look on his face, gave a little squeak of alarm, and fled, head down, in the opposite direction.

MacMillan ignored her and stalked over to Sherri. "Officer Willett," he said, "I have been thinking things over and I have decided that Eunice may have been right. That being the case, I want police protection."

*Of course you do,* Sherri thought. *Anything to make my life more complicated!*

Aloud, she suggested that they go back into the restaurant to discuss the matter. Guests had begun to leave in groups of two and three and she anticipated that in a few minutes there would be no one left but the kitchen staff to take an interest in their conversation. They could be private at the table she'd chosen. And she could record whatever he had to say to her.

MacMillan did not apologize for his behavior during his last interview, but he seemed inclined to be polite, almost pleasant, this morning. He went so far as to pull out Sherri's chair for her before seating himself.

"I'd like to get a few questions out of the way before we discuss whether or not you are in danger," Sherri said. She turned her little recorder on. "Can you tell me when and where you last saw your brother?"

"It was in the lobby," he said. 'Shortly after the power went out."

"Did you see him leave the lobby?"

"No," Phineas said. "I was more interested in peace and quiet than warmth. I retreated to my own room and went to bed."

"And you didn't encounter your brother elsewhere in the hotel?"

"I didn't encounter anyone. I went straight up to the second floor. I did not pass Go. I did not collect two hundred dollars."

Sherri ignored the snarky Monopoly reference. So much for the polite Phineas MacMillan. "So, what you're saying is that no one can vouch for your whereabouts."

"I slept alone, if that's what you mean. Although I could have had company, had I wanted it."

Sherri narrowed her eyes. "Mr. MacMillan, if someone was with you, it would be wise to tell me—that person could provide you with an alibi for the time in question."

"A gentleman never tells."

She didn't buy that Phineas was a gentleman, not for a moment. Was he laughing at her? Or was he just stringing her along? Or could it be that some unlucky female *could* actually vouch for his whereabouts?

"Let's switch topics to your speech at the supper," she said, abandoning one line of questioning to take advantage of the segue he'd inadvertently offered her. "It sounded to me as if you *told*, or at least hinted, a great deal."

"I'm afraid I don't remember all of the details," Mac-Millan said.

"You don't recall what you said about your associates and their families?" Sherri didn't bother to hide her amazement.

"I was making it up as I went along, trying to get a rise out of people." Phineas shrugged. "I didn't expect them to be so sensitive about a little ribbing."

"So, you're telling me that there is no written copy of your speech?"

"That is correct."

"That's too bad, especially if it turns out that you, and not your brother, were the intended victim."

Sherri reached into a folder for the notes Liss had made for her. "You said in your speech that pretty young girls were a commodity, especially if they play the bagpipe."

MacMillan smirked.

"To whom were you referring?"

"No one in particular. If someone took offense, it can only be because they had a guilty conscience."

"You didn't mean Amanda Tandy?"

"I don't even know little Mandy."

Sherri once again consulted Liss's notes. "You said something that upset Harvey MacHenry and then, a little later, you told him he should relax because you were 'done' with him."

MacMillan's laugh was unpleasant. "Eighty-plus years old and the man still hasn't learned how to take a joke."

"What joke? Do you think you could remember that much for me, Mr. MacMillan?"

Sherri realized she'd just sounded as crotchety as the man sitting across from her. She was supposed to remain cool, calm, and professional, she reminded herself. She must not let this odious man bait her.

"I said I'd heard he was planning to pay a visit to Helmsdale Castle," Phineas admitted. "What? No spark of recognition? I thought everyone knew that old story."

"Why don't you tell it to me." Sherri resented his attitude, which grew more patronizing by the minute, but she managed to keep her voice level. He was the one who wanted police protection. Let him prove he needed it.

"Helmsdale Castle is where the eleventh Earl of Sutherland and his wife were poisoned back in the year of our

Lord fifteen hundred and sixty-seven," MacMillan said. "The Earl of Caithness was behind the murders, and since MacHenry's mother was descended from—"

"Wait a minute. Are you trying to tell me that he got all bent out of shape because of something that happened hundreds of years ago?"

Again MacMillan shrugged. "Scots have long memories, Officer Willett. Harvey MacHenry is the SHAS genealogist. He likes digging up the skeletons in everyone else's closets. I just reminded him of his."

Sherri felt a sudden kinship with Alice, she of Wonderland fame . . . just after she fell down the rabbit hole. Logic was obviously not a requirement to join the Scottish Heritage Appreciation Society. "Let's move on to Mr. Bruce, shall we? You came right out and accused him of cooking the books."

MacMillan affected innocence. "Eye of the beholder, my dear girl. Or ear. I did nothing more than tell an old chestnut of an accountant joke. Some people are just oversensitive."

"You made several of those people very angry, Mr. MacMillan. Maybe angry enough to kill. We know that one of them mistook your brother for you and roughed him up a bit before the confusion was sorted out. That probably happened shortly after you last saw Phil and shortly before he was murdered."

At last, something seemed to rattle Phineas MacMillan. "This is the first I've heard of such an incident. Who—?"

"That's not important at the moment. Suffice it to say that there was a scuffle near the hotel gift shop. No one was hurt, but the incident clearly shows that your brother could have been murdered a little later by someone else who made the same mistake. Your sister-in-law may have been right. It could very well be that *you* were the real target."

He flicked an imaginary speck of lint off his trousers, pretending nonchalance. "Eunice certainly seems convinced that I was the intended victim. Then again, she was rather upset at the time. She may have been grasping at straws."

"Well, let's hang on to that particular straw for just a little longer, shall we? I understand that you also insulted two or three more people at the Burns Night Supper." Liss hadn't been able to identify one of Phineas's targets. "Can you give me their names, please?"

"I don't remember."

"You . . . don't . . remember?" Sherri leaned back in her chair and fixed Phineas with a hard stare. The man was unbelievable, and the most astonishing thing was that he showed no visible grief over the death of his brother—and a twin brother, at that. And no desire for revenge. In fact, he seemed to have no interest in discovering the identity of the killer. It was positively unnatural.

"I've told you already, Officer," Phineas said. "I was making it up as I went along. But if I upset someone as much as all that, I'm sure it will come out when you question him. Or her," he added as an afterthought.

Not the person who killed Phil MacMillan, Sherri thought. That individual would be very careful not to say a word about it. Not that she planned to question anybody. That was the state police detective's job, and he wouldn't thank her for trying to do it for him.

"So, what about my police protection?"

"I have one more question, Mr. MacMillan. Let's assume for a moment that it was not a case of mistaken identity, that someone really intended to kill your brother. Can you think of anyone who would want to do that?"

Phineas frowned. "Well, that *is* a puzzle, isn't it?"

"You hinted last evening that Phil might have faked the theft of his own brooch."

For a moment, MacMillan looked startled. Then he laughed. "So I did. I'd forgotten. Another off-the-cuff remark, I'm afraid. What is the expression? Oh, yes—I was just yanking your chain, Officer. Phil had his faults, but he was honest enough."

"So, no enemies you can think of?"

"None."

"What about his wife? Would she stand to profit by his death?"

"I don't see how. He was all but broke when he died."

"All right, Mr. MacMillan. Thank you. As for your request for police protection, you'll have to talk to the state police about that when they get here. I'm afraid the only thing I have to offer is advice. I suggest that you don't go wandering off alone and that you lock your door at night."

# Chapter Ten

Liss MacCrimmon had overlooked one salient feature of the gift shop when she'd given Russ Tandy the grand tour. It was Dan who reminded her that the former card room had a working fireplace. After breakfast, they set to work clearing out the display racks that had been artfully arranged in the unused hearth. Liss left the items on the mantel where they were. Dan brought in an armload of wood and kindling and in short order they had a cheerful blaze going. Once the temperature in the shop began to rise, Liss opened for business.

A slow but steady stream of customers trickled in. Everyone seemed to prefer rooms with fireplaces—the lobby, the lounge, the restaurant, the library—and word soon spread that the gift shop could be added to that list. In the first hour, Liss sold out of shawls and mittens, all hand knitted by a local lady. It was a pity there were no sweaters, she thought, but the sweatshirts with MOOSE-TOOKALOOK, MAINE across the chest did well. So did Liss's Scottish merchandise.

There was a short lull in business. Then Harvey MacHenry wandered by and, seeing that the shop was open, ventured inside. "Miss MacCrimmon, isn't it?" he asked.

"Call me Liss, please, Mr. MacHenry."

"Then do me the honor of using my first name, as well," he said with a courtly little bow. "It's Harvey. Like the classic Jimmy Stewart movie."

Liss laughed. Harvey MacHenry seemed like a nice old guy. She'd heard he was a bit irrational on the subject of his clan's history, but in a group like SHAS, that wasn't out of the ordinary. A lot of Scots indulged in ancestor worship.

"I feel I should apologize for my son's behavior here last night," Harvey said. "He's not usually so short-tempered."

"No apologies necessary. I know he was upset by Mr. MacMillan's comments. And worried about how you'd taken them, too."

"Poor Will. He frets. Thinks I'm going to keel over if he doesn't look out for me all the time. But really, the whole thing was a tempest in a teapot. MacMillan touched on a sore spot and I got a little overexcited and called him a bastard. That's not my usual style, I assure you. Then I felt a few twinges, but I popped one of my little magic pills and all was well." He patted the pocket of his shirt. A small round pill container made a slight bulge in the flannel.

"I gather you have a heart condition." Liss had a vague memory of her grandfather taking nitroglycerine every time he felt a chest pain. It must have worked. He'd lived to be ninety-six. She frowned, wondering if she'd gotten the name right. Wasn't nitroglycerine an explosive?

"It's under control," Harvey said, pulling her attention back to him. "Nothing to worry about." He picked up a kilt pin decorated with a clan crest and examined the workmanship more closely.

Liss hesitated. She'd promised to stay out of the murder

investigation, but she couldn't see any harm in satisfying her curiosity. "So," she said casually, "I take it that Will told you that he mistook Phil for Phineas."

Harvey set the kilt pin down and picked up another. "He did. He's very embarrassed about that."

By his mistake, or because he'd lost his temper in front of witnesses? Liss had to wonder.

Harvey abandoned the pretense of shopping and smiled at her. "I suppose you're thinking it strange that he'd risk upsetting me. I can tell. As it happens, Will didn't have any choice. I overheard Russ Tandy telling someone else about the incident this morning, before we went in to breakfast. Tandy seemed to find it amusing."

Liss felt relief wash over her. Talking about last night's ruckus was not something Russ would do if he knew Phil was dead, especially if he'd killed him. She hadn't seriously thought Gordon's brother capable of committing such a heinous crime, but after what had happened outside the gift shop, she'd had to include Russ's name on the short list.

"Such a pity," Harvey said, "that Tandy's brother, Gordon, is out of state. If he'd been at home, I've no doubt he'd have attended the Burns Night Supper and been on the spot to take charge."

"This is his area," Liss agreed, "but I didn't know he was a member of SHAS."

"He's not, but he came to the supper last year as his brother's guest. I had hopes of recruiting him, especially . . . well, no matter."

But Liss's curiosity was well and truly piqued. "Especially?"

"I suppose it's no big secret." Harvey wandered over to a display of paperback novels and gave it a spin so he could see the titles on the back side. "Did you wonder, perhaps, why Phineas MacMillan's speech was so full of vituperation?"

"I did, yes."

"We held a board of directors meeting last week. We're trying to attract new members. Younger members." He sent a wry smile her way. "That effort is not helped by having a president who is unsociable and prone to sarcasm. We voted Phineas out of office, effective at the end of the month."

"And replaced him with Russ Tandy?"

Harvey nodded. "Phineas did not take our decision well." He gave a little "what can you do?" shrug and continued his exploration of the gift shop.

Liss followed close on his heels. "So, you're saying Phineas's speech was a form of retaliation? That he was getting back at the other board members and at Russ by making those nasty remarks?"

"I'm afraid so. Phineas has grown very petty these last few years." Shaking his head, sadness in his eyes, Harvey studied Liss's face. "You dislike him, and I can understand that, but he wasn't always such a misogynist. He had a bad experience seven or eight years ago. It changed him. Made it hard for him to trust anyone, not just women."

"You'll forgive me if I don't feel too sorry for him."

"Not even over the loss of his brother?"

Embarrassment left Liss momentarily speechless. Total lack of sympathy under those circumstances was not an attractive trait. She wondered if Sherri had been right to suggest that she read too many mystery novels. Had she lost her capacity to feel sorry for the victims of crimes? Her focus had been on the challenge of finding clues and solving the puzzle. She was treating a real-life murder like an intellectual game. Appalled, Liss tried to tell herself that it was important to seek justice, to catch killers and other criminals and put them away where they couldn't hurt anyone else. But did a normal person really *want* to meddle in murder?

Harvey MacHenry seemed unaware of the turmoil his question had caused. He continued to examine the books on the rack, finally selecting a title by Clive Cussler to purchase. "I suppose you think my son could have had something to do with Phil's death," he said as she rang up the sale, "but I can assure you that we were together from the moment he returned to the lobby until this morning. And I think it unlikely, even if I couldn't vouch for him, that he'd mistake one twin for the other twice in one night."

"I'm sure you're right," Liss said, still wrestling with her conscience. Had she truly become heartless? Uncaring?

"Then again, Phil might have been the intended victim all along, in which case the police will concentrate on the obvious suspects. You know—who inherits and all that." He chuckled. "I suppose you're going to say that I watch too much television, but it seems only logical to look first at the victim's spouse."

"You think Eunice killed her husband?" In spite of her dismay at the way she'd reacted to Phil's murder, Liss couldn't stop herself from asking.

"In fact, I do not. I happen to know that Phil's death will put Eunice in a difficult financial position. She had no motive that I can see to kill him. None at all."

"How do you know so much about Eunice MacMillan's situation?" Liss asked.

"Oh, it's no secret that Phil made some bad investments. Eunice complained about that to anyone who would listen. And, behind her back, there was speculation that they'd have to sell their house, if they could find a buyer, to make ends meet. Still, Phil was a pretty sharp operator. If he'd lived, I suspect he'd soon have made the money back on the stock market or in some other manner. Eunice, though, the only thing she knows about money is how to spend it. With her husband gone, I wouldn't be surprised if she had to file for bankruptcy."

That was pretty much what one of the four SHAS ladies had said, too, when they'd been gossiping in the gift shop. Liss thought about asking Harvey more questions, then told herself, sternly, to keep out of it. She handed him his purchase and told him to have a nice day.

Not five minutes later, Phineas MacMillan wandered in. He inspected everything in the shop, then bought a tartan handkerchief. "I understand my brother stopped by here last night," he said as Liss rang up the sale.

"Yes, he did."

"And that there was a bit of trouble." Phineas didn't sound particularly concerned.

Liss had no idea what to say in response to his comment, so she didn't say anything at all. She supposed that by now everyone in SHAS knew about the incident.

"Will MacHenry could have followed Phil," Phineas said.

"And killed him later?" Liss shook her head. "I don't think so. They went off in opposite directions and Will spent the rest of the night with his father. Besides, by then Will knew that Phil wasn't you."

"Did he?" Phineas asked. "Did he really?"

Sherri rubbed her tired eyes and refilled her coffee cup. She was still sitting at the same table in the restaurant. The idea was to be available if anyone wanted to talk to her. And it was as good a place as any to go over the notes she'd made and prepare her report for the state police.

She was a little surprised when Richardson Bruce plunked himself down in the chair opposite her. "Is it true?" he asked. "Did someone strangle Phil MacMillan?"

"Where did you hear that?" Sherri asked.

"Everyone's talking about it."

Why didn't that surprise her? Sherri wondered how many more methods of murder would be making the rounds before the day was over. "As I said earlier, there was an unattended death. And yes, the deceased was Philip MacMillan. That's all the information I'm prepared to share until the medical examiner can evaluate the situation."

"Huh," Richardson Bruce said. "Poor Phil."

"Were you close?" Sherri couldn't resist asking.

"Not really. I knew his brother better." He shook his head. "It's a damned shame it wasn't Phineas who got himself killed. At least he wouldn't have left a widow and a mountain of debts."

Sherri's eyes widened. She waited, letting the words hang in the air until Bruce realized what he'd said. He blinked several times. Then he lowered his head onto his hands.

"Oh, my God. Is that what you think happened? Someone killed Phil by mistake?"

"It's a distinct possibility, Mr. Bruce. And I understand that there was no love lost between you and Phineas MacMillan."

"The man impugned my character," he said in a defensive tone of voice. "He all but called me a crook."

"And you were angry, weren't you, Mr. Bruce? Tell me, can you account for your whereabouts after the supper?"

He glowered at her. "I stayed in the lobby with everyone else until I went to bed."

"And when was that?"

"I have no idea. I wasn't watching the time."

Most people hadn't been. Nor had they been paying much attention to what other people were doing. Sherri was glad she wasn't the one who'd have to take statements from all of them.

"I do remember seeing the MacMillan twins talking to each other at one point," Bruce offered, "but that's all. I was staying as far away from both of them as possible. I'd had my fill of Phineas for one night. I have to say, though," he added, "that no one who knew them both could talk to Phil for more than three seconds and still mistake him for Phineas."

"Why is that, Mr. Bruce?"

He shrugged. "Mannerisms. Attitude." He gave a bark of laugher totally lacking in amusement. "Phineas has an annoying habit of calling people 'kiddies,' no matter how old they are."

Sherri had already noticed that tendency, although she was glad Bruce had reminded her of it.

Bruce started to rise. Sherri told herself she was not supposed to be interviewing suspects and that she should let him go. But she couldn't seem to stop the question from popping out. "Any truth in Phineas's jibe about you cooking the books?"

"Of course not." His face flamed. His hands gripped convulsively the back of the chair he'd just left.

"But you are an accountant by profession, I suppose?"

"You suppose wrongly. I'm a college professor. Medieval studies."

"Oh." She hadn't expected that. "Well, then, perhaps you did make an accounting error?"

"It does not require a degree in accounting to add a few columns of figures. There are no mistakes in the organization's books."

He met her eyes, but only for a moment. Did that mean he was hiding something? She gave in to the temptation to try to find out what it was. She asked more questions about the finances he handled for SHAS. The more he sputtered and denied, the more certain she became that he must have done something worthy of a cover-up. She kept at him and, five minutes later, he exploded.

"I am not a crook!" he bellowed.

So, Sherri thought, Mr. Bruce had a temper. That was one count against him. But was it enough to move him to the top of the suspect list?

And what did it matter? This wasn't her case. It wasn't her job to find Phil's killer. But she was finding that hard to remember, especially when the average person, including Richardson Bruce, believed that she *was* the one in charge.

"Sit down, Mr. Bruce," she said with as much authority as she could muster. "Let's go through last night's events one more time."

Although customers continued to keep Liss busy, she had been dimly aware of the wind dropping. She could no longer hear it howling. The sun came out, pale and anemic but still bright enough to make the crust of ice atop the snow glisten.

During a lull in business, when no one else was in the gift shop, Liss went to the window. She could actually see the landscape. The scenery was pleasant to look at, if she ignored the broken branches scattered about. Snow covered the back lawn almost to the top of the pretty gazebo at its center and extended into the woods beyond. Liss shivered, glad she was safe and warm inside the hotel.

No sooner had that thought crossed her mind than she realized that someone did not share her sentiment. In fact, there appeared to be *three* someones who did not. As she watched, they started across the slick white surface on snowshoes.

Behind her, Liss heard the shop door open. Two sets of

footsteps sounded on the wooden floor. They came to a halt a foot or two short of where she stood. "Lunch is about to be served," Dan announced. "Tricia is here to spell you so you can come with me to the restaurant and get something to eat."

"Sorry," Liss said. "I can't leave right now. I'm busy watching a low-budget version of *Prison Break*." She pointed to the three escapees. "I guess they got tired of waiting around."

Dan closed the distance to the window and gave a snort of disbelief when he saw what she was looking at. "I'd like to go home, too, but that's not a very smart way to do it."

"I can't imagine they'll get very far. They don't even have poles."

"From the look of it, none of them have ever been on snowshoes before, either," Dan said.

Tricia joined them. "What are you watching?" She blinked several times. "Is that Rhonda?"

"And Sadie and Dilys," Liss confirmed.

"Better known as the three stooges," Dan muttered.

On softer snow, assisted by trekking poles and with a little practice, they might not have fared too badly. Unfortunately, the hard shell left by a combination of sleet and wind had made the surface slicker than an ice rink. The snow was also littered with numerous hazards to navigation.

Rhonda's path took her on a collision course with a fallen tree limb. She looked up, saw the obstacle, and tried to back up. When the cleats on the bottom of her snowshoes caught on an icy patch, she wound up flat on her back.

Liss pressed closer to the windowpane. "I hope she's not hurt!"

"Not if the way she's flapping around is any indication."

Arms and legs flailing, Rhonda looked like a fish out of water—a big fish in a bright yellow winter coat, orange muffler, and knit cap.

Dilys moved toward her friend, but she slipped before she'd gone two steps. Windmilling her arms failed to restore her footing. She went down on one knee, hard, and at the same time her other leg abruptly broke through the crust and disappeared up to midcalf. She wriggled around, trying to free herself, but she was stuck tight.

Sadie LeBlanc, dressed in a heavy winter coat and wearing earmuffs, shuffled forward a few steps, weaving as she struggled to keep her balance. When she saw what had happened to her two friends, she froze as if playing Statues, apparently too afraid to try moving in any direction.

"I suppose we'll have to go out and rescue them," Dan said with a decided lack of enthusiasm.

"Looks that way." Liss reached for her coat, which she'd worn until the fire in the hearth had warmed the shop sufficiently for her to be comfortable without it. She shrugged into it and added a woolly hat and a pair of mittens.

Dan's coat was in his father's office. When he veered off to get it, Liss continued on into the hotel restaurant. If Sherri was still there, she'd get a kick out of the latest development.

Richardson Bruce nearly knocked Liss off her feet as he stormed out. His hands were curled into tight fists at his sides. He sent a venomous look over his shoulder, nostrils flaring, as he left. If he'd been able to breathe fire, Sherri would have been incinerated on the spot.

"Wow," Liss said, grabbing her friend's uniform jacket

off the back of a chair and handing it to her. "What did you do to him?"

"He didn't like some of my questions. Seems fair. I didn't like some of his answers. Where am I going?" She obediently zipped up her jacket.

"You need to see for yourself."

Dan was waiting for them in the lobby. Guests looked up, curiosity in their gazes, as the three of them headed for a door that led out onto a verandah. Joe Ruskin, equally curious, came out from behind the check-in desk.

"What's going on?" he asked.

"You'll be able to see the floor show from the window," Dan told his father. Then, in a voice filled with concern, he added, "You doing okay, Dad?"

Liss glanced sharply at Joe. His face was pale, except for the deep shadows under his eyes.

"I'm holding up," Joe said. "Nothing wrong with me that a good night's sleep and a win at Megabucks won't cure. Is that my housekeeping staff?" They'd reached the window that overlooked the drama unfolding on the back lawn.

"I'm afraid so."

"Where on earth did they get snowshoes?" Sherri asked.

"From the sports shop," Joe said. "That's the room next to the health club. The plan was to open it as soon as I came up with enough money to pay someone to run it. I figured we could rent out equipment to guests who don't bring their own. I've been buying up skis, snowboards, snowshoes, and ice skates for the last year or so, mostly through *Uncle Henry's Swap and Sell*, and storing them."

Muttering under her breath, Sherri pushed open the door. A blast of cold air rushed in. When Sherri went out, Liss gritted her teeth and followed close on her friend's heels. Dan was right behind them.

Sadie had put another dozen yards between herself and

the hotel. The modern aluminum snowshoes she wore had little metal cleats that acted like crampons to grab the surface of the snow and improve traction. She glanced back over her shoulder when Sherri shouted her name, but didn't stop her slow forward progress.

"Crazy woman," Sherri muttered. "It's not like she's going to get anywhere."

At her present pace, it would be days before she reached the village . . . if she didn't freeze to death first. Liss had a sudden vivid image of the three women turned into ice sculptures.

"Help!" Rhonda hollered. "Someone help me." She flopped and squirmed, unable to right herself. She couldn't turn over. She couldn't sit up. The snowshoes strapped to her boots weren't all that much larger than her regular shoes, but they were awkward enough to keep throwing her off balance.

Dilys didn't say a word, but her situation had not improved. That had to be an uncomfortable position, Liss thought, with one leg bent and the other stuck tight.

"Any ideas?" Dan asked.

"Leave them there?" Sherri suggested. "No. Forget I said that. It's not an option."

Behind them, the door opened again and Joe appeared, warmly dressed and armed with three snow shovels. He handed them out and kept going. "I'll fire up the small snowblower we use on the sidewalks, but I won't be able to get too close to them with that. You three will have to do the last part by hand."

Sherri sighed and pulled an old fashioned walkie-talkie out of her jacket pocket, using it to contact Pete and tell him she'd be a while.

"Where did that come from?" Liss asked when Sherri signed off.

"Joe Ruskin. He remembered that they used walkie-talkies during the hotel renovation and dug them out of storage." She managed a grim smile. "I get the impression that the basement is a rabbit warren of storage rooms. I guess we should be grateful Sadie smokes. Otherwise it might have been days before anyone stumbled across the body."

Liss blinked at her friend as she connected the dots. By the time she had all the lines drawn and had figured out that Sadie must have hidden a pack of cigarettes in that particular storage room, the noise from Joe's snowblower made further discussion impossible.

It took the better part of an hour to extricate the two trapped women and persuade Sadie that there was no way she was going to make it all the way home on showshoes. All three were in sad shape by the time they shuffled back across the icy surface to the verandah and from there into the hotel lobby.

"I'd kill for a cigarette," Sadie muttered. "It's nothing short of unconstitutional, this prejudice against smokers."

"Ran out, did you?" Liss asked without sympathy.

"That girl confiscated my property," Sadie whined, pointing a bony finger at Sherri.

Sadie's stash in the storage room, Liss supposed, was now evidence, as well as being part of the off-limits crime scene. The door was being guarded in shifts by Pete, Simon, and one of the cooks who worked for Angeline Cloutier.

Rhonda was no more grateful to be in out of the cold than her friend. She slapped Sherri's hands away when the younger woman tried to help her unbuckle her snowshoes. When she'd removed them herself, she clasped them tightly to her flat chest and looked ready to bite anyone who tried to take them away from her.

Dilys Marcotte followed suit. She struck a defiant stance—chin stuck out, hands on hips, and legs squarely planted—and glared at Sherri. "It's against the law to keep us here against our will."

"That's right," Rhonda agreed. "We've got rights."

"So does Mr. Ruskin," Sherri reminded them, glancing toward the check-in desk where Joe was once again on duty. "Not only were you running out on him in the middle of your shift, but you stole three sets of snowshoes belonging to the hotel. If he decides to press charges, I'll gladly arrest all three of you."

Sadie's jaw dropped. Rhonda moaned aloud.

"What on earth were you thinking?" Sherri demanded. "I thought I made myself very clear to Sadie about the necessity of staying put until the state police can talk to her. Aside from that . . . are you crazy? There's a sheet of ice on top of that snow. What if you'd gotten halfway home and then fallen? Who'd have rescued you then?"

Rhonda and Dilys exchanged a sheepish look, but Sadie was revving up for another attack. "It's none of your business what we do, Sherri Willett. I had nothing to do with what happened to that man in the kilt and you know it. There's no earthly reason to keep me here, let alone hold Dilys and Rhonda prisoner."

"Except common sense!"

"And your jobs." Dan spoke quietly, in contrast to Sherri's rising voice. He was saying the exact same thing, but coming from him it seemed to carry more weight. "Furthermore," he continued, "you were caught red-handed in possession of valuable hotel property." He took hold of the snowshoes Rhonda still clutched and tugged, jerking them free of her grasp. "I'll take these back now, thank you."

Dilys hastily relinquished the pair she held. Tears pooled in her eyes. "We just borrowed them," she whimpered. "We aren't thieves."

To Liss, Dilys's agitation looked genuine. So did Sadie's, but for a completely different reason.

"I need a cigarette," Sadie said irritably. "You've got no right to keep my property from me."

Again, Dan stepped in. "You light up, you'll be applying for unemployment bright and early tomorrow morning. I mean it, Sadie. You agreed to abide by the rules when you were hired. The hotel doesn't have that many of them, but that one's set in stone. It's a state law." He softened his voice again. "I know it's hard to quit smoking, but taking off on foot just because you're out of cigarettes wasn't a very smart move. If we hadn't brought you back inside, all three of you might have ended up frozen to death in a snowbank. It might have been spring before anyone found your bodies."

Sadie's face crumpled. Her gaunt features suddenly looked even more haggard.

"Suck it up, Sadie," Sherri advised with a total lack of sympathy. "Think of this as your chance to kick the habit."

Liss stared at her friend in shock. The murder must be preying on Sherri's mind more than Liss realized. It wasn't like her to be cruel.

Sadie aimed a dirty look at Sherri. "Come on, girls," she said to her companions. "It's time for our lunch break. With all the extra rooms we've got to clean, we need to keep up our strength." She stomped off toward the restaurant with the other two in tow.

No one moved or spoke until all that remained of Sadie LeBlanc was a whiff of her overpowering perfume—the scent she used to hide the stale cigarette smell that clung to her clothes and hair. Then Sherri sank into the nearest chair, her head in her hands. Her shoulders shook and she made an odd, choking sound.

Alarmed, Liss knelt beside the chair. "Sherri? Are you *crying*?"

A snort answered her. Sherri lifted her head so that Liss could see her face.

"You're laughing!"

"Oh, God," Sherri gasped. "I must be more exhausted than I thought. I don't know why I think this whole escape attempt is so funny."

"Because it kinda is?" Liss suggested.

Then she started to laugh, too, just as helpless to stop herself as Sherri had been.

# Chapter Eleven

"Feel better now?" Dan slanted a wary look Liss's way as they joined the line at the buffet table.

"Shut up." Pink tinged her cheeks, partly from laughing so hard and partly from embarrassment that he'd witnessed the jag she and Sherri had been on.

"Better laughter than tears any day."

"I think so, too. And yes, I do feel better. Laughter is cathartic. Relieves tension."

"Comic relief?" he suggested.

"Whatever. The upshot is that I'm hungry enough to eat a horse." She picked up a plate and utensils.

"I think we can do a little better than that." His father had gone all out to keep his imprisoned guests happy.

As Angeline Cloutier, their talented chef, had pointed out, better to use up what they had on hand than let it go bad for lack of refrigeration. There was no immediate danger of that, but eventually the generator would run out of fuel. Dan thought again of the great ice storm more than a decade earlier, when most of the state had been without power for the best part of a week. A repeat of that wasn't beyond the realm of possibility, although he fully expected everyone would be able to leave the hotel within the next day or two. After lunch, he intended to ask for volunteers to help clear the driveway. He was sure the town had a crew out already, working on the road at the entrance to The Spruces. They'd—

"Earth to Dan!" From Liss's tone, it wasn't the first time she'd spoken to him.

"Sorry. I was just thinking. Man, I wish we had some way to communicate with the outside world. I sure would like to know what's going on in the rest of the state. Or even just in downtown Moosetookalook."

"I know what you mean," she agreed. "But in the meantime, you should eat. Everything looks delicious."

She'd already piled her plate high. Dan followed suit, but by the time they'd found a table, he realized that those few moments of laughter hadn't had a lasting effect. Liss was brooding. "What's wrong?" he asked.

She sighed. "Is it so awful to want to find out who killed Phil MacMillan? I mean, it's not my job. I know that. But people talk to me, and—" She broke off and sent a sheepish smile his way. "Am I whining? Please tell me I wasn't whining."

Dan couldn't help but smile back at her. "Maybe a little bit, but I understand. I do," he repeated when she gave him a skeptical look.

"I've helped the police before. You know I have."

"I know. And I know it's cost you." He reached out to caress her cheek. A month ago, there had been a hell of a bruise there, acquired when she'd insisted upon involving herself in the search for a murderer. She'd almost become a victim herself.

"Dan—"

"It would kill me if anything happened to you. You know that, right?"

"I know."

"Then eat your lunch and let the professionals do the investigating."

Liss sighed and dug in, but her acquiescence lasted barely five minutes. "Can we at least talk about what might have happened?" she asked when she'd consumed less than half of the food on her plate. "You and me, I mean."

It took a valiant effort on Dan's part not to groan aloud, but somehow he managed. He shrugged instead. "Who dunnit, you mean?"

"I already have a list of suspects."

Of course she did. Seeing Liss's eager expression, Dan knew she wouldn't be able to let the mystery go. The intellectual exercise of it was like a drug. Then he realized something else. It was to his advantage to know what she was thinking. If she shared her ideas with him, then he'd be right there beside her if she got into any trouble.

"Good idea," he said.

"Okay. First a question. Do you think the killer made a mistake? That it was Phineas he was after when he killed Phil?"

"Maybe you need two lists, one for each possibility." Dan avoided answering the question directly. He had no idea if the murderer had killed the wrong man or not and, although he hated it that someone was dead, he didn't really care who the intended victim had been, so long as it hadn't been someone close to him. He flagged down one of the waitstaff and asked for paper and a pen.

"Almost everyone believes it *was* a mistake," Liss said thoughtfully. "I suppose that's why no one's particularly frightened, even though we're all trapped here, including the killer. Everyone assumes that Phineas is the only one who might still be in danger."

"Word got around pretty quickly that it was Phil who was dead," Dan observed. He remembered that Sherri had been careful not to mention his name when she'd made her public announcement that morning. "And there must be some people here who don't have any idea who was murdered or why. The skiers. The staff."

"I expect just about everyone is in the loop by now," Liss said. "You know how gossip works."

"I guess we should be glad the rumors haven't sparked wholesale panic."

"No, but you notice people are sticking together. Groups of two or three. Safety in numbers, you know?"

A sheaf of hotel stationery and two pens embossed with THE SPRUCES arrived along with refills on their coffee. Liss surrendered her empty plate, shoved aside the condiments, and started to write. She quickly made two lists. The one labeled "Phil" listed Eunice first, then Phineas.

"Why would Phineas kill his own brother?" Dan asked, reading upside down.

"Same reason as Eunice might—nearest and dearest are always suspects."

"So you don't have any specific reason to think either one of them did Phil in?"

"Other than their obvious lack of grief? No."

"Was Phil better liked than his twin?"

"He was less sarcastic, but I wouldn't willingly have spent time with either of them. Or with Eunice, for that matter. I think . . . I think maybe they fed off each other's unpleasant natures."

"Charming." Dan watched while she completed the second list, the one for Phineas MacMillan. This one was longer: Will MacHenry, Richardson Bruce, Russ Tandy, Tory Tandy, Harvey MacHenry, Lara Brown, and then a question mark.

"The people he insulted at the Burns Night Supper," Liss explained when she saw his puzzled expression.

"Shouldn't Phineas's nearest and dearest be on that list?" Dan asked. "Phil, I mean."

Liss frowned. "I guess he should, although I'm not sure what his motive would be. And I don't think Phineas has ever been married," she added, brow furrowing as she tried to remember that detail. "I guess that rules out a wife with a yen to be a widow."

"Maybe Phineas has been secretly lusting after Eunice all these years and finally snapped," Dan suggested with a straight face.

Liss gave him an incredulous look before she realized he was joking. Then she added both Phil and Eunice to Phineas's list. "Anything's possible," she conceded, "and Harvey MacHenry did hint that Phineas had his heart broken by a former sweetheart. Still, I think he said it happened seven or eight years ago, and I'm pretty sure Phil and Eunice were married longer than that."

After lunch, when Dan left to see about clearing the driveway, Liss headed back to the gift shop. She had to pass through the lobby to get there. Her steps slowed as she recognized Richardson Bruce.

He sat slumped in one of a pair of wingback chairs drawn up to the hearth. From the expression on his face, he'd just lost his best friend. This impression was so strong, and so at odds with the Richardson Bruce Liss had last seen storming out of the restaurant, that she stopped and stared.

What did she know about him? Liss searched her memory. She had done a fair amount of research on SHAS and its leading lights when she'd first agreed to act as liaison. The Internet was a gold mine of information, although how much was accurate was always open to question. Richardson Bruce was around forty and by profession a college professor who lived in South Portland. She thought back to her earliest conversations with the man. She'd gathered that he was unmarried, but hadn't he mentioned a dog?

She slid into the empty chair by his side, nodding politely to him before she stretched her fingers out toward the fire. If he'd talk to her, she might learn something that would be useful to the police. After a few minutes of silence she drew back hands that were now toasty warm and settled herself deeper into the chair.

"How are you doing, Mr. Bruce?"

"Well enough, Ms. MacCrimmon." There was a suspicious look in his heavy-lidded hazel eyes.

"Is there anything you need? We're all in an unfortunate situation—being stuck here by the storm, I mean—but the management of The Spruces wants everyone to be as comfortable as possible."

His mouth quirked. "Yes. I've noticed. There's a group playing charades in the library. What next? Simon Says?"

"I wouldn't know about that, Mr. Bruce. I just wish we hadn't lost phone service. I'm concerned about my two cats, and a quick call to my next door neighbor right now would be a blessing." When he didn't rise to the bait, she gave up on subtlety. "Are you worried about your dog?"

"I left Great Harry with a friend. He's fine."

Great Harry? What kind of name was that for a dog? "What breed is he?"

"Bulldog."

Liss tried to picture one of the barrel-chested, perpetually slobbering canines trotting alongside the slightly built Richardson Bruce with his ruddy complexion, receding hairline, and impeccable wardrobe. Even dressed down, as he was now, everything he wore was starched and pressed, not just the Oxford cloth shirt, but the blue jeans, as well.

They sat in silence, basking in the warmth from the fire, as Liss racked her brain for a new topic of conversation. She was a washout at this Mata Hari stuff. Probably just as well. The last thing she wanted was for Bruce to think she was flirting with him.

"We have a Bruce family in Moosetookalook," she said at length. "Eddie Bruce, the snowplow driver. Any relation?"

"Not that I know of. Are you on duty, Ms. MacCrimmon?"

"Liss, please."

"My friends call me Rich. Frankly, though, I'm not sure you qualify as a friend." He took off his glasses, produced a pristine white handkerchief, and made a production of cleaning the lenses. When he was satisfied they were spotless, he replaced the glasses on his nose and the handkerchief in his pocket, then leaned back in the chair and steepled his fingers on his chest. He peered at her with an inquisitive look in his eyes. "So, are you representing the hotel right now, or are you assisting the police?"

Liss forced a laugh. "Officially, neither. But I was the liaison for your group. I feel responsible for making sure you folks have everything you need, however long the duration of your stay."

She didn't think "Rich" knew she and Sherri were close friends, but he'd probably seen them talking together. Whatever Sherri had asked him, her questions had not gone over well.

Bruce shifted his attention away from Liss to stare at the fire. The low murmur of voices and the crackle of the flames, along with the welcome warmth, created a soothing atmosphere. He didn't seem so agitated now. Nor did he any longer look morose. But neither did he appear to be jubilant because he thought he'd gotten away with something . . . like murder. In fact, at the moment, he seemed suspiciously calm for an individual Liss knew to be habitually short-tempered.

"May I ask you something?" she ventured.

"Depends on what it is."

"Nothing major. I just wondered why you were so set on having the haggis made from a traditional recipe."

He regarded her solemnly, as if weighing whether or not he wished to be bothered to answer, but after a few more moments of silence, he relented. "I teach history. My specialty is medieval Scotland. My seminar students are required to prepare a fourteenth-century feast. They rarely get everything right, but that doesn't stop me from pushing for accuracy. As for this supper . . ." His voice trailed off and he shrugged. "It doesn't seem so important now, but I came here with high hopes for the menu. It would have taken very little effort to achieve perfection."

Liss considered that. She couldn't see that the exact ingredients in the haggis mattered that much, but everyone had their little quirks. "Was this year's Burns Night different from those in past years?" she asked.

He laughed. "It certainly was!"

"I don't mean because Phil was murdered. I was talking about the insinuations in Phineas's speech. Have the speeches and toasts always been so mean-spirited?"

Bruce's good humor vanished. "Not at all. That damn Phineas—" He broke off, scowling. "I don't wish to discuss this further."

*Drat*, Liss thought. She'd provoked him and now he clammed up completely. He stared fixedly at the fire, ignoring her. She might have been a piece of furniture for all the attention he paid her. She gave up and went back to the gift shop.

Tricia was waiting on Glenora Huggons, but there were no other customers. There was, however, an overflowing wastepaper basket. Liss hefted the large plastic container and headed for the basement. Pete was on duty again in front of the storage room door. He had his chair tipped back against the wall and was reading a magazine by flashlight.

Liss juggled the lantern she was carrying so that she could give him a finger wave and proceeded on down the hallway to the alcove that held a Dumpster and several industrial-size recycling bins. She set the lantern on the floor, lifted the lid of the one marked "mixed paper," and emptied her contribution into it. She'd just picked up the lantern and was about to head back upstairs when a bit of tartan fabric sticking out from beneath the lid of the Dumpster caught her eye. Curious, she held her lantern higher and used her free hand to hoist the heavy metal cover.

The fabric was part of the cover on the bag of the bagpipe Grant and Erskine had been fighting over. Liss had forgotten that Dan's sister planned to toss it in the trash on her way to her car. That afternoon—had it only been *yesterday* afternoon?—seemed eons ago.

Liss was about close the lid again when something suddenly struck her as odd about the discarded instrument. She took another look. The bass drone, the longest of the three, was broken in two. The larger of the sections lay across the bag, pointing entirely the wrong way, and the ferrule—the knob through which sound emerged—appeared to be cracked.

Really good bagpipes had drones made of very hard wood, difficult to break. This was a cheap model, but it had been intact when Liss had last seen it, and she doubted that Mary had done anything to damage it. Then she noticed the dark specks on the ferrule. Liss swallowed convulsively. That looked like blood. She peered at it more closely. And hair. Gray hair. The same color as Phil MacMillan's. Very carefully, Liss closed the lid of the Dumpster.

"Pete?" She had to clear her throat and try again when his name came out as only the faintest whisper. "Pete! Could you come here, please?"

Something of her anxiety must have been in her voice. She heard Pete's chair crash back down onto all four legs. Two seconds later he was standing at her side. She lifted the lid again and played her light over the bag and drones.

Pete gave a low whistle when he spotted the same things she had. Then he used his walkie-talkie to call Sherri.

When she'd taken a half dozen pictures of the bagpipe, Sherri placed it carefully inside a large paper bag and gave it to Pete to put in one of the lockers reserved for hotel staff. She stripped off the disposable gloves she'd used to handle it and reached for her audio recorder. Then she handed it to Liss. "Talk to the machine. Give me the scoop on this bagpipe."

Liss obliged, finishing up her account of the conflict between Erskine and Grant where it had ended for her, with Mary Ruskin Winchester's promise to toss the bagpipe in the trash on her way home.

"So, she'd have put it in this Dumpster?"

"I imagine so. The staff parking lot is just outside the door at the end of this hallway."

"Okay." Sherri took the recorder back and clicked it off. "Thanks. You can go back to the gift shop now."

"But I don't understand," Liss said. "I thought you said Phil MacMillan was killed with a skean dhu."

"Liss, you need to go. This is police business." It could hardly be "by the book" under these conditions, but Sherri was determined to keep as close to the rules as she could.

Liss looked like she wanted to argue, but what could she say? She knew Sherri was right.

When she'd gone, Sherri turned back to the Dumpster. She supposed she should declare it off-limits, too, and cover it with crime scene tape, but that seemed a little absurd. It had already been contaminated. Besides, it wasn't the Dumpster that was important.

She wasn't going to go back into the storage room to look for a small wound on the back of Phil MacMillan's head, either, but she could visualize all too well what must have happened. She'd wondered how a man of his size could be taken by surprise. His throat had been slit from behind and there had been no indication that he'd put up a fight. Now she knew why. He'd been hit over the head first, with enough force to break that drone. He'd been unconscious, or close enough to it to make no difference.

They'd been here in the basement, Sherri thought, victim and killer. Had it been mere chance that the killer had found the discarded bagpipe and seen its potential as a weapon? Maybe. In any case, Phil had been hit on the head. Then he'd been dragged into the storage room. Or helped to stagger in on his own and then shoved so that he landed on his face. Either way, all the killer had to do then was close the door, pull the skean dhu out of its sheath, drop down onto Phil's back, and slit his throat. He probably hadn't even gotten blood on his clothes or skin.

The killer could just as easily have been a woman, Sherri reminded herself. It wouldn't have taken as much strength or size to kill an unconscious or dazed man as it would one who was fully alert.

Then what? Put the bagpipe back in the Dumpster. Then rejoin the festivities in the lobby, behaving as if nothing out of the ordinary had occurred. Cold-blooded, Sherri thought. Or a sociopath.

An involuntary shudder ran through her.

Liss sat in the lobby feeling miffed. She had no idea what Sherri was thinking. Did she suspect Grant or Erskine, who'd done battle with that bagpipe? Maybe one of them had been the victim of the bad nose job Phineas referred to in his speech. A little embarrassment didn't seem like much of a motive for murder, but she'd heard of stranger things.

Maybe, Liss thought, she should ask around and find out just who it had been that Phineas meant. Richardson Bruce had left the lobby, but there were plenty of other people around. Two of the skiers were engaged in a lively debate over the best wax to use. Harvey MacHenry and his son were playing bridge with Elspeth and Maeve, two of the women who'd stopped in at the gift shop before the Burns Night Supper. Maeve had come back a second time to buy the floor-length tartan skirt she was currently wearing, one made of warm, thick wool.

In another of the pools of privacy created by pillars and high-backed chairs, Russ Tandy and his wife were talking quietly together as they sipped coffee. Or possibly hot cocoa. Angeline Cloutier had provided a continuous supply of both beverages since early morning. Russ could probably answer her question, Liss decided, but before she could join the Tandys and ask, a cry of alarm jerked her attention back to the bridge game.

Will MacHenry was on his feet, a look of anguish on his long, thin face. His father, Harvey, lay sprawled across the card table. Elspeth had her fingers pressed to his neck, feeling for a pulse. Unable to find one, she leaned closer, checking for signs of life.

"It's his heart," Will said in a choked voice.

"He's not breathing," Elspeth whispered.

Joe Ruskin came out from behind the check-in desk in a rush. He tossed a walkie-talkie to Liss as he ran toward the fallen man. "You. Call Dan. Tell him to bring the defibrillator."

As Joe started CPR, Liss fiddled with the unfamiliar

gadget, thinking that it was a good thing all she had to do was press TALK.

Dan had been outside. He still wore one of the light brown, one-piece snowsuits that were so ubiquitous in Maine at this time of year as he put the life-saving equipment to work. The hotel was prepared for medical emergencies, but no one had expected they'd need to deal with one for more than the fifteen or twenty minutes it normally took an ambulance to arrive. Everything was different now. They had no way to transport a patient to the hospital in Fallstown.

A few minutes after Joe and Dan managed to get Harvey breathing again, Sherri appeared. She took in the situation at a glance and reached for the portable police radio attached to her utility belt. When she turned it on it squawked, but after that there was nothing but static.

"Still dead," she muttered, glaring at the offending handheld. "If I could raise somebody, I could call for a helicopter to take Harvey to the hospital."

The tower had been damaged by the storm, Liss remembered. But surely fixing it was top priority. The repair crew must be having trouble getting through.

"He's holding his own," Dan reported, "but he needs to be seen by a doctor."

There were more than fifty people in the hotel, but not one of them was an M.D. or a nurse. They didn't even have a dentist or an chiropractor in the mix. Liss stared anxiously at the couch where Harvey now lay. He was breathing again, but he didn't look good. His son's face was a mask of agonized concern.

"Moosetookalook Family Practice is only a few miles from here," she said. "Dr. Sharon lives right next door to the clinic."

"It might as well be in the next county," Dan said. "We

can't use any of the cars. We've barely made a start on digging out, and the trees blocking the drive will take hours
to clear away. I don't even want to make a guess at how
bad things are on the other side."

"The clinic is less than a mile away as the crow flies."
Liss visualized the route, working the details out in her
mind. "We could cut through the woods."

"Do you have a snowmobile?" Sherri asked.

Dan shook his head.

"There's another way," Liss said.

"On foot?" Sherri gave her an incredulous look. "That's
crazy. We—"

Liss talked right over her friend's objections. "We have
snowshoes. Remember? And it's warmed up some in the
last couple of hours. The surface isn't glare ice anymore.
Traveling that way won't be fast, but someone from here
should be able to reach the clinic before dark. And Dr.
Sharon *does* have a snowmobile. Once he knows what the
situation is, he can ride his machine straight back to the
hotel."

For a moment no one said anything. Then Dan nodded.
"It could work, but I guarantee you it's not going to be
any walk in the park."

# Chapter Twelve

Dan checked their gear one last time. He wasn't happy about taking Liss with him to fetch the doctor, but she refused to let him go alone. She argued, rightly, that there were too many things that could go wrong on even a short trek cross-country. If they walked in a straight line between the hotel and the clinic, they wouldn't pass close to any houses. The terrain wasn't especially rough, but there were a lot of trees and branches down. It wouldn't take much to create a serious problem for a lone traveler.

Experimentally lifting first one foot and then the other, Liss seemed satisfied that the bindings attaching the light-weight aluminum snowshoes to her boots were secure. She'd already done a full ten minutes of warm-up exercises, and insisted that he stretch, too. That wasn't just the exprofessional dancer talking. They both knew the toll walking to town would take on them. They wouldn't end up lame, with painful feet and ankles, the way folks used to when snowshoes were huge, heavy, wooden affairs, but they could count on sore calf muscles for the next few days.

"We'd best get a move on," Liss said. "It isn't that long till dark and it's going to take us a while to get there."

Dan shouldered the backpack he'd filled with emergency supplies, especially bottled water, and gestured for her to go ahead of him.

To start, they followed the same route the three housekeepers had used on their aborted escape, moving out across the verandah and down a slight incline to the snow-covered back lawn. In the hours since they'd rescued Sadie, Rhonda, and Dilys, the sun had been out, softening the layer of ice that had once coated everything. Just at that moment, the surface of the snow was relatively easy to pass over on snowshoes. Unfortunately, that same sun was sinking fast in the western sky. Everything would start to refreeze as soon as it set.

They'd already decided to take turns breaking trail. It wasn't difficult, but it could be exhausting. Ahead of him, Dan watched Liss "stamp" the trail simply by pausing briefly after each step. This smoothed and compacted the snow, making it easier for the second person in line to walk on. She kept the lead until they entered the woods on the far side of the blocked driveway.

"Rest," he called.

She executed a turn by walking in a small semicircle and shifted both trekking poles to one hand in time to catch the small bottle of water he tossed her way. When she'd taken a long swallow and transferred the half-empty bottle to the pocket of her jacket, she paused to look back at the hotel. "Wow."

A glance over his shoulder showed Dan what she meant. Bathed in late-day sunlight, white walls and windows gleaming, The Spruces had a magical quality. Like a dream, he thought, not without irony. He stared for a moment longer, then turned his back on the vision and took the lead.

The Spruces sat on a ridge overlooking Moose-tookalook. The road twisted and turned its way down the side of a steep hill. Walking overland between the hotel and the town's center cut the total distance, but it wasn't a speedy way to travel. Even crossing level ground was slow going, and most of the terrain they had to cover was anything but flat. The occasional crack as an ice-laden branch broke off under the weight was a stark reminder that danger lurked above them as well as beneath their feet.

Dan had done a fair amount of walking on snowshoes as a kid—it was a much cheaper sport than skiing or snowboarding. It didn't take him long to get back in the rhythm. He rolled his feet slightly, moving with an exaggerated stride that was almost, but not quite, a run. After the first couple of times he kicked himself in the ankle, he remembered to lift each shoe slightly up and out and to keep his feet a little farther apart than they were when he had on regular shoes.

"I'm going to be bowlegged by the time we get to the clinic," Liss complained when they'd been walking that way for another twenty minutes. "And an icicle. A bowlegged icicle."

"Rest."

"There is some urgency about fetching the doctor," she reminded him.

"Arriving in such bad shape that he has to deal with two more emergency cases won't help anyone." Harvey MacHenry had regained consciousness just before they'd left. He'd looked like hell, but at least he'd been breathing and talking sense. Dan shared Liss's concern, but he wasn't about to risk her life to save MacHenry's.

Liss leaned on her poles, contemplating the rise of land ahead. It wasn't all that steep, but it was going to take extra effort to ascend. Dan considered the climb. He could go up first, making "kick steps" by kicking the toes of his snowshoes into the snow to make a rough staircase for Liss. Or they could both walk uphill sideways, the way skiers did. After a brief break, more water, and a little discussion, they elected to do the latter. They were both panting by the time they reached the top of the rise, but at least now their goal was in sight.

Lights showed here and there in the village. "Oil lamps and battery-powered lanterns," Dan said. "Not electricity."

Liss shot a quick, worried look at the horizon. The sun had very nearly set. A pink glow suffused both sky and land. "Good thing the doctor has a snowmobile. He'll need his headlights to find his way to the hotel."

"Good thing we planned to stay in town overnight and trek back tomorrow," Dan said.

To his mind, that was the best part of this expedition. Tonight, he could sleep in his own bed. Or, better yet, in Liss's. Their night in the tower suite hadn't been quite all he'd hoped for, but neither had she kicked him out. What was that old saw about adversity bringing people together?

"Time's a-wasting," Liss said, and started the descent.

She used a standard snowshoeing technique for going downhill called "step-sliding," running with exaggerated steps, but she was already tired and she wasn't used to this kind of exercise. Too impatient to be cautious, she slipped once or twice on the snow as she went.

"Slow down!" Dan shouted, and plunged after her.

Liss was halfway down the slope when one of her snowshoes caught on something hidden beneath the snow. Dan heard her give a yelp of surprise. Then she was falling.

He could do nothing but watch helplessly, his heart in his throat, as she landed on her backside with both feet up in the air. Her poles went flying. Then gravity took over. The incline was just steep enough that her efforts to get to her feet backfired. The struggle to rise sent her tumbling down again, and this time she kept going.

Liss rolled the rest of the way down the hill and landed

in an ignominious heap at the bottom. Once again, Dan heard her cry out. Then she lay ominously still.

His gaze glued to the silent, crumpled form, Dan found he couldn't get his breath. His pulse pounded in his ears. Worse, for an endless moment, he was unable to make himself move.

The thoughts racing through his mind were so terrifying that they paralyzed him. Had Liss hit her head? Why hadn't he insisted that she wear a helmet? Suddenly he was re-membering every case he'd ever heard about where some-one died from a simple fall on a bunny slope.

No. Not Liss. Nothing could happen to Liss. But why wasn't she moving?

Dazed and slightly dizzy, Liss watched Dan follow the trail she'd made as she tumbled down the slope. He used the fastest technique he knew—glissading. He sat down and slid on his butt until he fetched up right next to her.

"Ow," she said when he bent over her. Then she smiled to reassure him that she wasn't really hurt, just shaken up.

"Thank God you're alive," he whispered, and then, "Did you break anything when you landed? Did you hit your head?"

"I don't think so." Tentatively, she flexed assorted body parts.

Everything seemed intact. She was stiff and sore every-where, but that had been the case *before* she fell. She stretched, then lay still, staring up at the sky. It was the deep blue of twilight. Pretty soon it would be full dark. She lifted both arms toward Dan.

"Help me up. We have to get moving." Once on her feet, she looked around in mild confusion. "What hap-pened to my poles?"

Dan pointed back up the hill.

"Oh." Then she brightened. "Hey, look—we're on level

ground again. And that's Dr. Sharon's clinic just over there." The one-story brick building was no more than a quarter of a mile distant. "The worst is over."

Suddenly, Liss felt revitalized. Nothing like a jolt of adrenaline to perk things up. In short order, she was knocking on the doctor's door and explaining their sudden appearance to the startled physician.

"I'd take it as a personal favor if you'd check Liss over before you leave," Dan said when Dr. Sharon had agreed to take his snowmobile and go to the hotel. Liss made a face. Dan had been watching her like a hawk ever since her fall, alert for any sign of disorientation or wooziness.

"Head hurt?" the doctor asked. He was tall and lanky, with vivid blue eyes and a cheerful manner. A shock of prematurely white hair stood out around his head, as if he had a habit of raking his fingers through it.

"No headache," Liss assured him. "No dizziness. No blurred vision."

"Excellent." Dr. Sharon checked her pupils and ran his fingers over her head to look for bumps and scrapes, then pronounced her undamaged.

"I told you I was okay," she grumbled when the doctor had set off for The Spruces. "Stop fussing."

Once the roar of Dr. Sharon's snowmobile faded away, they set out to walk from the clinic to the village square, where both of them had houses and Liss had her business. The town plow had been hard at work clearing streets. They were able to make their way straight down Elm without snowshoes. Dan carried both pairs, together with his poles.

"I know you think I made too much of your fall," Dan said, "but here's the thing, Liss. For a minute there, I thought I'd lost you. Do you have any idea how that made me feel?"

Liss turned and tried to see Dan's expression. It was already too dark to make out any details. The moonlight was sufficient to show them the way home, but not much more.

"I didn't roll down that slope on purpose, but I'm sorry I gave you a scare."

They kept walking until they reached the square. Dan dropped the snowshoes and his trekking poles and caught one of Liss's gloved hands in both of his to bring her closer to him. "There's something I need to say to you. Something we need to get straight between us. It seems stupid to wait any longer to let you know what's on my mind."

She squinted up at him. She still couldn't see his face, but all of a sudden he sounded awfully serious. Her heart rate sped up and when she spoke her voice was breathy. "Okay."

"I want to marry you."

At her jerk of surprise, he tightened his grip.

"I'm not asking you yet. I just want you to think about the idea."

Suddenly Liss did feel dizzy and disoriented. "I . . . uh—"

"My timing is lousy. I know that. But I just—"

"Dan? Liss? Is that you?" Jeff Thibodeau, Moosetookalook's police chief, loomed up out of the shadows, lumbering toward them from the direction of the municipal building.

Dan released Liss's hand and went to meet Jeff halfway. Maybe it was just as well they'd been interrupted, Liss thought. She'd didn't have the slightest idea what to say in response to such a declaration. She wasn't sure what she'd have said if he'd actually proposed to her, either.

She followed Dan, but it took an effort to shift her focus away from him and onto Jeff. At least a full minute passed before she understood what Jeff had just said. He'd asked if Dr. Sharon had left yet for The Spruces.

"How on earth did you know we'd just come from the

clinic?" Dan asked after he'd assured Jeff that the doctor was on his way.

"We got the police radio back about ten minutes ago. Still no phone service, though. Anyway, Sherri filled me in on what's been going on up to the hotel. You folks sure have had a busy time of it." He sounded ever so slightly envious.

"Mr. MacHenry—is he—?"

"Still holding his own. I've asked for a LifeFlight helicopter to be dispatched. It should be on its way shortly, but Dr. Sharon will get there first. You two did good. Even if we'd known when the tower would be fixed, in a case like this, every minute counts."

Relief made Liss's knees weak. She leaned against Dan for support as Jeff went on talking. She caught only the highlights. Roads were blocked all over the place. The whole state had been hit hard by the storm. The hospital in Fallstown had power again, but phones and power were still out in most of Carrabassett County. Nobody knew how long it would be before those services were restored, especially with the weather so iffy.

"You covered a lot of ground in ten minutes of radio time," Dan said.

Jeff chuckled. "Wish I could take credit for being a miracle worker, but the CB radios never went out. I've been using the one in my truck to keep tabs on storm damage and weather reports."

"Note to self," Dan said. "Buy citizens band radio for the hotel. Are cell phones working?"

"Not so you'd notice." Jeff shrugged. Cell phone service was erratic in the mountains of Western Maine in the best of times. "The biggest problem right now is that there's another storm on the way. The town plow's working overtime as it is. I guess you saw that. But with this much snow it's going to take a while to clear the secondary roads. There are holdups with the roads the state DOT plows, too. Trees and power lines down and such. Add more snow and who knows how long it will take to dig ourselves out."

"What about Spruce Avenue?" Dan asked, naming the long, twisting two-lane road that led up to the hotel's equally long, twisting driveway.

"The wind really did a number on that. At least two big spruces are down. It'll be tomorrow before any vehicular traffic can get through. Probably not until late in the day."

"Same with the drive up to the hotel," Dan said. "We got started with the plow on Dad's pickup truck and with the chain saws this afternoon, but we didn't get very far."

Jeff slapped Dan on the back by way of commiseration. "We'll get through this. Everyone's pulling together. Come on over to the municipal building. It's cold standing around out here talking." He stamped his feet for emphasis, trying to keep them warm. "We've set up as a shelter. The generator's keeping everyone comfy. We've got hot coffee, too."

"Is my aunt there?" Liss asked. Margaret Boyd lived alone in the apartment above Moosetookalook Scottish Emporium and did not have a woodstove, a fireplace, or a generator.

"Sure is," Jeff said, "along with almost everybody else from around the square."

Liss looked with real longing at the single brick building in a sea of white clapboard, but now that she'd come this far, what she really wanted was to go home. "I need to check on my cats."

Jeff chuckled. "That Lumpkin's got enough body fat to keep him warm for a week. I bet he could go without food that long, too."

"Well, he shouldn't have to!" Liss knew she sounded a trifle defensive, but she couldn't help it. Just because Lumpkin had taken a bite out of Jeff's ankle once was no reason to say rude things about him. Lumpkin nipped *everyone's* ankles. Or at least he *had* been prone to do so. Liss thought she'd finally weaned him of that particular bad habit.

"You going back out to the hotel in the morning?" Jeff asked.

"Plan to," Dan answered for both of them. "I want to check out Spruce Avenue from this end. Then we'll use snowshoes the rest of the way." He stooped to pick up both sets and the remaining pair of poles.

"Be careful where you step," Jeff warned. "The temperature's dropped to right around freezing." Then he waved and headed back to the municipal building.

Liss heeded his advice and stayed alert for icy patches, otherwise known as black ice. They didn't have far to go, just down one side of the square and halfway along the next.

Now that Jeff was no longer present to act as a buffer, Liss suddenly felt self-conscious. Dan wanted to marry her but he didn't want to propose yet? Well, that was just dandy. How long was she supposed to wait for an actual proposal?

He seemed equally uncomfortable, and didn't broach the subject again. In fact, he didn't say anything.

When the silence started to become oppressive, Liss said the first thing that came into her head. "Do you suppose we could have gotten help more quickly if we'd walked out along the driveway and picked up the road?"

"I doubt it. I've seen the downed spruces from the hotel side. It would have been slow going just to get around them. If more trees are blocking Spruce Avenue, the way Jeff says, we'd have had to make even more detours."

"I doubt conditions will be much better tomorrow." Liss gave herself a mental kick. They were talking about the weather! Could they be any more trite?

"Probably not." Apparently oblivious to any undercurrents, Dan added, "I think I'll walk over to my brother's house after I take you back to the shelter. If Sam and I can round up a couple of chain saws, we can start clearing from this end at first light."

"I'm not going to the shelter."

That got his attention. "Liss—"

"I have wood. I have a fireplace in my living room. I can sleep on the sofa and be toasty warm. Heck, I even have a camp stove that runs on propane, so I can make myself coffee in the morning. I'll be fine."

"Are you sure you want to be alone?"

"I'll *welcome* being alone."

She winced. That hadn't come out right.

"Of course, I *won't* be alone," she blurted out. "Not with Lumpkin and the kitten around."

And that had sounded inane. Liss gave herself a mental head slap. Obviously, the mere mention of marriage had scrambled her brains.

"What are you really up to?" Dan asked.

"Nothing." No way was she going to admit that she wanted a block of time with no distractions so that she could think about what he'd said to her just before Jeff showed up.

"Try again."

*Casual,* she warned herself. *Keep it casual. Go with an answer he'll accept.* It wasn't hard to come up with one. She forced a laugh. "Okay. You caught me out. I want to take a look at the notes I made on the Scottish Heritage Appreciation Society. Three weeks ago, when I first agreed to help out with the Burns Night Supper, I did some research to familiarize myself with the organization. There might be something in that file that will help the police."

As she'd anticipated, Dan believed her. He didn't particularly like her explanation, but he bought it.

They stopped at her sidewalk, which hadn't been shoveled. Wading through deep snow to reach the porch kept Dan fully occupied and avoided any unfortunate comments he might have meant to make about her meddling in a criminal investigation.

Liss was out of breath by the time she turned her key in the lock. As she'd expected, it was pitch dark inside the house, but it felt at least twenty degrees warmer than it did outside. Dan fumbled in his pack for the flashlight he'd stashed there. He clicked it on and they followed the beam into Liss's living room.

"Candles, candlesticks, and matches are in the drawer under the television," Liss said, and Dan swung the light that way.

In passing, it picked out two pairs of green eyes. They were a welcome, if eerie, sight.

"Mama's home, babies," Liss crooned.

Dan made a sound of mild disgust as she knelt down and made kissing noises to try to tempt Lumpkin and the kitten to come to her. Neither did. From the feline point of view, she'd abandoned them, leaving them to starve to death in an unheated house.

When Dan found the candles and lit the first wax taper, Liss straightened. "You have food and kibble in your feeders," she reminded the two ungrateful cats. "And it isn't my fault that the power went out."

More candles flared to life, filling the room with a soft glow. "You know," Dan said, "candles aren't the best choice for light, especially with cats in the house. And if you're going to have a fire, you'll have to stay awake to keep an eye on it, which kind of makes it hard to get a good night's rest. Maybe you should reconsider going to the shelter."

"You have no romance in your soul," Liss complained.

She could have kicked herself. What a thing to say to a man who'd just—almost—proposed to her! But it was too late to take back the words, and apologizing would just make the situation more awkward. She waited a moment, thinking Dan might say something, but he kept mum.

Okay, she thought. If he was going to ignore her comment, then so would she. Right. They'd been talking about candles. The danger of open flames.

"I'll only use the candles when I'm right here and awake and can keep an eye on things," she promised. "I have a lantern and plenty of flashlights and oodles of spare batteries." In winter, it only made sense to keep such emergency gear on hand. Power outages, if not the rest of their current troubles, were a fact of life in rural Maine. "And you don't need to worry about the fireplace. I had it inspected when I had the chimney cleaned a couple of months ago. And I have a fire screen stored in the closet."

True, it would be the first time she'd actually had a fire in the hearth, but it wasn't as if she'd never heated with wood before. Even if she hadn't learned fire safety as a kid, she'd had last night and today at the hotel as a refresher course.

"If you're sure . . . "

"I'll be fine." She walked over to the thermostat on the wall and peered at the temperature by the light of the bright red Christmas candle she held on one hand. "Hey, it's all of fifty degrees in here. Practically a heat wave."

But when she shivered, Dan noticed. "You'd better go change out of those damp clothes."

"I plan to. Just as soon as you leave."

She also intended to take a quick sponge bath. She should have enough water in her emergency store, and it would feel very good to be clean and to put on fresh clothing. For the trek through the woods, she'd worn her pantsuit, together with a set of long johns she'd borrowed from one of the skiers. She'd found a pair of gaiters to wear with the snowshoes, to keep the snow out of her boots. They had kept her feet dry, but the rest of her clothing was decidedly damp. The distinctive smell of wet wool hung in the air. Fortunately, the long joins were made of some space-age material that kept moisture away from bare skin, because time and again she'd snagged her pant legs on branches. She'd accumulated a multitude of small rips in the fabric, but the underwear had done a good job of holding both sweat and snow at bay and had kept the cold from penetrating, too.

Still Dan hesitated to leave.

A yawn snuck up on Liss, so huge that her jaw cracked. She wasn't surprised. She hadn't had more than a couple of hours of sleep the night before. "Go, Dan. I'll be fine. I'll start a fire, find those notes, and curl up on the couch with the cats."

Who knew? There might even be something useful in the clippings and printouts. She'd collected a great deal of information about SHAS when she was preparing for her first meeting with representatives of the group. She'd just skimmed most of it back then. It would be worth her time to take another, closer look. Now that she'd gotten to know some of the members, anything significant ought to leap out at her.

Dan put his hands on her shoulders, instantly banishing all thought of SHAS. "Promise you'll dig out that fire screen *before* you start the fire?"

"I promise."

"And you'll snuff the candles? Once you curl up on that sofa, you'll be asleep inside of ten minutes."

"Yes! I promise! No candles. Fire screen. Now go!"

"In a minute." Slowly, he lowered his mouth to hers, giving her one very good reason to consider his almost-proposal in a positive light.

By the time they came up for air, Liss was clinging to him. Embarrassed, she stepped back. "Shoo. Scram. No fair dangling temptation in front of someone who's over-tired and stressed."

His face was shadowed in the candlelit room, but she thought his expression looked just a wee bit smug. "What I said earlier?" he whispered. "Think about it, okay?"

"Okay," she promised.

How could she not?

# Chapter Thirteen

When the helicopter had lifted off safely, Sherri turned to Pete and pantomimed wiping sweat off her brow. She had been spared dealing with a second death. There was every reason to be optimistic that Harvey MacHenry would make a full recovery.

Sherri glanced at her watch. It was only eight, but with the power still out she had a feeling that most people would opt for an early night. She hoped so. She was pretty close to collapsing from exhaustion herself.

On the other hand, it might be better if everyone partied all night and slept in tomorrow morning. The hotel's reluctant guests were getting antsy. She expected a stampede the minute they could get their cars out of the parking lot. The staff would decamp, too, with Sadie, Rhonda, and Dilys leading the pack.

Without much expectation of getting a signal, she fished out her cell phone. She stared at the tiny screen in surprise and pleasure. "Well, hallelujah!"

In a matter of minutes she was talking to her six-year-old son. His replies were scratchy and hard to hear, but sufficient to reassure her that he was okay. Even better was the news that where he was, halfway between Moosetookalook and Fallstown, the power had been restored. So had cable. Adam wanted to watch television. Sherri reminded him that it was already past his bedtime, but in the end she relented. He'd drift off in front of the screen and her mother would carry him to bed.

After an even briefer conversation with Ida Willett, who did not approve of coddling youngsters and reminded her daughter of that in no uncertain terms, Sherri went back inside The Spruces. Things were looking up, she told herself. Jeff Thibodeau, her boss, had relayed her report to the state police and they'd sent back word that they would arrive as soon as possible to take over the case. The downside was that it would probably be tomorrow evening before they could get through to The Spruces. Moosetookalook wasn't the only place that still had power outages and downed trees blocking roads. Heck, it might not even be the only community where there had been a homicide.

Sherri thought longingly of sleep as she headed for the conference room, but the nagging sense that there was more she could be doing wouldn't let her rest. Not yet. Not if everyone was likely to leave tomorrow.

She had left the notes she and Pete had accumulated, mostly from questioning people about the missing brooch, piled on the conference room table. Was there a clue somewhere in all that paperwork? Your average murderer, she reminded herself, especially one who killed on impulse, just wasn't very smart. If he or she had slipped up somewhere, said the wrong thing, been seen in the wrong place at the wrong time, then maybe she'd have more to offer the detective in charge than a dead body, a bloodstained skean dhu, and a broken bagpipe.

She was still going through the notes two hours later when Pete came looking for her.

"I have no idea what I'm doing," Sherri admitted. "And I don't seem to be getting anywhere."

"You're doing everything humanly possible," Pete assured her. "No one expects you to make an arrest. Your job was to preserve the scene, which you've done."

"Right. But this all started with the missing brooch, which *was* my case. God! Was it only yesterday afternoon? It feels like we've been here for days."

"So we're concentrating on the theft?" Pete asked.

"Sort of." Sherri stood, stretched, glanced at the coffee-pot, and looked away again. She was jittery enough without adding more caffeine. "The thing is, the theft almost has to be connected to the murder. It would be an awfully big coincidence if the two weren't related in some way. I've got a time line here somewhere."

After a brief search, she handed over a lined yellow pad. She had written down key events in the order they'd happened. A second page contained a list of suspects. She'd enumerated possible motives along with alibis for the time of the crime.

"I'm making lists," she said, shaking her head. "I've been hanging around Liss MacCrimmon too long. This is what all the amateur detectives do in those mystery novels she reads."

"It's not a bad idea," Pete said, flipping through the pages. "Think of it as a sort of mini murder board."

"Theft. Just the theft, remember?"

He handed the tablet back to her. "Why don't you summarize the case for me? Sometimes talking things through is even more helpful than writing down what you know." He pulled out a chair, turned it around, and straddled it.

Sherri thought for a moment. "It all started at approximately four yesterday afternoon, when Liss was on her way to meet with the MacMillans and saw Rhonda, Sadie, and Dilys heading for the basement to clock out." Her lips quirked into a fleeting smile. "She told me that she didn't notice any suspicious behavior from any of them. They were debating what men wear under their kilts."

"I'll give you an up close and personal viewing any time you like," Pete promised with a wink. "What's next?"

"The meeting in the private dining room. That lasted until around four-thirty. Then the MacMillans returned to their suite and discovered that their rooms had been searched. Meanwhile, Liss encountered two pipers bashing each other in the lobby and noticed Phil and Eunice, who'd just been in the gift shop buying toothpaste, watching them." She frowned. "That's odd."

"What is?"

"Neither Phil nor Eunice ever mentioned a side trip to the gift shop when they gave their statements. I only know about it because Liss told me."

"Might just be an oversight. They probably didn't think it was important."

"But that left their suite unoccupied longer. And it takes away Phineas's alibi, since he wasn't with them the whole time."

"Why would Phineas search his brother's suite?"

"No idea. He probably wouldn't."

"You can ask him. Tomorrow. After everybody's had some sleep."

Sherri rubbed her tired eyes. He was right. She needed sleep. But of its own volition, her gaze returned to the time line she'd drawn up.

Liss had witnessed an encounter between Richardson Bruce and Angeline Cloutier in the kitchen. Earlier, she'd seen the three housekeepers leaving. Those five, plus Grant and Erskine, the battling pipers, were likely in the clear for stealing the brooch. Also the kitchen staff, Dan's sister, and Liss herself. Sherri said so to Pete.

"Unless one of them made very short work of tossing the suite before heading downstairs. And maybe Bruce or Grant or Erskine deliberately created a scene, to give himself an alibi."

Sherri sighed. "You're not helping. I'm trying to *eliminate* suspects here."

Pete held up his hands in mock surrender. "Just trying to help."

"No. You're right. We have to consider all the possibilities. Eunice MacMillan said they left their suite by three-forty-five and got to the dining room ahead of Liss. Everyone I just mentioned *did* have time to steal the brooch, even Liss."

"And Phineas."

"And Phineas." She paused for a jaw-cracking yawn. "Moving on. After Phil and Eunice discovered that someone had been in their suite, they started to clean up before they realized that the brooch was missing." Sherri shook her head. "I still can't figure out why, as much as these people like to complain, they weren't going to report the fact that some unauthorized person had been in their suite while they were out."

"They said they thought they knew who was responsible," Pete reminded her.

"Yes. The practical jokers of the group, Eric Buchanan and Norbert Johnson. No joy there. They are among the very few members of SHAS who really do have an iron-clad alibi. Remember? They were hassling Tricia."

Pete, arms crossed on the back of the chair, looked relaxed, especially with his chin resting on his hands, but his eyes were alert. Sherri knew that, deep down, he wanted to find answers as much as she did. "We talked to the staff," he remarked. "Three from housekeeping. Three from the kitchen, plus the chef. Three who waited on tables at the Burns Night Supper. Dan and his dad. Tricia, and Simon from the bar." Simon had just relieved Pete on guard duty at the storage-room door.

"Lounge," Sherri corrected, since Joe wasn't around to do it.

Pete grinned. "Okay. Lounge. Storm gets worse. It's what? Ten at night? You and Dan go up to the private dining room to tell the SHAS people they gotta give statements and—boom!— the lights go out. Everybody files downstairs to the lobby. We talk to them. Thirty-two people at the Burns Night Supper. Twenty-five men and seven women."

"Plus the other guests, who were in the lounge or in their rooms when we lost power. They were all accounted for and in the lobby for at least long enough to pick up lanterns or flashlights and be apprised of the situation created by the storm. But we have no real idea how long anyone stuck around. We had no reason to keep track. The only person I can be fairly certain of is Sadie, since she decided to sneak a smoke before she went to bed. Until then, she stuck close to Rhonda. Dilys apparently turned in early."

"We know Phil MacMillan decided to go on walkabout, in the dark, by himself. He was last seen outside the gift shop. He might have been headed down to the basement to look at the pool."

"Missed opportunity there. If he'd drowned, we might have thought it was an accident." She sighed. "We don't even know exactly when he died. The gift shop incident took place around midnight. That's the best guess, anyway. No one was paying much attention to clocks, probably because they all stopped working when the power went out."

"So how did Phil end up in the storage room with his throat cut?" Pete asked.

Sherri shuddered, remembering. "You know what? Let's not go there. It isn't my case. And to tell the truth, I think I *prefer* to deal only with less violent crimes."

"Amen to that," Pete agreed. "You couldn't pay me

enough to investigate homicides. Give me a run-of-the-mill domestic dispute any day."

Sherri fought another yawn. It was definitely time to get some sleep. Her brain was so fuzzy it could pass for a dust bunny. She stood, swayed, and made no objection when Pete rushed to her side and put his arm around her.

"I hear the tower suite's available tonight," he said.

"Yeah?"

"Want to take a trip back to the nineteenth century? Four-poster bed. Claw-foot bathtub."

"We're already in the nineteenth century," she murmured sleepily. "No forensics. No quick and easy way to verify anything, not even fingerprints."

But that four-poster did sound appealing.

Liss dreamed she was back in the gift shop, waiting on the women of SHAS. Such interesting names they all had: Elspeth, Maeve, Eunice, Glenora, Tory, and Lara. She frowned in her sleep. Wasn't there another wife in the group? One she hadn't met?

She'd call her Susie, Liss decided in her sleep, and felt a rush of pleasure at having picked a name so easily. It was no simple matter to find the right name.

In Liss's dream, Susie bought the tourmaline ring, even though Liss repeatedly told her that it wasn't for sale. Even Glenora Huggons, she of the bright green cat's eyes, tried to talk Susie out of it. It did no good. When Susie stuck the ring on her finger and walked out of the gift shop, Liss abruptly woke up.

The black kitten was sitting on her chest, her furry face only inches from Liss's nose. Liss stared into her bright green eyes, blinked once, and asked, "Glenora?"

The kitten cocked her head.

"Do you like that name?" When a cheerful chirrup answered her, Liss laughed. "Well, then, Glenora it is."

Lumpkin, Liss's large yellow Maine coon cat, made his way up from the foot of the sofa, where he'd been keeping her feet warm. Shoving the much-smaller Glenora aside, he bumped against Liss's shoulder, demanding equal attention. She scratched him behind the ears. After a moment, he snuggled in closer, sprawling across her stomach. At first she thought he was being affectionate. Then she realized that he wasn't nuzzling her chest. He was chewing on the zipper at the front of the fleece hoodie she'd slept in for extra warmth. Worse, he was drooling.

"This is *not* cute," she informed him, pushing him off the sofa where all three of them had spent the night. "You have quite enough bad habits already."

She might have weaned Lumpkin of biting ankles, but he still chewed on leather—shoes, handbags, jacket sleeves— and he stole food right off her plate if she didn't keep her eye on him during meals.

She'd slept well, Liss realized. No one had disturbed her. Not Aunt Margaret. Not Jeff Thibodeau. And not, to her secret disappointment, Dan Ruskin. Before she'd sacked out in the living room, Liss had managed that sponge bath she'd hoped for and had eaten well on assorted items from her refrigerator that would probably have spoiled if she hadn't consumed them. The cats had helped her dispose of those leftovers. All the while, she'd listened for Dan's return, but there had been no sign of him. Finally, too sleepy to keep her eyes open any longer, she'd put the fire screen in place, snuffed all the candles, and drifted into peaceful slumber.

Without thinking, Liss swung her legs off the sofa and stood up, only to fall back onto the cushions with a yelp of pain as her calves screamed in agony.

She'd forgotten all about the previous day's unaccustomed exercise on snowshoes. Gingerly, Liss massaged her instep, her ankles, and her legs. She did a few stretches, still sitting on the sofa. Only then did she make another attempt to stand. The aches were still there, but they were no longer crippling. She walked a few steps, did a few more stretches, and decided she'd was less sore than she might have been. She grimaced at the prospect of putting the snowshoes back on to trek all the way back to the hotel, but decided not to think about that just yet.

When she'd bundled herself into the wool bathrobe she'd left near at hand, Liss realized that even though her fire had burned down to coals, her living room was still comfortably warm. It had helped that she'd closed all the doors.

After a quick, cold trip to the bathroom, she started coffee in an old drip pot, using the two-burner propane stove she'd unearthed from the cellar the night before. She was grateful now that she'd kept the few pieces of camping gear she'd found in the house when she'd inherited it.

"Come on, Lumpkin. Come on, Glenora. Din-din." They were both right there, underfoot, as she opened a can of cat food, served up two portions, and emptied a small bottle of water into a separate dish.

While they ate and Liss waited for her coffee to brew, she surveyed the neighborhood from the vantage point of her bay window. In the morning light, the world looked peaceful and pretty. She had a wonderful view of the square, with its monument to the Civil War dead and its gazebo. The latter was the twin of the one at The Spruces. Only the tops of the swing set and the jungle gym showed in the playground area, and the merry-go-round and the slide were completely covered by snow, but someone had already shoveled the paths. On the far side of the square, people were heading home from the temporary shelter in the redbrick municipal building.

The smell of freshly brewed coffee drew her away from the window and reminded her that she had work to do before Dan collected her. When she'd poured the steaming liquid into an insulated go-cup, she took one last look outside, zeroing in on Dan's house. She saw no sign of activity there, meaning he was probably already out and about.

Turning her back on Moosetookalook, Liss settled herself in the middle of the living room rug with her research on SHAS. There was no point in lugging everything back to The Spruces. She'd go through the computer printouts, clippings, and notes before they headed back.

The more she'd thought about it, the more Liss wondered if there *was* something she'd missed. With the contents of a thick file folder spread out around her, she sipped and read, drank more coffee, and read some more. She'd polished off half the liquid in her oversized cup before she realized it.

A black streak flashed past, just at the edge of Liss's vision. A second later, she heard a loud, sharp sound, a cross between a hiss and the snap of an electric shock.

"Will you two cut it out!"

Both of them ignored her. Lumpkin's lip curled into an expression of feline contempt. He had not been happy about sharing his house with another cat in the first place. He was even less crazy about being confined with Glenora in one room, even if it was warm and contained cat food, water, and a king-size litter box.

Glenora, bent on mischief, prepared to make another pass at Lumpkin by shifting her slight weight to her forepaws and wiggling her bottom in the air.

Liss's spot on the floor was dead center between them.

The kitten dashed directly across the papers, sending pages skittering in every direction. Torn between laughter and frustration, Liss watched Glenora stop short an inch in front of Lumpkin's face, leap straight up, turn in the air, and sprint to the left before the older cat could lift a paw to swat at her. Lumpkin made that strange noise again—

Liss decided he was spitting—heaved his bulk upright, and lumbered after his tormentor.

"Play nice," Liss ordered.

She *thought* they were just playing. She hoped they were. Unless Lumpkin accidentally sat on Glenora and smothered her, it seemed unlikely either of them would come to any harm.

Resigned to being at the center of their game, and glad she'd taken Dan's advice about the candles, Liss started to gather up the scattered sheets. She froze, eyes riveted to the photograph that accompanied one of the many newspaper items she'd copied. She'd been right to look at the material again. She *had* missed something!

The photo had been taken some years back. Liss hadn't written the date on the page, but the people in it looked a decade younger than they were now. The MacMillan twins stood side by side, big grins on their faces. Eunice MacMillan hovered next to her husband. And there, on Phineas's right, identified as his fiancée, was a thinner, dark-haired, smiling Dilys Marcotte.

With a cheery fire providing warmth and the bright morning sun streaming through east-facing windows, Sherri studied Phineas MacMillan. He sat alone at one of the smaller tables in the hotel restaurant at The Spruces, cautiously sipping from a steaming cup of coffee and about to chow down on bacon and scrambled eggs from the breakfast buffet. If he was concerned about his safety, he gave no sign of it. Neither did he seem to be particularly grief stricken or depressed by his brother's death. He'd brought a book with him—a James Patterson novel— and appeared to be so absorbed in reading while he ate that he didn't hear their footfalls. Either that or he knew Sherri and Pete were approaching and chose to ignore them.

"Mr. MacMillan? A word with you?"

With exaggerated care, he marked his place with a strip of tartan cloth, placed the novel on the table, and lifted his head to fix her with a bland stare. "Good morning, Officer Willett. Deputy Campbell."

He didn't ask them to sit down, but Sherri pulled out one of the empty chairs at his table and took a seat across from him. Pete remained standing. Deliberately, she let the silence build. MacMillan resumed eating breakfast, apparently savoring every bite of his food.

He was a cool customer. She'd give him that. "I have a question for you, Mr. MacMillan. After you left the private dining room on the mezzanine following your meeting with Ms. MacCrimmon, where did you go?"

Instead of replying, MacMillan picked up his cup and took a long swallow of the black coffee it contained.

"Even small details can be important," Sherri continued, "and your brother's brooch is still missing." She had to remind herself to be polite. Bad dreams and general anxiety had wrecked any chance of a good night's sleep. She was just as tired and on edge as she had been the night before.

"I went straight back to my room," MacMillan finally replied.

"Not up to Phil's suite?"

"No." He frowned. "He and Eunice went to buy shampoo, didn't they?"

"Toothpaste."

"Yes. Well, they hardly needed my help for that. You, on the other hand, seem to need a great deal of assistance. It was rather inept of you, don't you think, to allow Phil's killer to walk right out the door like that?"

"I beg your pardon?" Sherri couldn't believe what she was hearing.

"Listen up, kiddies," he said, including Pete in a disdainful look. "The man who murdered my brother is no longer here."

Pete cut in before Sherri could find her voice. "The murderer hasn't escaped, Mr. MacMillan. No one has—"

"No one?" His eyebrows shot up. "I beg to differ. Dan Ruskin went into town. Liss MacCrimmon went with him. And both Harvey and Will MacHenry were airlifted out."

Sherri sank back in her chair, flabbergasted. "Which one are you accusing?"

"Why, Will MacHenry, of course. If he was fool enough to mistake Phil for me once, he could easily have done so a second time, especially down in that dark basement. Furthermore, if MacHenry were still on the premises, I'd be renewing my demand for police protection. As it is, there's no need."

"What makes you so sure it was Will MacHenry who killed your brother?" Pete asked. "Do you have proof?"

"I have common sense. I considered the matter and came up with the solution you people should have thought of long before now. Do you know where Will went after the incident in the gift shop?" He paused to give Sherri time to answer, and when neither she nor Pete said anything, he went on. "I thought not. The Tandys, so I'm told, stayed in plain sight in the lobby, but you only have Will's father's word for it that he and his son were together in their room. If the old man dies, Will won't even have that lie to save him."

Sherri opened her mouth and closed it again. His reasoning literally left her speechless.

"Interesting theory," Pete said. "Even more interesting is that no one can vouch for you, either, Mr. MacMillan. We have only your word for it that you went straight to bed after you left the lobby."

Phineas MacMillan seemed to find this observation amusing. "Ah, I see. You think I killed my brother. But why would I? There's no advantage to me in Phil's death." Shaking his head, he stood. "If you have no more questions, I believe I'll adjourn to the library. Perhaps there I'll be allowed to read my book in peace."

# Chapter Fourteen

The buzz of chain saws filled the morning air, nearly drowning out the sounds made by the town plow. Dan, his brother, Sam, and several other Moosetookalook men had been working since dawn to limb and section the fallen trees blocking the street. It was sweaty, back-breaking work, and as Dan lugged yet another three-foot log to the side of the road to be picked up later, he couldn't help but remember the bit of rural wisdom that said wood warmed you three times: once when you cut it, once when you split it, and once when you burned it.

He deposited his burden against the snowbank the plow had made and sank wearily down on top of it. Logs made good places to sit, too. He took off his hat—a billed cap with ear flaps that looked a little silly but was just right for the kind of weather they had in those parts—and swiped at his brow with his sleeve. A cold wind riffled his hair, making him shiver. Nothing like being overheated and chilled to the bone at the same time!

"Hey! No goofing off on the job!" Sam yelled, but he had a good-natured grin on his face.

"Yeah, yeah. I'm coming." Dan pushed off from the log, feeling the movement in every muscle, but especially in those he'd overworked the day before on that cross-country snowshoe hike.

He hoped Liss wasn't hurting too badly.

He'd deliberately stayed away from her the previous night. He hadn't wanted to pressure her, not after telling her he intended to propose. Besides, he'd had to talk to Sam and then he'd gotten roped into an impromptu meeting of the Moosetookalook Small Business Association at the municipal building. Dan smiled to himself. He didn't envy Margaret Boyd the task of telling Liss she had yet another item to add to her to-do list.

He glanced at his watch. Another hour and he'd go get Liss and head back to the hotel. The driveway at The Spruces would still be partially blocked, but they could use their snowshoes to walk around the remaining fallen tree. The rest of the way should be clear. He'd talked to his father earlier and been told that volunteers from among the guests were hard at work on their end.

Jeff Thibodeau turned up just as Dan was about to rev up the chain saw once more. From the expression on Jeff's face, he wasn't bringing good news.

"That other storm? It's definitely going to hit us," Jeff said.

"How bad?"

Jeff shrugged. "The meteorologists are saying that their computer models don't agree, but their best guess is another ice storm. Sometimes I wish they'd go back to having bouncy weather girls guess at what's coming. They were just as accurate as all this newfangled equipment and a lot more fun to watch."

"Well, if I get a vote, I say no ice or high winds, just light snow."

"From your mouth to God's ear," Jeff agreed.

Liss reached for the phone sitting on the end table. There was still no dial tone. She was about to hunt up her cell and try that when she heard a knock at the front door.

"Liss? You in there?" Aunt Margaret's shout had Liss scurrying out of the living room and into the foyer to let her in.

Margaret MacCrimmon Boyd was a slender woman of nearly sixty with light gray hair and a cheerful disposition. She talked a mile a minute, and by the time they were back in the warmth of the living room she'd already given Liss an update on the weather and told her how much she regretted having left the hotel the night before last.

"You know I'd have stayed if I'd known I wouldn't be able to get back to work the next morning."

"And what good would that have done?" Liss asked her. "I'm glad you weren't stuck there with the rest of us. Besides, who would have checked on my furry babies if you hadn't been home?"

"There is that," Margaret conceded, reaching down to stroke Lumpkin.

"Jeff said you stayed the night at the municipal building."

"It seemed the sensible thing to do. There's no heat in my apartment. When Jeff told me where you were, we thought you might join us." She looked around, taking in the newly stoked fire, the camp stove, and the cat dishes. "Obviously, you had no need for the shelter. You're all snug and cozy in your own little cocoon."

"*We* thought?" Liss asked as she poured two cups of coffee from the fresh pot she'd just made. "As in you and Ernie?" Margaret had been spending most of her free time since her return to Moosetookalook with Ernie Willett, Sherry's divorced father. Liss didn't see the attraction herself—Ernie was something of a curmudgeon—but if he made her aunt happy, she was in favor of the relationship.

"We, as in the Moosetookalook Small Business Association." Margaret shrugged. "Well, we were all there, weren't we? Or most of us were. So we ended up discussing what to do about some of our current problems. Once Dan Ruskin showed up, that made the meeting official, him being the president of the MSBA and all."

"Did Dan talk to his brother?" Liss asked.

"Oh, yes. Chain saws all around this morning. Dan said to tell you he'd be by as soon as he has a better take on road conditions. But to return to the MSBA. We've decided to advertise online to recruit new businesses that will fit in with Moosetookalook's image. Sell the town as an ideal place for a craft store or an art gallery or a photographer's studio to relocate. We might even offer some kind of incentive to anyone willing to open up shop in one of the vacant buildings on the square."

Liss set her mug aside. There was something in her aunt's tone of voice that warned her she was talking about more than just putting an ad on a real estate site. The sudden impulse to run and hide was nearly overwhelming.

"We voted to have you look into the matter," Margaret continued. "You're already on the committee, and as the most computer literate among us, you're the obvious choice to handle this new project."

"I'm also, apparently, the only one who wasn't there to object to being volunteered for the job."

"That, too," Margaret admitted.

Liss sighed, but she knew when she was licked. "I'll do what I can, but not today. Aside from the fact that I can't go online until the power comes back on, right now I need to get back to the hotel. I have some information that may help solve this murder."

Her aunt stared at her, thunderstruck. "Murder? What murder?"

\* \* \*

Dan had walked only a block in the direction of Liss's house when he met Margaret Boyd coming the other way. She was carrying a pair of snowshoes—the traditional kind, not the lightweight aluminum models Dan and Liss had used. They were made of wood and had to be at least five feet long. Margaret was panting a little by the time he reached her.

"Let me take those."

"Thanks. They were my husband's, and I think they belonged to his father before him."

For their age, the snowshoes were still in great condition. Even the leather bindings appeared to be in good shape. "You planning to go somewhere on these?" Dan asked.

"Back to the hotel." When he lifted his eyebrows, a stubborn gleam came into her eyes. He recognized that mulish look. He'd seen it often enough on her niece's face. "Why didn't you tell me there'd been a murder?" she demanded.

"There wasn't enough privacy while we were all together in the municipal building." He turned around and headed back to the work site. There was no sense carrying the snowshoes all the way to Liss's and back again.

"Well, I suppose I forgive you, then," Margaret said, trotting along beside him. "How's your father coping?" Margaret and Joe had been friends for a long time, and she'd always been one of his biggest supporters on the hotel project, even investing her own money in the venture.

"Taking it one day at a time, as always."

Dan had been trying to emulate his parent, but with only partial success. As long as the hotel was cut off, no new guests could check in. Meanwhile, they were losing money hand over fist on the guests who were stuck there. Since their extended "vacation" at The Spruces was not their choice, they could hardly be charged for their food and lodging.

"Liss didn't tell me much." Margaret gave him an eager look that invited him to share what he knew.

"Liss and I don't know much."

"Oh." She sounded disappointed. "Well, anyway, after Liss told me about Sadie finding a body, she described this strange dream she had. She's named the kitten Glenora."

Dan wasn't sure he followed Margaret's train of thought. "Is that important?"

"I suppose not, except that it shows how much this murder is preying on Liss's mind. Glenora Huggons is one of the SHAS people."

They'd reached the log Dan had earlier used as a bench. Sam spotted them and headed their way, walkie-talkie in hand. This wasn't the time to be talking about Phil MacMillan's murder, Dan decided. Once again, there were too many people around. Dan had given Sam the basics the previous night, but he didn't want to go into more detail, not even with his brother.

"Look, Margaret, let's wait till we're back at The Spruces to discuss this, okay? And you'd better wear the snowshoes I had on yesterday to get there. I'll use the ones you brought."

"Thanks." She sent him a sheepish smile. "They are kind of heavy."

They were also going to make walking around the remaining fallen tree much more of a challenge, but he'd manage. "Okay, then. If you'll wait here at the work site, I'll go get Liss and we'll be back in a few."

He was already retracing his steps toward the town square when she called to him. "Wait, Dan! Liss isn't at the house. She said she'll meet us here as soon as she can."

Slowly, Dan walked back to where Margaret stood. "And where, exactly, is she?"

"She was going to Rhonda's to pick up a change of clothes for her."

Dan frowned. "I didn't know Liss and Rhonda were friends."

"They aren't, as far as I know."

"Then why—?"

"She didn't say. I swear, the two of you are turning into the most closed-mouthed individuals I've ever met! You really should have told me about the trouble at The Spruces last night. I'm sure we could have found a quiet corner where no one could overhear."

"I didn't want to worry you." He still didn't.

While Sam and Margaret greeted each other, Dan peered down the street, hoping to see Liss hurrying toward them. There was no one in sight. He tried to tell himself he had no reason to be concerned about her, but he still felt uneasy.

The hell with it, he thought. If she didn't like him interfering, that was just too bad. He headed for the Snipes house. He wasn't quite running, but it was a fast walk.

"Well, well. If it isn't little Liss MacCrimmon. Haven't seen you in a dog's age."

"Hello, Mr. Snipes. Hello, Rodney. Hello, Norman," she added as his two sons appeared in the doorway behind him.

They were not an appealing sight. Rhonda's husband, known by one and all as "Cracker," could best be described as slovenly. He wore an old pair of sweatpants, paint spattered and full of holes, and an even older and more ratty-looking sweatshirt with the sleeves cut off above the elbow. It did nothing to hide rolls of belly fat.

Cracker's oldest son, Rodney, was only a few years

younger than Liss, but he was already starting to resemble his father. Liss remembered him as a brat, the kind of boy who delighted in pulling girls' hair and shooting people with water pistols. The youngest son, Norman, didn't look much like his father or brother. Instead, he bore a strong resemblance to a ferret.

At least they were already up. She would have hated to see what any of them looked like when they first rolled out of bed.

"You're lettin' the heat out," Cracker Snipes said, gesturing for Liss to enter.

She accepted the invitation, though not without a few second thoughts, and followed the three men into the kitchen. They had a woodstove. The entire downstairs of the house was wonderfully warm. They were using it for cooking as well as heating. A kettle full of hot water steamed on the back section, and on the front a cast-iron fry pan contained the remnants of Canadian bacon and scrambled eggs.

Rhonda would have a huge cleaning job to do when she got back. Not only had her menfolk left their dirty dishes lying around, but heating with wood was always messy. A trail of small bits of bark marked the path from the wood pile in the shed to the stove. No one had bothered to dig out a broom and dustpan and sweep them up.

"So, Liss," Rodney said. "What brings you here?"

"I came to pick up a change of clothes for Rhonda and one for Dilys."

Cracker's brow furrowed. "Why the hell isn't Rhonda home where she belongs? If she can send you—"

"There's no way to get cars out of the hotel parking lot right now," Liss said hastily, "not with all the trees that came down across the driveway and the road. I hiked out yesterday on snowshoes and I'll be going back in the same way later this morning."

"Rhonda coulda walked out." He sounded more sulky than angry, for which Liss was grateful.

She considered telling him that his wife had indeed tried to get home the day before, but thought better of it. That would require far too much explaining. "Rhonda is needed at the hotel," she said instead, "what with all the guests being stuck there, too. Think of all the overtime Joe Ruskin will have to pay her to stay on."

"There is that." Cracker Snipes immediately looked more cheerful.

"If you're anxious to see Rhonda, I'm sure the three of you would be a welcome addition to the crew trying to clear the road. And the sooner the way is open, the sooner she can come home."

None of them rushed right out to help. Cracker didn't even escort Liss to the master bedroom to collect clothes for Rhonda. He just pointed the way. "Upstairs. First door on the left. And Dilys's room is the second on the right."

Liss was not surprised to discover an unmade bed and piles of dirty clothing on the floor of the room Rhonda and Cracker shared. She ignored the debris as she foraged for underwear, clean slacks, and a blouse and bundled them into one of the two plastic bags she'd brought with her.

The first door on the right obviously led to the room Rodney and Norman shared. It featured bunk beds, more piles of dirty clothes, and a stack of magazines of the sort that local stores sold only when their covers were concealed by plain brown paper wrappers. She wondered if there was anything more the Snipes family could do to become a veritable cliché among stereotypes.

Once inside Dilys's room, Liss needed only a few minutes to gather up a change of clothing and stuff the items into the second plastic bag. Then she went back to the door to make sure that no one had followed her upstairs.

As soon as she was certain that the coast was clear, she began to search the small bedroom. She told herself she was looking for the missing brooch, but after finding the link between Dilys and Phineas in her notes on SHAS, she also kept an eye peeled for anything that would link the housekeeper to the MacMillans.

It didn't take long to go through Dilys's belongings. The woman traveled light. She had no jewelry at all. Then, just as Liss was about to give up, she noticed the bookmark Dilys had used in the romance novel by Debbie Macomber that she'd left on the bedside table. It appeared to be a newspaper clipping, and so it proved when Liss cautiously opened the dog-eared paperback—stamped on the flyleaf with the name of a used book store in Portland—and examined it.

There was no date, but Liss knew the item had probably been published no more than a month or two earlier. It announced that the Scottish Heritage Appreciation Society had selected a newly opened hotel called The Spruces as the site for its next Burns Night Supper.

Taking the clipping with her, Liss went back downstairs. She considered a quick exit, slipping out before anyone noticed her, but she'd been brought up better than that. Besides, she had a question for Mr. Snipes.

With a sigh, she straightened her shoulders and headed for the kitchen. She stopped short in the doorway. Cracker and his sons had been joined by two other men. Liss knew them only in passing, but that was sufficient to realize that they weren't the most savory characters in town. All five were playing poker. They'd set up a card table next to the woodstove, where it was nice and hot, with the result that they were all in shirtsleeves or T-shirts except for Cracker, who had stripped down to a sleeveless undershirt. For someone Cracker's size, it was a bad fashion choice.

"Uh, I'll be going now," Liss said. "Thanks for your help."

"Yeah. Fine." Cracker scowled at his cards. "I'm out."

"Uh, Mr. Snipes?" She waited until he looked her way. "I'm just curious. How long has Dilys been living here?"

Cracker reached into the bucket full of snow he'd placed close to his chair and pulled out a can of beer. Apparently he *could* do more to make himself into a stereotype! It didn't seem to matter to him that it was not yet ten o'clock in the morning. He popped the top and took a long swallow before he answered. "Two weeks, give or take."

"Oh. Somehow I thought she'd been in town longer than that."

He shrugged. "She'd been nagging Rhonda to help her get a job at the hotel for a couple of months. Can't figure why she'd want to work there. She had a perfectly good job in Portland that musta paid a lot better."

"Probably got laid off," Norman suggested.

Rodney leered at Liss. "Probably just got—"

Before Rodney could complete that thought, a loud banging at the front door interrupted him. It was followed by Dan's voice, shouting. "Liss? You in there?"

"Who's that?" Cracker demanded.

Annoyance made her voice sharp. "It's Dan Ruskin. I have to be going now. Thanks again for your help, Mr. Snipes."

She managed to head Dan off before he could do something disgustingly macho like break down the door. It was not the first time he'd arbitrarily decided that she needed to be rescued. She brushed past him without speaking and stomped down the front steps and out into the street. When he caught up to her, she turned on him and glared.

"Do you really think so little of me that you believe I can't look after myself? I went there to pick up a change of clothes for Rhonda and Dilys. It was not exactly a high-risk mission!"

"I'm not going to apologize," Dan said. "Rodney Snipes has an unsavory reputation with women." They headed for the work site, walking in silence for the first two blocks. Then Dan added, "I always wondered if it was because his mother named him after a character in *Peyton Place*. Norman, too."

Liss caught herself smiling and hastily pursed her lips.

"Ever see the movie?" he asked. "It was shot here in Maine, you know. Camden, or maybe Rockland. Someplace on the coast. All those towns along U.S. Route 1 look the same to me."

Liss glared at him. "Don't try to distract me. You know I hate it when you get overprotective. You *know* that. I've looked out for myself for a long time."

"And now you don't have to. What's so wrong about me not wanting anything bad to happen to you? It's only natural to want to protect someone you love. It doesn't mean you can't take care of yourself, just that I want to . . ." As she stared at him in amazement, he searched for the right word. He grinned at her like a little kid who'd caught his first fish when he found it. "I want to be your backup."

Frowning, Liss considered the idea. And the fact that he'd just said he loved her. Sort of. Then she noticed that he was holding his breath.

"Okay then."

"Okay. Good."

They continued on toward the work site, walking side by side.

Liss got the distinct impression that Dan would do exactly the same thing all over again in a similar situation, but somehow that no longer bothered her quite so much.

"Dan?" She waited until their eyes locked. "I'm glad you came after me. I *was* feeling just the teensiest bit uneasy about being in that kitchen with five beer-swilling, poker-playing lowlifes."

Then she told him what she'd discovered about Dilys Marcotte.

Sherri clicked off her cell phone and smiled. During the last few hours, between the phone and the police radio, she'd been able to access a surprising amount of information. Things were finally beginning to come together.

Although she knew she should probably leave further investigation to the state police, the stolen brooch *was* her case. It wasn't out of line for her to pursue it. And if it happened to overlap with solving a homicide, then that was just—what had her father called it when she was a kid? Oh, yes—the fickle finger of fate.

What Sherri had learned, among other things, was that Eunice MacMillan did stand to benefit financially from her husband's death, but not in a way that was at all suspicious. The mortgage on her house would be paid off by the insurance policy banks always insisted upon taking out, and there might be other life insurance, but a great deal of money would not be forthcoming. As a likely motive for Eunice to dispose of her spouse, that one wouldn't fly. There might, however, be another reason for her to want to get rid of him.

Tagging Pete for backup, she explained what she wanted to do and then went in search of the not-very-grief-stricken widow. They found her in the library, ensconced in a chair close to the warmth of the fireplace.

Sherri snagged a straight-back chair and hauled it over to place next to Eunice. Pete followed suit.

"Ms. MacMillan—a word?"

Eunice glared at them. "I'd like a word with you, too, Officer. What is the holdup here? When can we leave? And why haven't the state police arrived yet to conduct a proper investigation into my husband's death?"

Pete fixed Eunice with a stern stare. "You don't get to ask questions," he said. "You answer them or you face charges of obstructing justice."

"Please, Deputy Campbell, let's not get off on the wrong foot." Sherri used her most soothing tone of voice, good cop to his bad. "I'm sure Ms. MacMillan wants to cooperate. After all, it was her husband who was brutally murdered."

If Eunice was at all intimidated by Pete's bluster, it didn't show. Eyes full of resentment, she folded her arms across her bosom, crossed her legs at the ankles, and braced her back against the plush upholstery of the chair. Defenses up, Sherri thought, and decided to take this as a sign of progress.

"Now, then," she said, whipping out a pen and notebook—the batteries in her audio recorder had finally died—" would you like to tell us why your husband claimed a valuable brooch was stolen when he knew all along that it had not been?"

Surprise showed briefly in Eunice's eyes, but she wasn't about to admit to anything. "I don't know what you are talking about," she said in a huffy voice.

Sherri remembered how Eunice and Phil had seemed to be at odds when she and Pete first interviewed them about the theft of the brooch. That made sense to her now. Feigning astonishment, she drawled, "Do you mean to say that you weren't aware that your husband was attempting to commit insurance fraud?" Sherri leaned closer to the other woman. "You see, according to my sources, a man fitting your husband's description sold that particular piece of jewelry, that brooch he reported stolen, to a upscale jewelry store in downtown Waterville just over three weeks ago."

# Chapter Fifteen

Sherri sprang to her feet when Liss entered the conference room. Before she could stop herself, she blurted out, "I think I know who killed Phil MacMillan!"

She clapped both hands over her mouth. So much for keeping civilians out of the loop! Well, she had *tried* to go by the book. These were extraordinary circumstances. And Liss wouldn't rat her out to the state police. It might not be professional to be so pleased with her deductions, or to want to share them, but both reactions were perfectly natural.

Sherri couldn't prove anything yet, but she was certain Eunice was guilty. Why else would the woman have stormed out of the library after answering only a few of Sherri's questions? She'd even uttered that hackneyed phrase, "I'm not saying another word until I talk to my lawyer!"

Liss stared at her in amazement. "How on earth did you find out about Dilys?"

"Dilys?" Momentarily confused, Sherri blinked repeatedly, trying to adjust her thinking. "Dilys Marcotte? What does she have—?"

"She's the murderer."

"Dilys? No way."

"Wait till you see." Liss tried to take off her coat and

get something out of the pocket of her jeans at the same time. With an inarticulate sound of frustration, she finally managed both. She was grinning from ear to ear when she thrust a piece of paper into Sherri's hands.

It had been folded several times and there was something tucked inside—a newspaper clipping. Sherri scanned the page, a printout of something Liss had found online, then looked at her friend for an explanation.

"I had that in my folder on SHAS," Liss said. "Don't you think it's highly suspicious that Dilys never mentioned that she knew either twin, let alone that she was once engaged to Phineas?"

The photograph showed a younger and much more slender Dilys Marcotte. She had been a blonde when the picture was taken, but when Sherri looked closely she could see that it was undeniably the same woman who now worked as a housekeeper at The Spruces.

"She deliberately hid the connection," Liss went on. "In fact, she's been very careful to stay in the background, unlike Rhonda and Sadie. I think she was trying to avoid being recognized."

Slowly, Sherri nodded, remembering how flustered Dilys had been when she'd encountered Phineas MacMillan in the vestibule. She ducked her head and scurried away. And just before that, she'd told Sherri that she'd never met Phil. Clearly, that had been a lie.

"Why didn't any of the other SHAS members spot her?" Sherri asked. "Looks like she must have known several of them. The old-timers, anyway."

"That's not so surprising," Liss said. "Not only did she keep a low profile, but Dilys has changed a good deal since this picture was taken. Besides, as a housekeeper, and even as a waitress at the cocktail party, she'd have been almost invisible. Guests in hotels pay as little attention to staff as they do to the furniture. Unless they have a reason to complain about them, of course. Dilys could easily have gone unrecognized, particularly if she was *trying* to be inconspicuous."

"It could be just a coincidence that Dilys Marcotte and Phineas MacMillan crossed paths again at The Spruces." Sherri was willing to give Dilys the benefit of the doubt, since she had a better suspect in mind for Phil's murder. "And wouldn't most women who run into a former fiancé years later, when they're older and heavier and working in a menial job, prefer *not* to be recognized?"

"Read the clipping."

Sherri skimmed it. "So?"

"I found that in Dilys's room at the Snipes house."

Sherri winced. "You searched Dilys's belongings?"

"I didn't mess up any evidence."

Sherri waved the clipping. "Hello? What do you call this? You removed it from Dilys's room. Now we have only your word that it was ever there."

"Oh." Liss's face fell. "Sorry."

"It's a little late to worry about it now." Resigned to explaining yet another breach in protocol to the state police, Sherri slipped the clipping and the printout into a fresh file folder and labeled it with Dilys's name. "We'll just have to hope this doesn't turn out to be critical to building a case. Tell me what you think it means."

"Isn't it obvious? Dilys's engagement ended badly and she wanted revenge. She was a woman scorned. She meant to kill Phineas but mistook one twin for the other. Cracker Snipes told me that Dilys has only been in Moosetookalook for a couple of weeks. She moved here *after* she read that news item about the Burns Night Supper. She took a job at the hotel specifically so that she would be here at the same time as Phineas."

"Well," Sherri allowed, "her actions certainly seem suspicious, but wouldn't she be able to tell the twins apart? It was *Phil* who died, don't forget, and I've got a pretty good reason to suspect—" She broke off before she named Eunice. She'd said way too much already.

Liss glared at her. "What's the big deal about sharing information?" she demanded. "I've helped the police out before."

Sherri waffled. Her friend had a point. Liss's insights, flawed though they often were, had been useful in the past. Besides, she could tell Liss what she'd found out about the brooch if she wanted to. That was her case. Sherri absently rubbed her temples, where a headache continued to throb. If she was honest with herself, she'd admit that she'd been dying to share everything she'd found out with an appreciative audience.

Quickly and concisely, Sherri brought Liss up to date on what she'd discovered about Phil's sale of the piece of jewelry he'd claimed was stolen. "Eunice did answer a few questions before she lawyered up," Sherri added. "Very reluctantly."

"She admitted that Phil was trying to defraud the insurance company?" Liss asked.

Sherri nodded. "When Phil realized that someone had been in their suite while they were out, he decided to take advantage of the situation. Eunice didn't approve. That's why she continued picking up after the intruder."

"But she still claims someone *was* in their room? They didn't make up that part, too?"

"She says not. I don't know if I believe her."

Liss pondered this for a few minutes while she fixed herself a cup of coffee. "So, you think she killed her husband because . . .?"

"It's the simple, logical explanation. As a widow, she doesn't stand to profit all that much from his life insurance policies, but she does shed a husband who was screwing up her life. He'd lost all their money on bad investments. They were facing bankruptcy. His attempt at fraud could well have put them both in jail."

"Only if he were found out. How could she know that you'd be so good at your job?" Liss sat opposite Sherri at the conference table. She let Sherri bask in her praise for about a minute and a half before she burst the bubble. "You're jumping to one heck of a conclusion."

"My theory makes as much sense as your scenario," Sherri objected. "Dilys as a crazed killer out for vengeance? Give me a break."

"It wouldn't hurt you to question Dilys about Phineas. Maybe talk to Phineas about her. He'd be the one who'd know if she had reason to want him dead." She took a sip of coffee, made a face at the bitter taste, and set it aside. "If you don't want to do it, I'll be happy to."

"Okay. Okay." Sherri held up both hands in surrender. "I'll follow up on your lead. But you have to promise me you'll let me handle it. No interfering in police business, Liss. I mean it."

Liss mimed crossing her heart and zipping her lips.

Sherri glanced at her watch. "It's already lunchtime. Let's head for the restaurant. Both Dilys and Phineas will probably be there. One thing is sure—everyone in this crowd likes to eat."

A hard left as they exited the passage that led to the offices and conference room took them into a plush vestibule. On its far side was the restaurant. Sherri and Liss paused at the entrance, scanning the lunch crowd for Phineas or Dilys. Richardson Bruce shoved rudely past them, but since there were a couple dozen guests ahead of him in the buffet line, he was forced to stop short only a few feet inside the door.

"I don't see either Phineas MacMillan or Dilys Marcotte," Sherri said just as her cell phone rang. She glanced at the readout. "It's the state police. I've got to take this."

"I'll stay here and keep an eye out for Dilys," Liss volunteered.

"Do not question her on your own," Sherri warned before she headed back to the privacy of the conference room. "Or Phineas, either. I hate to keep repeating myself, but this is police business."

By the time Sherri finished her conversation with the state police officer who would be taking over Phil Mac-Millan's homicide, nearly three-quarters of an hour had passed. She returned to the restaurant to find that Liss had been joined by Dan and Pete, and that they, and almost everyone trapped in the hotel, had already finished lunch. Only a few people remained, chatting over coffee. Only one, Rhonda Snipes, came in after Sherri did.

"Did Dilys or Phineas show up?" Sherri asked as she joined her fiancé and her friends.

"No sign of either of them," Dan answered. "Maybe they ate earlier. Or maybe Phineas had something sent up. Dad insisted we offer room service today, although he's hoping no one will want to eat in an unheated bedroom."

Tricia Lynd, who had been bussing the next table, stopped at Sherri's elbow on her way back to the kitchen. "I couldn't help overhearing. Are you looking for Phineas MacMillan?"

"Do you know where he is?" Sherri asked.

"No, but I saw him just a little bit ago. He was in the vestibule. He was heading this way, but he ran into Mr. Bruce, who was on his way out of the restaurant. They talked for a minute or two and then they both walked away. I guess Mr. MacMillan changed his mind about having lunch."

"Did they go somewhere together?" Sherri asked.

Tricia shook her head. "Mr. Bruce went toward the lobby, but Mr. MacMillan veered off near the service elevator." She frowned. "Of course, the elevators aren't working with the power out, so I guess he must have been headed for the stairs. Or maybe the offices."

"He might have been coming to see you, Sherri," Liss suggested. "I bet Richardson Bruce overheard us say we were looking for Phineas. Remember? Bruce went into the restaurant just before you took that call."

"If Phineas was trying to find me, he didn't look very hard." Sherri abandoned her salad and stood. She wasn't very hungry anyway. "I think I'd better have a word with Richardson Bruce."

Her quarry was still in the lobby, seated in one of the wingback chairs near the fire. Sherri thought about telling Liss to make herself scarce, but decided it hardly mattered at this late date.

"Mr. Bruce," Sherri said in a no-nonsense voice that usually got results, "would you mind telling me what you said to Mr. MacMillan in the vestibule near the dining room a little while ago?"

Bruce had the grace to look embarrassed. "I, uh, told him you were looking for him. And for someone named Dilys Marcotte. I, uh, overheard you say so. Just before your phone rang."

Liss had certainly pegged that correctly. How much more, Sherri wondered, had she got right? "And why, exactly, would you go out of your way to warn him?"

"If you must know, I was trying to annoy him. Don't you think he deserves some payback for his insinuations about my honesty? I saw a chance to needle him—give him a hard time because the police were after him. It's not often anyone can rattle Phineas MacMillan, least of all me."

"So he was . . . alarmed by what you told him?"

"He was some startled," Richardson said, relishing the memory. "And then he just took off. Are you going to arrest him for something? That would really make my day."

"At the moment, I'm not going to arrest anyone, Mr. Bruce. Except, possibly, you yourself, for interfering in an investigation."

Bruce sniffed. "I was just trying to get a rise out of Phineas. No harm in that."

"I don't suppose he said where he was going?"

Bruce shook his head.

"Are you thinking what I'm thinking?" Liss asked when she and Sherri were back in the conference room.

Sherri dry-swallowed two aspirin but doubted they'd do anything to relieve the constant pounding in her head. "I haven't a clue what you're thinking," she admitted. But the proof was piling up that she was not cut out to handle a murder investigation on her own.

"Isn't it obvious?" Liss asked. "What sent Phineas running off without his lunch wasn't hearing that you wanted to talk to him as much as it was the mention of Dilys's name. He didn't know she was here. What do you want to bet he went looking for her?"

Sherri reached for her walkie-talkie. "That's not good. If you're right and Dilys killed Phil, thinking he was Phineas, then the last thing Phineas should do is confront her. We need to find them both before he gives her the opportunity to correct her mistake."

Sherri alerted Margaret, Sam, and Joe to be on the lookout for Dilys and Phineas and then dispatched Pete to look for them in the two areas where most of the hotel's guests had been congregating, the lobby and the restaurant. "Check the gift shop, too," she said into the walkie-talkie.

Joe Ruskin had arranged for Tricia to work there all afternoon, freeing Liss from the responsibility.

"I have an excuse to go up to the guest room Dan assigned to Dilys," she reminded Sherri. "I brought a change of clothes back from town for her." She retrieved the two plastic bags she'd left in the corner of the conference room when they'd gone to lunch.

"Okay. Yes—good idea. But take Dan with you. He can use his passkey to get into her room. She might be in there and not answer a knock."

For once, Liss didn't even think of objecting to having a big, strong man along to protect her. But as they headed upstairs, it suddenly dawned on her that Sherri didn't really believe that Dilys had killed once and might kill again. More than that, Sherri expected Dilys's hotel room to be the *last* place she'd be. Sherri was humoring her! Still, she went through the motions and, as she'd anticipated, there was no one in the room Dilys had slept in for the last two nights. Liss came away from there still carrying her two plastic bags.

"Does Dilys have a locker?" she asked Dan on their way back downstairs. "Someplace to store her purse when she's working?"

"All the employees do. I can open it, but I think we'd better leave that to Sherri, don't you?"

Liss jiggled the plastic bags. "I just want to leave Dilys's clothes there."

"Sure you do." But he led the way to the locker room and opened the one that had Dilys's name taped to the front.

Like the hotel room, it was empty. Disappointed, Liss deposited Dilys's possessions inside. Then, while Dan went to report their lack of success to Sherri, Liss took the other bag to Rhonda. The matriarch of the Snipes family had been in the dining room when they left it to go in search of Richardson Bruce. She was still there, sitting in a corner by herself, hunched over a cup of tea.

"Have you seen Dilys?" Liss asked when she'd given Rhonda the change of clothing and received a surprised "thank you" in return.

"Not since before lunch. Was everyone okay in town? My family?"

"Uh, sure. The place was nice and warm from the woodstove."

Rhonda stared hard at Liss's face, then sighed. "Let me guess—guzzling beer and playing cards, all three of them?"

"Uh—"

"Never mind." She started to get up.

"Wait, Rhonda. Sit, please. Can I ask you about Dilys?"

"What about her?" Reluctantly, Rhonda resumed her seat.

"She's your cousin, right?"

"Distant."

"Did you see much of her before she moved into your spare room?"

"Once in a while. Not often."

"Did she ever say why she wanted to move to Moose-tookalook?"

"Said she had a fancy to work at a grand hotel." Rhonda shrugged and took a sip of her tea. "Lot of nonsense, that was. A job's a job, and cleaning up strangers' messes is the same no matter how ritzy the surroundings are."

"What about the group staying here, the Scottish Heritage Appreciation Society? Did she ever mention them to you?"

Rhonda shook her head, but she eyed Liss with increased wariness.

"Did Dilys have a purse with her?"

"A purse? What kind of question is that?"

"Her locker is empty. We just wondered if—"

At that, Rhonda gave a screech and sat up straight. "What were you doing snooping in her locker? Those are supposed to be private."

"Now, Rhonda, you know management reserves the right to open employee lockers. I assume that's why Sadie hid her cigarettes elsewhere."

But Liss's words had no effect. Instead of calming down, Rhonda became more agitated. She shoved her chair away from the table and came to her feet in a rush. Her teacup overturned, spilling the dregs onto the snowy white tablecloth. "What's going on here? Why are our civil rights being violated?"

Liss gaped at her. Civil rights? Where had *that* come from? "We're trying to discover who killed Phil MacMillan, Rhonda. That's all."

"MacMillan?" A stricken look on her face, Rhonda abruptly plopped back down in her chair. "That's who was killed? MacMillan? I didn't know. No one ever said a name."

"You know, then, that Dilys was once engaged?"

Face pale, hands trembling as she automatically righted her empty teacup, Rhonda nodded. "Dilys was going to marry some guy named MacMillan, but he called it off at the last minute. She was bitter about that. Who wouldn't be? Is he the one Sadie found?"

"No. Dilys was engaged to Phineas MacMillan. It was his brother, Phil, who was killed."

"Phil. That's right. I remember now. Dilys blamed the brother—Phil—for breaking them up. He faked some pictures. Made it look like Dilys was running around on her fiancé. She told anybody who'd listen that she'd like to kill that sonofabitch."

Realizing too late what she'd just said, Rhonda's eyes went wide, but she could not call back the damning words.

So, Liss thought, maybe the murderer didn't make a mistake, after all. Maybe it was Phil Dilys had intended to kill all along.

# Chapter Sixteen

Sherri had mixed feelings about bringing civilians into the search for Dilys and Phineas, but she didn't see that she had much choice, especially after Liss repeated her conversation with Rhonda. If she didn't look for the woman, Liss would go hunting for Dilys on her own. On the other hand, two officers of the law simply couldn't canvass the entire hotel by themselves. That being the case, Sherri felt justified in gathering her troops together in the conference room—herself and Pete, Liss, Dan, and Joe, and Sam and Margaret, who had come back from town at the same time as Liss and Dan.

"I'm trying to locate Dilys Marcotte," Sherri announced. "It looks as if Phineas MacMillan, upon discovering that Dilys, to whom he was once engaged, was in the hotel, went looking for her. Now they're both missing."

"Phineas could be dead," Liss said.

Sherri scowled at her, but she supposed they all had a right to know the rest. "It's possible Dilys is the one who killed Phil. *Possible*. So be careful."

"Maybe she didn't kill anyone. Perhaps Phineas realized he made a terrible mistake by breaking up with her and you can't find them because they're off somewhere having spectacular make-up sex."

Everyone turned to stare at Margaret Boyd, showing an interesting variety of facial expressions.

"What? It could happen."

Sherri cleared her throat. For all she knew, Margaret was right. "Whatever the reason for their disappearance, I want them both found, especially Dilys, and the sooner the better. If that means knocking on every door, so be it."

Dilys had lied about knowing Phil. She might well have held back other information in an effort to protect herself. Sherry really needed to talk to her.

"At least we don't have to worry about her leaving the hotel," Dan said.

They all looked out the window. Sleet battered the glass. The second storm had blown in as predicted and showed no sign of letting up any time soon.

They started with the basement—storerooms, the break room and locker room, the health center, and the room that contained an indoor pool. Most of the doors were locked and they had to use the passkeys Joe Ruskin provided to open them. Dilys had a passkey, too, Sherri reminded herself. She could be anywhere.

"It's too cold to spend much time down here." Liss shivered in spite of the warm sweater she'd brought from home. Sherri had on her uniform jacket to ward off the chill.

"But this is where Phil was killed," Dan said, joining them. The rest of the search party was right behind him. Over by the crime scene tape, Simon the bartender watched them, curious to know what they were up to, but too far away to overhear what they were saying.

"Why was Phil down here?" Margaret asked.

"To meet somebody?" Liss suggested.

"Why would he agree to meet anyone, particularly

Dilys, in the basement?" Sherri wondered aloud. "I could see it if it were Phineas, but—"

"No, that won't wash, either. They all had rooms. There's no good reason for any guest to be down here. Not Phil. Not Phineas. Not even Dilys. Certainly not Eunice."

Sherri sent a quelling look Liss's way. "Who besides you heard Phil say that he was going to check out the pool?"

Liss's brow knit as she tried to remember. "It was after Will MacHenry scurried off, so only Russ and Tory were still with me."

"Will had gone? You're certain?"

"Yes, I'm sure of it. And anyway, we all knew by then that it was Phil, not Phineas."

"But Phineas thinks Will MacHenry is the killer," Sherri confided. "He came right out and told me that I'd let a murderer escape when I allowed Will to accompany his father to the hospital."

Dan weighed in. "Taking a swing at someone because he upset your elderly, ailing father is a far cry from killing him for it."

"It would make more sense if Phil had been murdered by mistake for Phineas *after* Harvey MacHenry collapsed," Pete said. "But he wasn't."

Margaret cleared her throat. "I hate to speak ill of anyone, but Will has had his . . . problems in the past."

Once again, they all turned to look at her.

"What kind of problems?" Sherri wasn't sure she wanted to know. She had too many suspects already.

"Oh, you know—brawling, drunk driving, resisting arrest. The usual kind of thing a young man with too much money and not enough sense will do. But all that was ages ago. He hasn't been in a bit of trouble since that time he spent six months in the county jail."

"Exactly how long ago are we talking about?" Sherri asked.

"Oh, let me see. It must be a good twenty years by now. The whole experience was probably good for him. What do they call it—scared straight?"

Sherri wondered if Phineas knew about that incident. She decided he did not. Otherwise it would have been featured in his before-supper speech.

Back on the main floor of the hotel, they opted to search in the west wing first: the lounge that overlooked the pool, the music room, the library, the game room, the gift shop, and the business center, where computers and printers—none of them working at the moment—were available to guests. On the other side of the lobby, in the east wing, they searched the offices, the restrooms, the restaurant, and the kitchen. No one they encountered had seen either Dilys or Phineas.

The mezzanine contained function rooms, including the small, private dining room that had been used for the Burns Night Supper, and a ballroom. It was eerily quiet on that level. No one had any reason to be there. The search went quickly and turned up nothing.

"How many guest rooms?" Sherri asked as they reconvened at the stairwell next to the elevators and headed up to the next level en masse. Without power, using the stairs was their only option. Lanterns and flashlights still provided the only illumination.

"One hundred and forty," Dan said.

"That many?" Sherri repressed a groan. This was impossible. It would take forever to go through all the rooms, and for what? She had no proof of any wrongdoing. Besides, what was to say that their quarry wouldn't go down another flight of stairs while they were climbing up this one?

"It's not so bad," Dan said. "We're not using the rooms in either wing. Those sections are closed off from the rest of the hotel on the second and third floors to save on heat."

"What about the tower rooms?" One at each corner contained a fourth-floor suite, and there were fourth and fifth-floor suites in the tower at the center of the hotel.

"Two of the corner towers are closed off, too. So we have fifty-six fewer rooms to search—only eighty-four doors to knock on."

But Liss didn't buy the math. "A killer isn't likely to obey a KEEP OUT sign."

"Suspect," Sherri corrected her. She glanced at Dan. "Exactly how are those sections closed off?"

"Wooden pocket doors. Locked."

"But they can be opened with a passkey, right? And Dilys is on the housekeeping staff, so she has a passkey. We'll have to take a look at the rooms in those wings, too, if we don't find Dilys and Phineas elsewhere first." Sherri decided to leave them till last, though. If there was no heat in those areas, no one with any sense would try to hole up there.

Determined to be organized and thorough, even though she still wasn't convinced that Liss's theory was correct, Sherri checked to make sure that each of her searchers had a walkie-talkie before she gave them their assignments. "Margaret, I want you watching the stairwell at the east end. Joe, you take the west stairs. The rest of us will go door-to-door. If someone answers a knock, ask to come in. If no one's there, go in with a passkey. Don't forget to look in the bathrooms and closets of empty rooms."

"What about under the bed?" Liss asked.

Sherri wondered if that was sarcasm. She decided it was

not. Liss was a straightforward person and rarely managed to be subtle.

The hunt continued to be time-consuming and frustrating. A few people were in their rooms, but most were empty. Nowhere did anyone spot any sign of Dilys or Phineas, and no one they encountered recalled seeing either of them since well before lunch. The searchers moved on to the third floor.

Liss rapped on the door of Eunice MacMillan's suite. She knew that Sherri had not abandoned her theory that Eunice had killed her husband, and she certainly hadn't exonerated the woman of complicity in Phil's scheme to defraud his insurance company. If Eunice wasn't in, Liss decided, maybe she would take the opportunity to search the premises. After all, she had Joe Ruskin's permission to enter any room in the hotel. She hardly needed Eunice's okay, let alone a search warrant. At least she didn't think she needed one. Sherri probably knew exactly what constituted illegal search and seizure. She wouldn't approve of Liss's plan. Then again, she didn't have to know about it, not unless Liss found something. She was just about to stick her passkey in the lock when Eunice opened the door.

"Oh, it's you," Eunice said in voice icier than the storm outside. "What do you want?"

"I'd like to come in, Ms. MacMillan."

"Why?"

"I have a few questions for you about Dilys Marcotte."

Eunice jumped back as if she'd stuck her hand in a electrical socket. Her voice rose to a shriek. "Dilys Marcotte? What the hell does that little tramp have to do with anything! That conniving gold digger is long gone."

"I'm afraid that's not quite true," Liss said. "Do you want to discuss this in the hall?"

Reluctantly, Eunice waved her inside. The blanket abandoned on the sofa told Liss that Eunice had been huddling under it for warmth. Reluctant to go back downstairs where Sherri could get at her? Since she'd told Sherri that she wouldn't answer any more questions until she'd consulted a lawyer, that seemed a logical conclusion.

Without waiting for an invitation, Liss plunked herself down in a comfortable armchair and waited for Eunice to sit. Instead, the other woman scooped up the blanket and flung it around her shoulders.

"What's this nonsense about Dilys Marcotte?" she demanded.

"Dilys works at the hotel."

Eunice's expression was one of disbelief. "Surely not. I'd have recognized her."

"Her appearance has changed in the last few years and she's been careful to keep a low profile." How much more, Liss wondered, should she tell Eunice? It had to be enough to provoke her into talking. Suddenly inspiration struck. "Dilys may have been the one who entered your suite while you were meeting with me before the Burns Night Supper."

A fascinating sequence of emotions played across Eunice's features, but chief among them was confusion. She'd lied about the brooch being stolen. Had she also made up the story about someone searching the suite?

"I'm told," Liss said, repeating what she'd learned from Rhonda, "that it was your husband who caused Phineas to break his engagement to Dilys."

Eunice tugged the blanket more tightly closed and settled herself on the sofa with her legs curled beneath her. "Dilys Marcotte," she said, "was only after the trust fund."

"Go on."

"There's not much to tell. Phil and Phineas inherited a trust fund from their father. It was split evenly between the two of them, and the principal was sufficient to allow both of them to live comfortably on the interest. However, the way it was set up, there was a big payout when each of them married. That, of course, reduced the principal. Phil and I benefitted from that provision. Phin's engagement meant he'd get his share, after which the interest on what was left would be much less." She shrugged. "Phil didn't want to take a cut in pay, so to speak, so he started rumors about Dilys. Attacks on her moral character. Her associates. You know the sort of thing."

"Lies?"

"I don't know if the stories were true or not, and I don't care. Phil came up with some photographs—Dilys leaving a motel room with another man. He said he'd hired a private detective to follow her. Whatever the truth of the matter, Phineas believed Phil's story, and the pictures. That was all that counted. In fact, Phil's plan worked even better than he'd hoped. After that, Phineas stopped trusting anyone and he vowed never to marry, which suited Phil very well."

A shrink would have a field day with this family, Liss thought, and even a layperson like herself could see that Phineas had probably been taking out his bitterness on innocent bystanders in that speech at the Burns Night Supper.

"What happens to the trust fund now that Phil's dead?" she asked.

"I inherit Phil's share," Eunice admitted.

Sherri would like that—more motive for Eunice. Time to leave, Liss decided. She thanked Eunice for her time and headed out, intending to go straight to Sherri. Perhaps her friend had picked the right suspect, after all. That trust fund gave Eunice an excellent reason to kill her husband.

Sherri had just come out of one of the rooms on the third floor when she recognized the man walking toward her. It was Phineas MacMillan. Surprise had her going completely blank for a moment. He seemed even more startled to see her.

"Ah, were you looking for your sister-in-law?" Sherri asked when she could string words together coherently. Eunice's suite was just a few doors down. Liss was just leaving it.

"Oh, er . . . yes." He didn't sound very certain.

Liss saw them, recognized Phineas, and for once contained her impatience when Sherri sent her a warning look. She gave a little wave, then headed in the other direction, but she went no farther than the stairwell, where Margaret Boyd was standing guard.

Sherri pulled herself together and ignored the two women. "Could I talk to you a minute, Mr. MacMillan?"

He flashed her a bright, toothy smile at odds with his usual surly manner. "Certainly. How can I help you, Officer?"

She led him to the elevator foyer, furnished with two chairs nobody ever seemed to sit in and a table topped with a vase of artificial flowers. Liss and Margaret hadn't moved. They stood by the exit, eyes glued on Sherri and Phineas. Sherri made a little shooing motion behind Phineas's back, hoping they'd take the hint and make themselves scarce. Liss and her aunt obligingly strode off down the hall, heading away from the elevators. But they stayed in sight.

Once Phineas was seated, Sherri didn't beat around the

bush. "I'm relieved to see you safe and sound, Mr. Mac-Millan. I take it you didn't find Dilys Marcotte?"

Although the emergency lights along the corridor shed very little light, Sherri thought she saw Phineas tense.

"What are you talking about? I haven't seen Dilys in years."

Sherri frowned. Richardson Bruce had told Phineas that she, Sherri, was looking for him. Hadn't he also said that he'd told Phineas she was also looking for Dilys? Yes, she was sure of it. Bruce had said Phineas had been "some startled" by this news. And that was when he'd taken off, presumably to hunt for Dilys.

"Where have you been for the last couple of hours?" she asked.

"Wandering. Exploring this lovely old hotel."

Just like his brother, Sherri thought. And look what had happened to Phil! "And you didn't run into Dilys?"

"Do you mean to tell me that Dilys Marcotte is in this hotel?"

"No one told you she was here?"

"I should think I'd made that obvious. No, no one told me. And to tell you the truth, I'm having difficulty believing it. How could she be here without my noticing her? There aren't that many of us here, you know."

"She works at The Spruces, Mr. MacMillan. As a housekeeper. She was also one of the waitstaff at the cocktail party before the Burns Night Supper."

He shook his head in denial. "I can't believe this. Where is she? I—"

Sherri stopped him from rising by catching the sleeve of his sweater. "There's something you'd better know before you go looking for her. It's possible that Dilys is the one who killed your brother."

"Nonsense!" But he appeared shaken by the suggestion. He made no further effort to leave.

"At the moment, we don't know where she is. That being the case, it might be a good idea if you stayed close to other people."

She didn't need to say that he might be Dilys's next target. He got the message. Uncharacteristically meek, he agreed. "I'll go back down to the lobby. Or to the lounge," he amended, making a weak attempt at humor. "I believe I could use a drink."

Sherri walked him to the stairwell. MacMillan descended the first few steps, then turned back, frowning.

"Officer Willett, you say you don't know where Dilys is now?"

"That's right. We've been looking for her, but she's staying out of sight. She could be anywhere in the hotel."

"Or out of it. I know this sounds mad, given the current weather conditions, but I could have sworn I saw someone setting out across the back lawn on snowshoes not twenty minutes ago."

Sherri watched Phineas until he was out of sight at the bend in the stair before she pulled out her walkie-talkie and ordered everyone back to the conference room.

When they'd exchanged information and Liss had taken her scolding for talking to Eunice on her own, she voiced an objection to Sherri's report. "I don't buy that idea that Dilys took off cross-country. It's sleeting outside! In fact, I'm not sure I believe anything Phineas MacMillan said."

"If Dilys did leave, there's no way we can go after her," Dan said, "but I don't think we should jump to conclusions, either. We should finish searching the hotel."

"I think I know where she is," Margaret said. Liss's aunt was just full of surprises today. "After Sherri and Mr.

MacMillan settled in for their little tête-à-tête by the elevators, I took a stroll down to the east end of the hall. I thought something looked a bit odd about the pocket doors, so I checked. They weren't just unlocked, they were open by a good inch."

Liss wondered how she'd missed that. Probably, she decided, because she'd been brooding about Eunice, thinking that, after all, she probably was a better suspect than Dilys Marcotte.

They reconvened in a truncated section of hallway blocked by the wooden barrier of the pocket doors. The doors themselves were swallowed by shadows. At first even the beam of Sherri's powerful flashlight failed to provide enough illumination to tell if they were tightly closed or not. Liss had to advance all the way down the short corridor before she spotted the gap.

Sherri reached for the knobs on either side and gave a start of surprise when the doors slid apart at her merest touch. "If Dilys used her passkey to open these doors, she may have been in the east wing all along."

"Hiding out?" Liss asked.

"Could be. Although, if that's so, I'm surprised she didn't take the precaution of locking up again after herself."

"And what is she hiding *from*?" Margaret asked. "She has no reason to think you suspect her of anything, does she?"

"Maybe she overheard Richardson Bruce tell Phineas that I was looking for them both." Sherri peered into the icy darkness of the closed-up wing.

Liss ran through the hotel's floor plan in her mind. The kitchen and one section of the restaurant were on the first floor in this wing. She'd been in both rooms and didn't remember seeing any stairs. If Dilys was in this part of the building, she was cornered. All they had to do was flush her out.

"We need more light," Sherri said.

While they'd been searching, the sun had set. That happened far too early at that time of year. It wasn't even five o'clock yet.

"And I need my coat." Liss shivered in her woolly sweater. "It's almost as cold in there as it is outdoors."

"I'll go get it, dear," Margaret offered, and slipped away from the group.

Sherri was already bundled up in her dark blue police-issue jacket, but now she took the gloves out of her pockets and put them on.

"We have everything shut off in that section," Joe said. "No water. No power. No heat."

"No other exit?" Sherri asked.

"There's a stairwell at the far end of this hallway, just outside the tower room. It goes straight to an outside door on the first-floor level."

"That could be how Dilys left," Pete speculated, "assuming Phineas is right about seeing a person fleeing from the hotel on snowshoes."

Liss cocked an ear. The ice storm was still raging. Periodically, over the course of the last hour, she had heard the ominous crack of breaking branches.

Joe scratched his head. "There's no access from that stairwell to the mezzanine or the basement, but someone could come out on the second floor by way of the pocket doors right below us."

Sherri promptly dispatched Joe and Sam to guard them. "Use your walkie-talkies to alert me if you hear any sound at all coming from the other side," she instructed, "and don't get in the way if someone comes out."

"Maybe I should be down there," Pete suggested after the two civilians were on their way.

"I need you here." Sherri contemplated the length of the corridor.

Liss followed the direction of her gaze. There were a lot of rooms. A lot of places to hide.

"Are you sure all this is necessary?" Margaret asked, returning with Liss's coat, an extra sweater for Sherri, and more flashlights. "I mean, you don't actually know that Dilys has done anything wrong. And surely she's not the only suspect."

"Even if she hasn't, she's gone missing. That's cause enough for concern when there's already been one murder on the premises."

Sherri removed her jacket, put on the sweater, and shrugged back into the outer garment. Then she sent Margaret down to join Joe and Sam at the pocket doors. When the older woman had gone, Sherri drew in a deep breath, made a megaphone of her hands, and shouted through the open pocket doors. "Dilys Marcotte. If you're in there, please come out now."

No one answered.

"Is anyone in there?" Sherri called.

Silence.

With a sigh, Sherri turned to her remaining searchers— Liss, Dan, and Pete. "I guess we have to do this the hard way. Check every possible hiding place. Every room. Every closet."

"Wait a sec," Liss objected. "If Dilys did kill Phil and is hiding in here to avoid arrest, then she's not likely to calmly turn herself in if we find her."

"That's why I told Joe and Sam not to try and stop her if she bolts."

"Is she dangerous?" Dan's brows knit together in concern. "I don't like the idea that she might hurt one of us, or my father or brother."

"Or my aunt," Liss added.

Sherri took a deep breath. "I do not believe anyone is in any danger from an overweight, out-of-condition, middle-aged woman, but it pays to be cautious. If you don't want to help search, just say so."

"You can't get rid of us that easily," Liss said.

# Chapter Seventeen

Snug in warm outerwear, armed with extra flashlights, Liss followed Pete and Dan into the east wing of The Spruces. Sherri came last, locking the pocket doors behind her.

"We'll split up," she said, "and meet in the tower room at the end of the hall. Don't take any foolish chances. And . . . thanks." She disappeared into the first room on the right-hand side. Pete entered the one just beyond.

Liss started to unlock the first door on the left, then glanced over her shoulder at Dan. "All of a sudden I'm a little nervous." True, as Sherri had said, they were looking for an overweight, out-of-condition, middle-aged woman. But she had left out one adjective—desperate.

"Fine with me if we do the first few together. You can watch my back."

Feeling foolish and relieved at the same time, Liss nodded. She even let Dan go into the room ahead of her. It was a perfectly ordinary room, with doors leading to a bath and a closet. It was also unfurnished.

"Are you still renovating in here?"

"We have a couple of things left to do. This is the oldest part of the hotel." Dan stood in the center of the empty room, shining his flashlight at the walls and contemplating . . . something.

"What are you looking at?" Liss asked.

"I never fail to be impressed by the sheer mastery of nineteenth-century craftsmen. My brother and I replaced every window in the hotel to make the place more energy efficient, but we took pains to save the interior woodwork. You just don't see molding like that anymore."

Liss made an appreciative murmur, but her knowledge of architectural features was minimal.

"The wood in some of these rooms, including this one, still needs to be stripped and refinished. The old wallpaper has to come off, too." He shone the flashlight at his feet. "The hardwood floorboards are just begging for attention. It's a real pity that we'll end up covering them with wall-to-wall carpeting."

"Even in historic hotels, guests expect some modern amenities," Liss said. "I've got to admit I'm not fond of a cold, bare floor first thing in the morning. So, this section of the hotel dates from 1910?" She ran one hand over the cabbage roses in the wallpaper, wondering if it, too, could possibly be a century old.

"Actually, this wing of the hotel predates that. The first incarnation of The Spruces was up and running by 1890, but it was a pretty small operation. It was 1910 when the owners took a stab at becoming a 'grand hotel' like the Poland Spring House or the Mount Washington Hotel over in New Hampshire. In its heyday, The Spruces had two hundred guest rooms. We reduced that number to a hundred and forty by combining some of them to make suites and by adding private bathrooms to the ones that didn't already have them. But I guess this isn't really the time for a tour-guide spiel."

Liss smiled in the semidarkness. In spite of all the craziness going on around them, she'd never felt more connected to Dan Ruskin than she did right now. Hearing him talk about a topic he loved had calmed her as nothing else could have.

"I don't mind the history lesson. You don't usually say much about the hotel, unless it's to tell me what kind of wood was used in the wainscotting."

"I don't want to bore you. Besides, The Spruces is Dad's baby, not mine."

Liss let that pass. She knew how much of himself Dan had invested in the renovations. He was a fine craftsman. That was evident everywhere there was wood. And there was a lot of wood at The Spruces.

"We need to search the closets and the bath," he reminded her.

No one was hiding in either, but someone had opened up the clothesline strung across the 1980s-style bathtub. Several rags had been draped over it.

"Laundry day?" she asked.

"Those probably got wet cleaning something," Dan said, "but they shouldn't have been left here. Nor should that," he added, pointing to a stepladder that had been folded and propped against the wall. Liss suspected that a Ruskin Construction employee was going to catch hell the next time Dan saw him.

They moved on to the next room. It was the twin of the first, and even emptier. When Liss inspected the bath, she couldn't help but glance at the small metal fitting from which the over-bath clothesline unrolled. This one was empty. The line had been removed.

"I think it's okay to split up now," Liss said after she came out. "I'm over the jitters."

"You sure?"

She nodded. "I'll be fine." She patted her pocket, where the walkie-talkie Sherri had given her resided. "And I'm not exactly out of contact." No one would have any difficulty hearing a good scream, either.

Dan went into the third room on the left. Liss went ahead to number four. She shone her heavy-duty flashlight into every corner and sighed. Nothing. Not even any furniture. Not even drapes or a carpet.

"This could get monotonous," she muttered and stepped inside to check the bath and the closet. "Ah, clothesline intact!" Perhaps if she made a game of the search, she wouldn't have to think too hard about the fact that they were looking for a suspected murderer.

Slowly, the four of them worked their way along the hall until they reached the octagonal room at the back corner. A stairwell was situated just to one side of its door. While Dan went up to inspect the tower room, Liss, Sherri, and Pete headed down. They would follow the same pattern to check the rooms on the second floor, working their way back to the pocket doors where Joe, Sam, and Margaret waited.

Somehow, this level seemed even darker. And colder. All three of them went into the octagonal guest room first. Like its twin upstairs, it yielded nothing of interest, although it was furnished. When Sherri and Pete turned left out of the door, Liss went right.

Her footsteps echoed as she moved along the wood-floored corridor. In spite of her warm coat, she felt chilled to the bone. She tried to shake off the feeling of impending doom as she went through the first door. Obviously, she'd seen one too many promos for bad horror movies. This room was much like all the others she'd searched, except that on this level the renovations were complete and carpet, drapes, and furniture had been installed. Everything looked perfectly normal. But when a faint scraping sound reached her from the hall outside, Liss almost jumped out of her skin.

"Get a grip," she muttered. That had to have been Dan, leapfrogging to the next room. "Dan?" she called softly.

Apparently he was already inside and couldn't hear her.

Although she'd already searched dozens of unoccupied rooms without incident, that single odd sound set Liss's nerves jangling. She couldn't seem to stop thinking up worst-case scenarios. If she was right about Dilys, the four of them were playing cat and mouse with a killer. Since this was the oldest section of the hotel, it probably contained any number of nooks and crannies where a person could hide, places that weren't readily apparent to the searchers, especially when those searchers were hampered by poor visibility.

Cautiously, half expecting Dilys to spring out and bash her over the head as she had struck down poor Phil MacMillan, Liss stepped back out into the hall. The heck with this, she thought. She headed for the room next door instead of the one beyond. She'd hook up with Dan again. They'd search the rest of the rooms together. Safety in numbers was not a cliché. It was a truism.

But Dan was not in the room she entered, nor was he in either of the next two. Liss beat a hasty retreat and shone her flashlight up and down the deserted hallway. The beam of light raked over an unbroken line of closed guestroom doors before it touched, briefly, on the wall next to the stairwell. No Dan.

But there had been something odd about one section of paneling.

Frowning, Liss brought her light back to the anomaly. Curiosity outweighed fear as she moved cautiously closer, sweeping the beam over the area that enclosed the underside of the staircase.

A scene from the first Harry Potter movie played in her head as she examined the wall. Poor Harry's bedroom in his aunt and uncle's house had been a cabinet—or was it called a cupboard?—under the stairs. Could there be a similar storage space tucked into this area? Liss crouched down until she was sitting on her heels. She ran one gloved hand over the wood. If there was a seam or a latch or a knob, she ought to be able to feel it.

A moment later, her searching fingers encountered a rough spot. Her excitement grew as she explored more carefully. There *was* some sort of latch. It was set right into the wall, so that it was nearly invisible, but she could just make out the shape of it if she squinted. She fumbled a moment longer and was rewarded with a sharp clicking sound. A triangular section of paneling creaked loudly as it swung toward her.

Liss scrambled out of the way, grinning as she retreated. This was so classic—the secret passage. Well, secret closet. But still—

Such giddy thoughts came to an abrupt end as the beam of Liss's flashlight revealed what lay inside the space under the stairs. Liss's eyes widened and she gasped. Then she lost her balance and landed on her backside. At floor-level, she was face-to-face with Dilys Marcotte.

Dilys wasn't hiding. She'd been hidden. Bound and gagged, she'd been wedged into the hidden closet.

She didn't respond in any way to the sound of the door opening or Liss's exclamation of shock and surprise. Liss stared at her, unable to tell if she was still breathing. Dilys's knees were tucked up under her chin and her hair had fallen forward to hide her face.

Liss stretched out one trembling hand to feel for a pulse. Dilys jerked when Liss touched her. Liss yelped. Then she yelled for Sherri and Pete. Dan burst through the stairwell door a moment later.

Dilys was more hindrance than help as Sherri and Liss attempted to free her from her prison. She squirmed and grunted and, when she finally tumbled out into the hallway, she glared at them balefully over the top of the handkerchief that had been stuffed into her mouth.

She wasn't hurt, Liss realized. She was madder than a wet hen. Well, why shouldn't she be? Someone had bound and gagged her and rammed her bodily into a storage space barely big enough for a child, let alone a grown woman. Liss removed the gag. She dropped it on the floor and hastily scrambled out of the way when Dilys began to sputter and cough.

Sherri, meanwhile, still struggled to undo the ropes that bound Dilys's hands and feet. "Hold still, Dilys," she muttered. Finally, exasperated, she extracted a folding knife from her utility belt and sliced through the bonds. "What *is* this stuff?"

"Clothesline," Liss said, belatedly recognizing it. "From one of the bathrooms."

Dilys flailed at Sherri and Liss as they tried to help her to her feet.

"Are you injured?" Sherri asked.

"Do you need a doctor?" Liss added.

"What I need is that son of a bitch's head on a platter," Dilys croaked.

"Phineas did this to you?" Sherri asked.

Of course he did, Liss thought, suddenly aware that the handkerchief that had been used to muffle Dilys's cries for help was one of the tartan ones from the hotel gift shop, probably the same one she'd sold to Phineas MacMillan on the day after the murder.

"Phil," Dilys managed to say between paroxysms of coughing. "Phil."

"Don't try to talk just yet, Dilys," Sherri said in a soothing voice. "I know this has all been a terrible shock to you. Don't worry. We'll sort it all out."

Dilys shook her head violently. "It's horrible. Unnatural. How could one twin kill the other?" Then she burst into tears.

"We need to get her someplace warm," Sherri said, exchanging a worried look with Liss over Dilys's head.

Pete, who had been on the walkie-talkie, tucked it away. "Good news," he said as he scooped Dilys up into his arms. "The power just now came back on in the main part of the hotel. Which room was Dilys using? I'll take her straight there."

Liss told him, and by the time they reached the pocket doors at the end of the hall, Joe had them unlocked. Dilys's room was just down the hall.

Liss caught Sherri's arm to hold her back while Pete went on ahead. "Where's Phineas?" she asked. "If Dilys was tied up—"

"He must be the one who left her here?" Sherri grimaced. "I should have twigged to this possibility sooner. When I talked to him, he claimed he didn't even know Dilys was in the hotel, but Richardson Bruce had told him she was here. I knew he was lying. I just never thought—" She broke off, shaking her head. "The thing is, people lie to the police all the time, and it's usually for some stupid but perfectly harmless reason."

"Are you going to arrest him?" Liss asked. Phineas's guilt seemed pretty cut and dried to her.

"I'm going to talk to Dilys first. See if she can fill in some gaps for me."

"Isn't it obvious? He left her there because he needed to put in an appearance, to stop our search. Once we gave up looking for her, he meant to come back and kill her, too. Why else would he have made up that preposterous story about seeing someone leave the hotel on snowshoes?"

Her expression grim, Sherri gestured toward the open door to Dilys's room. "Let's ask Dilys, shall we?"

"No one's doing anything until poor Dilys has a chance to catch her breath," Margaret said, blocking their way. Bustling around the room, she fussed over the thermostat, complained when the heat didn't come up fast enough and, as a temporary measure, bundled Dilys into no fewer than three warm blankets. Then she sent down to the kitchen for a pot of tea.

With an efficiency that impressed Liss, Sherri yielded Dilys's care to Margaret but took charge of everyone else herself. She handed her cell phone to Pete, instructing him to get hold of the state police and bring them up to speed. She sent Joe and Sam back down to the first floor of the hotel.

"Find Phineas," she instructed, "but don't do anything. One of you should keep an eye on him while the other comes back here to tell me exactly where he is."

Then she swore softly.

"What?" Liss asked. She kept one eye on Dilys and Margaret, impatient to ask the housekeeper what had happened to her.

"Some by-the-book cop I am! I left the clothesline and that handkerchief behind in the east wing." She glanced toward Pete, but he was still on the phone, talking in a low voice to the trooper who was nominally in charge of the case.

"I'll go get them," Dan offered. "I have something else to do in that wing anyway. There's a broken window in the tower room that needs to be repaired. That's what took me so long getting down to the second floor. I had to rig up a temporary fix."

"Don't handle the evidence more than you absolutely have to," Sherri called after him.

"Aren't you supposed to have little plastic bags to hold stuff like that?" Liss asked.

"In a perfect world, I'd not only have evidence bags and fancy gadgets, but also a whole crew of forensics experts to back me up. Plus a state-of-the-art lab to test things in. Haven't you ever watched *Bones*?"

"Too gory," Liss told her. "I'm more a *Murder, She Wrote* kind of gal."

Liss was pleased when her wisecrack made Sherri smile. She had begun to worry about her friend. For all Sherri's efficiency, her eyes were bloodshot and her color ashen. Lack of sleep combined with too much responsibility could do in even the healthiest, most capable individual.

When the tea arrived, Liss was glad to see that it had come in a large pot and that there were three cups with it. Satisfied, Margaret cleared out and Pete left to see if he could locate Phineas, since neither Joe nor Sam had returned. Somewhat to Liss's surprise, Sherri did not insist that she go, too. When Sherri plunked herself down at the foot of Dilys's bed, Liss grabbed the desk chair and moved it closer to the two of them.

When they'd first found her, Dilys's face had been pasty white. Now a bit of color had returned to her cheeks and her breathing was steady. She'd stopped crying, although the tracks of tears still stained her cheeks. Considering what she'd been through, Liss was amazed that she was as calm as she was.

"Okay, Dilys," Sherri said when all three of them had teacups in hand. "I need you to tell me exactly what happened to you. Was it Phineas MacMillan who tied you up?"

Dilys's eyes immediately filled. "No."

Liss and Sherri exchanged a startled look. If not Phineas, then who?

"Was there someone else in that closed-up wing?" Sherri asked. "Did Phineas have a confederate? Eunice, maybe?"

Dilys answered with a bleat of hysterical laughter. The hand holding the teacup shook visibly. She set it back in its saucer with a loud clatter. Before the hot liquid could spill all over her, Liss rescued it and set the cup on the bedside table next to her own. Dilys swiped at her streaming eyes with both hands. Sherri raided the bathroom for a handful of tissues. Dilys noisily blew her nose.

"All right, Dilys," Sherri said with badly concealed exasperation. "Let's try this from another angle. Who tied you up?"

Dilys sniffled, crumpled the tissues in her hand, and drew in a shaky breath. "Phil MacMillan."

"*Phil*? Dilys, I think you're confused. Phil—"

"No, *you're* confused." Dilys sat up straighter and glared at both Sherri and Liss. "Do you want to hear my side of this or not?"

"Yes, we do, Dilys," Sherri said in a tight voice.

Liss studied Dilys's face. Was the woman delusional? Had she been hit on the head?

"Let's start at the beginning, okay?" Sherri suggested. "Keep everything in order?"

"Go all the way back, Dilys," Liss said. "Back to when you and Phineas were engaged to be married."

Dilys turned on her, eyes narrowed. "How do you know about that?"

"I saw an old picture in a newspaper. It showed you with the twins and Eunice. I also found the clipping about the Burns Night Supper in your room at Rhonda's house. I know you only came to Moosetookalook because you wanted to be here that night. What did you plan to do, Dilys?"

Dilys wrapped the blankets more tightly around herself. "I'll tell you everything, okay? I will. It's just . . . hard."

Sherri patted her arm consolingly, although Liss could tell she was running out of patience. "Take your time," she said.

*Just not too much of it*, Liss thought. If this were a mystery novel instead of real life, she'd already have peeked at the ending.

*   *   *

It didn't take Dan long to retrieve the length of thin, strong clothesline and the handkerchief. They were right where Sherri and Liss had let them fall when they'd freed Dilys—in front of the closet under the stairs. Dan tucked both into one of the capacious pockets in his jacket.

He'd stopped at a utility closet for supplies on his way back to the east wing. Armed with a sheet of heavy-duty plastic and a staple gun, he headed up the stairs to the fourth-floor tower room. One of the windowpanes had been broken by the storm. Struck by a flying branch, most likely. Sleet had been pouring into the room earlier, when he'd gone up there to search for Dilys. He'd plugged the hole with rags, but that wouldn't keep the elements out for long.

Sturdier repairs weren't difficult to make, but the job required all his concentration. He was working by the dim light of a lantern placed on the floor. It hadn't seemed worth the effort to go down to the basement and throw the breaker switch to turn power back on in this wing, not for a simple job like this one.

He was careful not to damage the window frame as he fastened the plastic securely in place. The biggest challenge came from random gusts of wind and the cold. It was so intense that his fingers felt like icicles even with gloves on. In spite of the adverse conditions, he finished up a quarter of an hour later and stood back to examine his handiwork. The small flashlight he'd had in his pocket confirmed that the result wasn't pretty, but it would do.

The octagonal tower had large windows in all eight sides. They looked out over the surrounding mountains. If the sky had been clear and it had been daylight, Dan would have been able to see halfway to Mt. Washington in neighboring New Hampshire. Even on a wretched night like that one, his memory provided a picture of that view on a bright summer's day. Once work was finished in this room and its twin in the west wing, they would be a real draw for guests, just as the other two tower rooms and the suites in the central tower already were.

Dan wasn't sure how long he stood there, contemplating the hotel's future, before he was jerked back to his surroundings by a squawk from his walkie-talkie. Pete's voice filled the room. "Dan? You still in the east wing?"

He depressed the TALK button. "I'm just finishing up repairs on a bit of storm damage in the tower room. Tell Sherri to hold her horses. I'll be there in a minute with her evidence."

"You see anything of MacMillan?"

Dan frowned. In the east wing? "Not a trace. Did you lose him again? That's getting to be a bad habit."

"He isn't where he said he'd be," Pete replied. "I'm headed back to the second floor to see if Sherri has finished taking Dilys's statement. Meanwhile, you'd best get down here."

"On my way."

Dan hooked the walkie-talkie back onto his belt and looked around for his staple gun. He'd put it down on the floor and it had promptly been swallowed up by shadows. He'd just spotted it when he heard a faint sound behind him. He turned, aiming the flashlight toward the door. The beam revealed nothing but bare floor and empty space.

"Is someone there? Liss?" It wouldn't surprise him if she'd come looking for him. That was Liss all over—too impatient to wait for anything.

But the silhouette that shifted out of the greater darkness near the bath was far too bulky to be Liss MacCrimmon. Dan swung his light over and up. For an instant, teeth gleamed white in the flashlight beam. Then something flew in Dan's direction.

He tried to duck, but his reaction time was slowed by

disbelief. His brain had registered that the object was another flashlight—one of those high-powered, long-handled ones that were way too heavy for ordinary household use—but he didn't have time to get out of the way before it struck him, hard, on the side of his head.

He felt a moment of pain. Then everything went black.

# Chapter Eighteen

———————

"I did come to Moosetookalook because of the Burns Night Supper," Dilys confessed. "I knew Rhonda had a job at the hotel and I figured she could get me in. I wanted to see Phineas again." She sighed deeply.

"What were you planning to do?" Sherri asked.

"I didn't have a plan. Not really. I just hoped I'd have a chance to talk to him without Phil around. I . . . I wanted him to know that Phil lied about me. Phineas wouldn't listen at the time, and I didn't have any proof anyway."

"Do you now?" Liss asked.

"Yeah. A couple of months ago, I ran into the photographer Phil hired to fake those photos of me coming out of a motel with some guy. He told me the whole story, but I figured it was too late to do anything about it. Then, just after my cousin had been telling me about this great new job she had, I saw that item in the newspaper. It seemed like fate." Dilys swabbed at her eyes. "A chance for a little payback, maybe, but mostly I just wanted to set the record straight. I wasn't after Phineas MacMillan's money. I really thought I loved him back then. And I wasn't some cheap little tramp who cheated on him!"

"Whew," Sherri said, scribbling notes to herself. "Okay, Dilys, let's fast-forward a bit. You're at the hotel. Working. All three of the MacMillans had checked in by around three. You didn't get off till four. Did you see Phineas that afternoon?"

"Oh, I saw him all right. He and his brother and Eunice walked right past me in the hall and none of them gave me a second glance." She looked ready to turn into a fountain again.

"On the third floor?" Liss asked. "On their way down to meet me?"

"I don't know where they were going, but they all came out of three-twelve just as I was coming down from cleaning the fifth-floor tower room. I . . . I was caught off guard. I backed up into the alcove where the ice and snack machines are, but Phineas . . . he looked right at me." Her voice rose to a wail. "He used to swear he'd love me forever and he didn't even recognize me!"

Sherri looked sympathetic, but that didn't stop her from pressing for more information. "Did you see Harvey MacMillan?"

Liss sent a startled glance her way. What did Harvey have to do with anything?

"I didn't see anyone else," Dilys said.

Sherri gave a dismissive little wave. "No, I guess you wouldn't have. Forget I mentioned it. Harvey was people-watching through the peephole in his door and all he saw was an unidentifiable shadow, but that must have been you. What happened next, Dilys? Did you by chance go into Phil and Eunice MacMillan's suite?"

Dilys hung her head. Her answer was barely audible. "Yes."

"Why?"

"Since all three of them came out of that door, I thought maybe it was Phineas's room. I don't know exactly what I had in mind to do. I was upset that he didn't recognize me, but I guess I was a little bit relieved, too, because his brother was with him, and I didn't want anything to do with Phil. I thought if three-twelve was Phineas's room, I could wait in there until he came back. Then I could talk to him alone. But as soon as I got inside the suite, I saw Eunice's things scattered around and I knew I'd made a mistake."

"But you didn't leave right away, did you?" Liss asked.

Dilys was silent for so long that she thought the housekeeper might not answer, but at last she took another deep breath and resumed her story. She kept her head down, as if ashamed, and fixed her eyes on her hands, which she held tightly clasped in her lap. She'd discarded the blankets. The room was now comfortably warm.

"I don't know what came over me. But, like I just told you, it was Phil who sabotaged my engagement to Phineas. And suddenly I just felt so *angry* with him. I pulled the cushions off the sofa and threw them across the room. Then I went into the bedroom and grabbed the pillows from the bed and tossed them on the floor, too. I know that sounds pretty lame, but I was just so frustrated. I had to do *something*."

"So a few pillows? That's it?" Pencil poised over notebook, Sherri waited.

Dilys shook her head. "When I looked around, I saw how neatly Phil MacMillan had all his things arranged. Just so. All very orderly and organized. Suddenly I wanted to do something that would really piss him off. I thought about smashing his laptop, but somehow that didn't seem personal enough."

"You could have *stolen* his laptop, or other valuables," Liss suggested. "Stashed them in your housekeeping cart."

Dilys looked offended. "I'm not a thief. And I didn't appreciate being questioned about some stupid missing property when I came back to the hotel later that evening. If someone stole something from Phil MacMillan or from anyone else in this hotel, it wasn't me."

Liss kept silent. Both she and Sherri knew very well that Dilys hadn't taken the brooch, but Sherri said only, "Will you tell me what else you did do while you were in the MacMillans' suite?"

Dilys worried her lower lip. "There were some papers stacked on the desk. I tossed them onto the floor, too. And I pulled some clothes out of the closet and stomped on them—Phil's good plaid and a spare kilt. And then I dumped that fancy after-shave of his right down the drain."

"Okay. And then?" Sherri seemed certain there was more.

Liss suspected there was, too, since she'd watched Dilys become steadily more agitated as she made her confession. She'd never before seen anyone literally wring her hands, but Dilys was.

"It was the papers," Dilys whispered. "I didn't notice until I was on my way out, but the pile of papers I'd knocked over had been stacked on top of a passport. Hiding it. And there was another paper beneath the passport. The paper had Phin's name written all over it. His signature, I mean. That stopped me dead. I couldn't think why such a thing would be there in Phil's room."

"Please go on, Dilys," Sherri said when the older woman abruptly stopped speaking. "Liss, give her a fresh cup of that tea."

"I'm okay." But Dilys took the cup Liss handed her and drank half of it in one gulp.

"Whose passport was it?" Liss asked.

"Phineas's. And tucked inside was Phineas's driver's license."

Liss felt her eyebrows lift. "Why would Phil have his brother's documents?"

"That's what I wondered. It kinda spooked me, finding them. That's when I got out of there. Fast. It was time for me to go off shift anyway. I was supposed to meet Rhonda and Sadie. I . . . I just left. I decided to forget I'd ever gone into three-twelve."

"But you left the pillows and papers and clothes all scattered around," Sherri pointed out. "That was enough to betray the fact that someone had been there."

"I wasn't thinking."

"Why did finding the passport and driver's license upset you?" Liss asked.

"I . . . I don't know, exactly. But it stood to reason that Phil was probably up to no good." Dilys gave a short, humorless laugh. "He was always up to something. I thought about it after I got back to Rhonda's place. I decided maybe he had Phineas's papers because he was trying to set his brother up to take the blame for something *he'd* done. Phil, I mean. So, by the time I came back to the hotel that evening, I'd made my mind up to talk to Phineas, no matter what, and tell him what his brother did to us all those years ago and tell him about the passport, too. I figured if I stuck around after the cocktail party, I could maybe take him aside and talk to him. But then we got hauled in for questioning." She sent a resentful look Sherri's way.

"So you never got the chance to talk to Phineas, after all?" Sherri asked.

"Not then. But after the power went out, everyone was in the lobby, at least for a little bit, and when Phineas went off on his own, I followed him. I caught up with him near the stairs by the freight elevator and persuaded him to come and sit with me on that padded bench in the vestibule outside the restaurant. I had to tell him who I was." Bitterness underscored her words. "And then, of course, he didn't want to listen to a word I said. He started to leave, so I just blurted out what I'd seen in Phil's suite. That got his attention!"

"So he didn't know that his brother had his passport and driver's license?" Liss was starting to have difficulty keeping all the details straight. Her fingers itched for a yellow lined pad and a felt-tip pen so she could make a "who knew what when" list.

"He said Phil *couldn't* have them. He even pulled the wallet out of his sporran to show me his real driver's license."

"So the one you saw in Phil's suite was a fake," Sherri murmured, still scribbling.

"It must have been, and that's what Phineas thought. He got really ticked off about it, too."

"How long were you and Phineas together in the vestibule?" Sherri asked.

"Not long. No more than ten minutes. Phineas was finally willing to listen, so I told him what Phil had done with hiring that photographer and all. But he said the past didn't matter. And he told me that he'd prefer it if I didn't bother him again. He said that he certainly didn't intend to acknowledge that he knew me." She looked down at the white blouse and black slacks she'd been wearing ever since the cocktail party. "I suppose he could tell by my clothes that I worked at the hotel. It was pretty clear he thought I was beneath his notice."

"Did anyone see you together?" Sherri asked.

"I don't think so."

"Do you know what time it was when you talked to him?"

Dilys shook her head.

"Which of you left first?" Sherri asked.

"I did," Dilys said. "I came here, to my room, and stayed here."

"And which way was Phineas going when you last saw him?"

"He was just standing there, in the middle of the vestibule, looking like he wanted to strangle his brother."

Liss and Sherri exchanged a speaking glance. Phineas could have told Sherri the truth. He could have been heading for his room and gone there directly after he talked to Dilys. The stairs by the freight elevator led to the second floor.

They also led to the basement, where his brother had later been found murdered.

Phineas's conversation with Dilys had given him reason to be angry with his brother. Add to that the lie he'd told Sherri about not knowing that Dilys was in the hotel, and Liss was convinced they'd found Phil's murder.

"Near as I can figure," Sherri said, "Phil must have been at the gift shop at about the same time you were talking to Phineas. Very soon afterward, Phil was dead."

"No," Dilys said. "You've got it wrong."

Confused, Sherri cocked her head. "It was Phineas at the gift shop? Phineas who fought with Will MacHenry?"

Liss started to object. She *knew* that had been Phil. She'd gotten a good look at his bow tie. But Dilys spoke up before Liss could remind Sherri of that.

"I don't know anything about Will MacHenry. I don't even know who Will MacHenry is. You still don't get it. I talked to Phineas *before* the murder. That part is right. That's the one thing I'm absolutely sure of." Dilys leaned forward until her eyes locked with Sherri's. "Because the body in the storage room isn't Phil MacMillan. Don't you get it? It's Phineas who's dead. And *Phil* is the one who killed him."

Dan shifted, trying to find a comfortable position on the cold floor. He was trussed up like a turkey. With his hands tied behind him, his arms were forced back at an unnatural angle. His shoulders ached and his fingers had gone numb.

At least he wasn't gagged. And unlike the turkey, his feet were free. And he was still alive. He really, really hoped he was going to stay that way. He didn't want to end up dead. He had a lot he wanted to do yet with his life, not the least of which was spend the rest of it with Liss MacCrimmon.

Dan had no idea how much time had passed since he'd been knocked out, but he did know that his captor was nervous. MacMillan paced from one window to the next in the octagonal tower room, watching the storm.

That was why he hadn't taken off for parts unknown, Dan decided. He had to wait till the weather cleared. But why take a hostage? If he'd just stayed in the shadows, Dan would have gone back downstairs and been none the wiser.

No, he supposed, that wasn't strictly true. MacMillan must have heard Pete say they couldn't find him. It would only be a matter of time before they started a new search.

MacMillan had killed his own brother. Dan found that hard to believe, but what other conclusion was there? He couldn't imagine ever being mad enough at Sam to murder him, and they'd been plenty mad at each other on occasion. And weren't twins supposed to be even closer than regular brothers?

MacMillan started to turn his way. Dan quickly closed his eyes. Somehow it seemed safer to pretend he was still unconscious.

Footsteps came closer, then moved away again. He risked a peek through half-closed eyes. MacMillan was back at the window.

This was absurd, Dan thought. There had to be something he could do to improve his situation. For one thing, he didn't want Liss to come looking for him and walk straight into trouble.

He tried moving his hands. He had a little mobility. And his right thumb was touching the walkie-talkie attached to his belt. If could wiggle his fingers a little closer and hit the TALK button and hold it down, then he'd be broadcasting everything that happened in this room—not just what he said, but his captor's words, too. It was worth a try.

"Until this afternoon, I thought that the dead guy *was* Phil," Dilys said. "I figured Phineas killed him because of what I told him. That's why I was so desperate to get out of here the next day."

"You convinced Rhonda and Sadie to leave the hotel with you on snowshoes so you could get away from Phineas?" Liss asked a second before Sherri could.

Dilys nodded. "I was trying to avoid the man I *thought* was Phineas. The surviving twin. I was afraid he'd see me as a threat, since I knew about the passport and all. I was scared when he cornered me in the locker room at noontime today. But when I saw him close up, I realized that he *wasn't* Phineas. That's when I really panicked."

"Did he know you recognized him?" Sherri asked.

"I don't think so. I tried not to let on."

"You're sure he didn't guess? Why else would he kidnap you?"

"I . . . I don't know. All I know is that as soon as he was sure there was nobody else around, he grabbed me and took my passkey and opened the pocket doors and dragged me into the east wing and tied me up." Her voice rose higher with every word.

Liss believed her. All of it, including the fact that Phil had been pretending to be Phineas. He'd even adopted Phineas's annoying habit of addressing people as "kiddies."

"Do you suppose Phil planned to kill Phineas all along?" she asked Sherri.

"Can you think of any other reason why he'd have copies of Phineas's passport and driver's license?"

"He's a monster!" Dilys sobbed. She grabbed Liss's arm in a bruising grip. "He told me he was going to see to it that I was blamed for the murder. That he'd make my death look like a suicide, like I'd killed myself out of guilt for killing Phil."

"And Rhonda would have confirmed that you'd told her that you'd *like* to kill him," Liss murmured.

"He was gloating when he tied me up. I bet if he'd known I was in the hotel to begin with, he'd have set me up to take the blame for the murder right from the start." Dilys shuddered convulsively.

"But why?" Sherri asked. "Why did Phil want to take Phineas's place?"

"Phil was in financial trouble," Liss mused aloud, "but there was a trust fund. If Phil took Phineas's place, then that money would be his, plus he'd have a clean slate. No bankruptcy in his future. No debts to settle."

"But why kill Phineas here? And why in such a brutal way?" Sherri's complexion took on a greenish tinge, making Liss glad she'd never had to look at the body herself. "Dilys, did Phil say anything to you about what his original plan was?"

Dilys shook her head.

But Liss was remembering something else. "Suicide," she whispered.

"What?"

"Remember? When I first heard how he'd died, my first thought was *skean dhu—just big enough for a Scot to slit his own throat with.* And I *thought* that because only that afternoon, Phil and Eunice made sure I overheard them bantering about Phil being the one who kept his skean dhu sharp while Phineas's was always dull."

"That doesn't make sense. If a death is ruled a suicide, life insurance companies won't pay up."

"Trust fund," Liss repeated. "Maybe he didn't care if he left Eunice broke."

"He doesn't care about anybody," Dilys said. "He'd have killed me as easy as he'd lop the head off a chicken." She looked as if she might be sick.

"You need to rest," Sherri said. "Don't worry. You're safe now." She stood and Liss followed suit.

"You're leaving me here alone?" Panic sent Dilys's voice up an octave.

"Pete Campbell will stand guard right outside your door until we have Phil MacMillan in custody. You have my word on it."

Dilys still looked terrified.

"We could find Rhonda for you," Liss offered.

But Dilys shook her head. "No thanks. I don't think I'm up to explaining all this to her just yet. My cousin's a little slow on the uptake on her best day."

Back in the hall, Sherri used her walkie-talkie to contact Pete and ask him to meet them on the second floor. Then she sagged against the wall to wait for him. "It's a pretty crazy story."

"But you believe her."

"How can I not? Somebody tied her up and stuffed her in that closet."

"Phineas is missing," Pete reported, jogging toward them. "If you were hoping to talk to him again, you're out of luck."

"No," Sherri said. "Phineas is dead. Phil is the one who's missing."

Pete gave a low whistle and listened in amazement as Sherri repeated everything Dilys had told them.

"He has to be somewhere in the hotel," Sherri added. "The storm's still going strong. It's not fit weather out there for man nor beast."

"Got that right," Pete said. Suddenly struck by a thought, he asked, "Did Dan get back with the clothesline and that handkerchief? Last I heard, he was on his way out of the east wing, but that was a while ago."

"We haven't seen him," Sherri said. She tried the walkie-talkie, but there was something wrong with it.

Pete fiddled his with his unit, but got no better results. "It's acting like someone's TALK button is stuck."

Liss tried not to panic, but she had a bad feeling about this development. It wasn't like Dan to disappear, not when he had to know she'd worry.

Ten minutes later, Liss's worst fear was confirmed. A voice came over the walkie-talkie, faint but distinct.

"Stop playing possum, Ruskin," Phil MacMillan said. "I didn't hit you that hard."

# Chapter Nineteen

L iss listened in growing horror as Phil's voice faded in
and out. He was pacing toward Dan, then away, muttering to himself. Most of his words were too indistinct to
catch.

"Dan must be holding the TALK button down," Pete
said.

"Do you think they're still in the east wing?" Sherri
asked.

"Must be. It he knocked Dan out, he couldn't carry him
far. Dan was making repairs to the room at the top of the
tower. They're probably still there."

Well out of reach, Liss thought. Phil MacMillan was
trapped, but so was Dan.

Then, clearly, they heard MacMillan say, "What the
hell? Let go of that!"

A loud thump followed. Then silence.

"He spotted the walkie-talkie," Pete said.

Liss's chest tightened unbearably at the realization that
Dan's danger had just increased tenfold.

Sherri's hand shook as she held up her own walkie-
talkie. "I can talk to him. Tell him we'll negotiate for
Dan's safe release. But then he'll know for certain that
we've been listening. I . . . I don't think he's rational."

The walkie-talkie suddenly crackled back to life and

Sherri had to clench her fingers around the unit to keep from dropping it.

"I know you're there," Phil said, "so listen and listen good. You try anything and I kill Ruskin. I've got nothing to lose. You hear me?"

"I hear you, Mr. MacMillan," Sherri said. Her voice had only a slight tremor.

"As soon as the storm clears, I'm getting out of here."

"Whatever you say, Mr. MacMillan, but be advised that the driveway is barely passable."

"Get it cleared!"

Dead silence followed. He'd turned off his unit, ending further communication.

"Trees are out of the way," Pete said. "Just a matter of plowing and sanding."

"We can't let him take Dan with him!" Liss's voice rose the same way Dilys's had.

"Take it easy." Sherri took Liss by the shoulders and gave her a hard shake. "We need clear heads. Panic won't help. The first thing we need to do is contact the state police. They have people who are trained to handle this kind of thing. Meanwhile, we don't do anything to set MacMillan off. And we don't go looking for them." She waited until Liss met her eyes. "Got it?"

"Got it. But you can't let them leave the hotel."

Visions of high-speed chases, car crashes, and flaming vehicles filled her mind. She took several deep breaths, fighting to get herself back under control. Sherri was right. Panic was bad. She'd be no good to anybody, least of all Dan, if she couldn't think straight.

She leaned against the wall while Sherri made her phone call. She didn't even try to listen in. Any state police negotiator was miles away, and there was no phone in the unfinished tower suite. Of course she knew they couldn't go rushing in to rescue Dan without putting him at greater risk, but there had to be *something* they could do.

"Eunice," she said aloud.

Sherri had just ended her phone call with the state police. The scowl on her face changed into an expression of mild confusion. "What?"

"Eunice," Liss repeated. "I'm going to go talk to her. Maybe she knows something that will help us persuade Phil to turn himself in."

Five minutes later, Sherri and Liss were standing in front of Room 312. "Remember what I said," Sherri reminded Liss. "Let me handle this. You're too emotionally involved."

"And you're not?"

"Dan's my friend. You're in love with him. Big difference."

Sherri had been watching Liss closely. She'd never seen her friend so shaken, and they'd been through a lot together. Sherri had a feeling that if she didn't keep an eye on her, and include her where she could, Liss would go charging into the east wing in spite of her promise, too impatient—and too afraid of what Phil might do to Dan—to wait for the hostage negotiator to take charge.

Sherri pounded loudly on the door of the MacMillans' suite. "Open up, Ms. MacMillan!" she shouted. "This is the police."

A weak smile flickered across Liss's face. "I bet you've always wanted to say that."

"Of course I have," Sherri agreed, glad to see even a brief return of Liss's usual lighthearted outlook on life.

The sound of muffled footsteps on the other side of the door killed the moment.

"Yes?" Eunice kept hold of the door with one hand

while she brushed tangled hair out of her face with the other.

"It's about your husband, Ms. MacMillan." Sherri pushed past her, using enough force to make Eunice stagger back a few steps.

"My husband is dead."

Sherri reached the middle of the suite's living room and turned, one hand resting lightly on her holster. "No, he's not. Shut the door, Ms. MacMillan, unless you want all your friends in SHAS to hear."

Eunice closed the door.

"Have a seat, Ms. MacMillan." Sherri's tone made it clear this was an order and not a request.

Eunice sat on the edge of the sofa, her hands tightly clasped in her lap. She looked from Sherri to Liss and back to Sherri, her eyes wary. Liss perched on the arm of the chair opposite.

"Jig's up, Ms. MacMillan. We know your husband killed his brother."

"What nonsense is this?" Eunice's attempt to look insulted was not particularly convincing.

Sherri hesitated. If Dan weren't in imminent danger, she wouldn't be talking to Eunice. This wasn't her job. She'd catch hell for not waiting for the state boys to arrive, let alone for trying to badger Eunice into answering questions. But Eunice had already cut short a previous interview by threatening to lawyer up. Sherri couldn't let her get away with that a second time. Not when Phil had Dan. Her job wasn't worth a friend's life.

She read Eunice MacMillan her rights.

"You're arresting me? You've got a lot of nerve. You have no—"

"Your husband has taken a hostage, Ms. MacMillan," Sherri said.

"No, he wouldn't—" Eunice broke off, realizing too late what the wording of her protest had given away.

"You needn't try to deny that your husband is still alive, Ms. MacMillan. Dilys Marcotte can tell the difference between Phil and Phineas just as easily as you can."

Eunice seemed to wilt before their eyes. She sagged against the back of the sofa, her face contorting as silent tears coursed down it.

Sherri almost felt sorry for her, but she didn't have time to indulge the other woman. "Snap out of it, Ms. MacMillan. I need you to answer my questions. Think of the bright side. If you help us persuade your husband to release Dan Ruskin, things will go easier on you."

"Why would he listen to me?" Eunice continued to sob.

That was not what Sherri wanted to hear.

Liss had restrained herself so far, letting Sherri do all the talking, but now she leaned over and, a bit awkwardly, patted the other woman on the shoulder. "You're his wife, Eunice. His helpmeet. His partner. I'm sure you have more influence with him than you realize."

"A lot you know." Eunice swiped at the moisture on her face. Her voice was brittle and full of bitterness. "He married me for my money. It's always money with Phil. You wouldn't believe how furious he was when he asked Phineas for help . . . financial help . . and Phineas flat-out refused."

"Is that when Phil decided to kill his brother and take his place?" Sherri asked.

Eunice stared into space for a long moment. Then she drew in a deep breath and turned a sharp-eyed gaze on Sherri. Clearly, she was no longer wavering on the verge of an emotional breakdown. Sherri had to wonder if she ever had been.

With icy-cold clarity, Eunice MacMillan laid out her

price for cooperating with the police. At the top of the list was immunity from prosecution.

Sherri kept her face expressionless and her voice bland and boldly told a blatant lie. "That can be arranged, Ms. MacMillan, if you'll help us right now by telling us all you know. We don't know how much time we have before the storm lets up and Phil tries to leave the hotel."

Eunice studied her a moment longer, then nodded.

Sherri hid her relief. Bluff and double bluff. Eunice didn't know as much as she thought she did about how those things worked. Thank goodness television cop shows usually got it wrong! Sherri didn't have any authority to offer any kind of a deal, but as long as Eunice thought she did, as long as she believed that Sherri could keep her out of jail, she'd answer questions. Now Sherri just had to ask the right ones and hope that Eunice knew something that would help rescue Dan.

"Is your husband armed?" she asked.

Eunice shook her head. Sherri heard Liss's small sound of relief.

"Not even Phineas's skean dhu?"

Eunice frowned. "Maybe. I don't know. Phineas kept it dull, so it hardly matters."

That didn't mean it was *still* dull, Sherri thought, or that it couldn't be used to stab someone, but she kept those thoughts to herself. Eunice might have control of her emotions, but Sherri wasn't so sure about Liss.

"The state police negotiator will probably want you to talk to Phil. Will you do that?"

"It won't do any good. If he's taken someone hostage, he's obviously gone off the deep end. I should have seen it coming."

Liss had stood as much as she could. "Wasn't that obvious from the moment he started planning to murder his twin brother and make it look like suicide?"

"Suicide?" A flicker of surprise showed on Eunice's otherwise immobile face. "It was going to be an accident, not suicide. Phil was going to drown Phineas in the hotel pool. Why else would he have arranged for Phineas to meet him in the basement?"

The whole story tumbled out then, in more or less coherent form. Sherri thought she had the gist of it. Phil's plan had been to kill Phineas and make it look like an accident, identify the body as Phil, and take Phineas's identity, gaining Phineas's share of the trust-fund income and all Phineas's other assets for himself. Originally, however, they'd intended to kill Phineas on his way home from The Spruces. In a car crash.

Dilys's search of their suite had thrown a spanner in the works. Phil, thinking that it was *Phineas* who'd been there and that he'd found the passport and driver's license while Phil and Eunice were buying toothpaste, had moved up the timetable. He'd studied the hotel literature, seen that there was a pool, and made plans accordingly, even to visiting the gift shop to let people know that he was headed that way.

"What went wrong?" Sherri asked. "How did he end up slitting his brother's throat?"

Eunice winced at the blunt question but, now that she'd started her story, she seemed determined to finish it. "Phil told me afterward that Phineas was acting all suspicious. Well, he would, wouldn't he, after what he found in our suite? Anyway, Phil couldn't get him to go near the pool. After a couple of minutes of arguing, Phineas said he'd talk to Phil in the morning. He said he had something he had to do first. Then he turned his back on Phil and headed for the stairwell. That's when Phil noticed the Dumpster and remembered the quarrel we'd witnessed earlier. He told me it was serendipity. Suddenly he just knew that old bagpipe would be in there, and that it would have lots of fingerprints all over it. He fished it out and hit Phineas over the head with it."

"But then it would look like murder," Sherri said.

"Yes." Eunice almost smiled. "After that speech Phineas gave, it made perfect sense. There would be lots of suspects. Phil said it all fell into place as he was dragging his brother through the first unlocked door he found. He finished the job in there."

"But how on earth could he expect to get away with such a thing in this day and age? Twins don't have the same fingerprints, do they?" Liss blurted out the questions, then sent Sherri an apologetic look. Sherri shrugged. She'd like to hear Eunice's answers to those questions herself.

"Phil said no one would question the identification if I made it. That's why we kicked up such a fuss and demanded to see the body." Eunice glanced at Sherri. "But you wouldn't let us into the storage room. Phil was furious about that, even hours later when we got together to make sure we had our stories straight. He'd taken so much trouble with the body, you see."

"I'm not sure I do," Sherri said.

"Well, neither of them wore rings, so that wasn't a problem, but Phil took Phineas's wallet and key card out of his sporran and put one of the keys to our suite in. You never even looked, did you?"

Sherri shook her head. She'd been trying too hard to preserve the crime scene.

"Phil used his own skean dhu and took Phineas's. And since Ms. MacCrimmon here called his attention to them, he swapped bow ties. Thank goodness they both wore clip-ons."

Phil MacMillan, Sherri thought, was even more cold-blooded than she'd imagined. Or a lot crazier. "So, he knocked Phineas out, made the necessary exchanges, and then slit his brother's throat. Have I got that right?"

Eunice nodded. Liss was looking rather ill. Sherri hoped she could hold it together for a few minutes longer. She had more questions to ask.

"Why complicate matters with that business of the stolen brooch?" she asked.

Eunice gave a disdainful snort. "That's Phil all over. Can't resist the chance to make an extra buck. I told him it was a mistake to bring the police in. Look at what happened. If you hadn't already been here asking questions about the brooch, there wouldn't have been anyone to stop us looking at the body."

She was right about that, Sherri thought. Civilians would undoubtedly have moved the body and disturbed the crime scene. Added fingerprints. Phil's would have been found, but as he was supposed to be the dead guy, no one would think anything of that. Would an autopsy have revealed that the body was Phineas and not Phil? Sherri was almost certain it would have, meaning that Phil's grand plan had been flawed from the beginning, but she could see how Phil might have convinced himself that it would work.

"Then Dilys Marcotte turned up," she said aloud.

Eunice's eyes went even colder. "Damn that Phil. He should have told me about that development. We could have figured something out."

"Instead, he grabbed her, locked her in a closet, and planned to go back later and kill her. He told her he was going to make it look like a suicide. As if she'd killed herself out of remorse for murdering Phil."

Eunice snorted again. "I take it she got away."

"She was found. And now Phil has taken another hostage. What will persuade him to let Dan Ruskin go unharmed?"

"Money," Eunice said promptly. "Lots and lots of money."

Talking to Eunice had been a waste, Liss thought. Oh, yes, they now knew what had happened to Phineas and why. Eunice had neatly wrapped up several loose ends. But she had been useless as far as being able to suggest a way to rescue Dan. Even if they had pots of money to offer him, Phil must know he had nowhere to run. The state police were on their way. They'd be at the hotel in less than an hour.

The storm had finally petered out. Joe and Sam were even now clearing the driveway and laying down sand. Any minute now, Phil MacMillan would try to slip out of the hotel with his hostage. Liss was half out of her mind with worry.

For the first time, she really understood what Dan had gone through every time she'd been in danger. Now that his life was at stake, she found that she could not imagine her life without Dan in it, nor did she want to. He *had* to come through this crisis safely.

"There has to be a way to rescue Dan," she said for what felt like the hundredth time. She was with Pete and Sherri in the conference room. Waiting. They'd been waiting for hours, hoping Phil MacMillan would contact them. The walkie-talkies remained ominously silent.

"There's no way we can sneak up on MacMillan in the tower suite," Pete said. "He'd hear us coming. And he's got a clear shot down the stairwell to an outside door when he's ready to leave."

"We don't believe he's armed," Sherri said, trying to sound reassuring.

"Except for Phineas's skean dhu."

"We don't know—"

"We don't know anything!" Liss exclaimed. She felt like

screaming in frustration. Pulling at her hair. All those things cartoon characters did to show they were upset. "How long now till the state cops get here?"

"Forty minutes, give or take." Sherri had been keeping a line open to the negotiator, hoping they'd have a chance to use his skills. She got regular updates.

Liss's heart sank. Even with lights and sirens, a cruiser could only travel so fast on roads that were still dangerously icy. "MacMillan will be long gone well before they arrive. He's only been waiting for the storm to wind down to make a try for his car."

"Then they'll go after him. And they'll set up roadblocks."

Liss did not find either of those prospects comforting. A high-speed chase wouldn't be good for anyone. And roadblocks would be useless when there were so many different back roads Phil could take. Those would be more dangerous, too, still covered with black ice. Dan would be badly hurt if Phil crashed his car.

Everything Eunice had told them made Liss more certain that Phil MacMillan was teetering on the edge of reason. And even if he was sane, a man who'd slit his own brother's throat would hardly hesitate to kill a virtual stranger.

Liss had never felt so helpless. There had to be something she could do, something to stop Phil before he took Dan from the hotel.

She tried to visualize the stairs they'd have to use. Joe Ruskin had mentioned earlier that they ended in a small, closed-in foyer that backed up against the kitchen, one with no access to the first floor. A fire exit led directly out onto the back verandah. From there Phil could easily reach the parking lot where he'd left his car.

A stray thought tugged at Liss's memory. She tried to catch it, but it proved elusive until she pictured herself and

Dan sitting at the small table in the kitchen just before the Burns Night Supper.

"Oh, my God," she whispered.

"What?" Sherri and Pete both turned to stare at her.

Liss didn't answer. She was already running as fast as she could for the kitchen.

Dan was dizzy. He was having trouble breathing around the wad of fabric MacMillan had stuffed into his mouth—the same handkerchief he'd used to gag Dilys. It didn't help that Dan's arms were still fastened at an awkward angle behind him, with what he supposed was another length of retractable clothesline. They hurt like blazes. His shoulders remained in their sockets, but it wouldn't take much of a twist to dislocate one or both of them.

MacMillan took a firm grip on one arm and hauled him to his feet. Dan whimpered like a little baby.

"Walk ahead of me. No funny business." He showed Dan a skean dhu just like the one he'd used to kill his brother, bringing that damned little pig sticker up to Dan's throat and pricking him with it.

Dan wondered if falling down the stairs would be funny. He could barely keep his balance. The railing was no use to him without his hands free. He descended slowly, shuffling his feet to feel his way. It didn't help that it was so cold and dark. He was half frozen and supposed MacMillan must be, too. Their only light came from MacMillan's flashlight, the one he'd used to coldcock Dan.

After what seemed like eons, they reached the bottom. MacMillan glanced over his shoulder, but it was too dark to see much. Reassured that no one was lurking in the small, enclosed entryway, he shoved Dan toward the door.

Dan thought again about tripping. If he fell, he'd drag MacMillan down with him. But if there was no one around to follow up on the move, all he'd succeed in doing was getting himself killed. Same with trying to knock the knife aside and run. He couldn't open the door without the use of his hands. The only escape route was back up the stairs. He wouldn't get far. He'd probably lose his footing and tumble back down and break his damn neck.

Forget that! More than anything, Dan wanted to live. He had plans, most of which centered around Liss Mac-Crimmon.

Thank God she wasn't the one in danger this time. He took some small consolation from that fact.

*Think positive*, he told himself as he moved in tandem with his captor toward the door. A dead hostage was no good to anyone. It was in MacMillan's best interests to keep him healthy.

Until it wasn't.

They reached the threshold. MacMillan only had two hands. He needed four if he was going to open the door while keeping the knife at Dan's throat, a grip on Dan's arm, and a hold on the flashlight. He peered through the glass. There didn't seem to be anyone around. Dan wasn't sure what he hoped for. A swat team with sharpshooters sounded good. But barring that, he hoped the police on the scene—Sherri and Pete—would have sense enough not to try to stop MacMillan from leaving.

MacMillan tucked the flashlight into his armpit and used that hand to fumble awkwardly with the knob. He had to lean out around Dan's body to see what he was doing. Dan ended up standing sideways in the tiny foyer, in a perfect position to see something move just at the edge of his peripheral vision.

His eyes widened but he managed not to cry out as a large dark object swung past his face and struck the back of MacMillan's bent head with a dull thunk. At almost the same moment, Dan felt himself being shoved out of the way. He landed hard on his butt, wrenching both shoul-

ders painfully. The instant agony in his upper arms over-
rode everything else. For the second time that day, the
world went black.

Liss tossed aside the cast-iron frying pan she'd used to
knock out Phil MacMillan and threw herself down beside
Dan's motionless body. Before tears blinded her, she saw
the dried blood on his face and the ghastly paleness of his
skin. Frantic, she ran her hands over his chest, up to his
throat, desperately seeking a pulse.

It was there. Strong. He wasn't dead.

Then she saw the small cut, one obviously made by a
skean dhu, and she wished she'd hit Phil MacMillan
harder.

Tears filled her eyes. She blinked away the moisture as
she fumbled with the makeshift gag MacMillan had used.
The tartan handkerchief he'd bought in the gift shop fell to
the floor in a soggy lump.

Behind her, Liss heard Pete and Sherri emerge from the
hidden doorway.

"Is he dead?" Sherri asked.

"No," Liss said.

A moment later, Pete gave the same answer with regard
to Phil MacMillan.

"Good." Handcuffs clicked shut around MacMillan's
wrists.

Liss tried to turn Dan over so that she could release his
arms. He was too heavy for her, but her efforts brought
him back to consciousness with a yelp of pain.

"Sorry!"

"Liss?" He sounded dazed.

"It's okay. Everything is okay now."

"She remembered the hidden doorway from the kitchen,"
Sherri said as she helped Liss prop Dan up and untie him.

"And apparently she grabbed a weapon on her way through."

Angeline Cloutier's shout reached them through the still open door. "I want that fry pan back!"

Liss started to shake. She scooted sideways to let Sherri finish dealing with Dan's bonds, bracing herself against the wall as the reality of what she'd just done sank in. "I could have killed him," she whispered.

"He could have killed me," Dan corrected her. "You saved my life."

"Up we go," Pete said, and eased Dan to his feet.

Dan rolled his shoulders—very carefully—and winced, but then he reached out a hand to Liss. "Come on. Let's go find someplace warm and celebrate being alive."

She wouldn't let him help her up. She could see he was hurting. And as soon as she was on her feet, she went up on tiptoe, took his face in both her hands, and kissed him full on the mouth. Their lips were still locked when the slamming of car doors from the parking lot announced the arrival of the state police.

"I can't believe that only sixty-four hours have passed since this all began!"

It didn't seem possible, Liss thought. It had been just about four o'clock on the twenty-fifth when she'd eavesdropped on the three housekeepers. Now it was eight in the morning on the twenty-eighth. The state police had just taken Phil and Eunice MacMillan away.

"Not even three full days," Dan marveled, "and less than sixty hours without power. Things could have been far worse."

"What part? Doing without creature comforts or nearly losing you?"

She was trying to sound flippant, but the effort fell flat.

Remembering how close Dan had come to getting himself killed made her voice tremble and her hands shake. She wanted to take him home, surround him with love, and never let him out of her sight again.

And that, she thought, would be a bad idea. She knew firsthand how annoying it was to have someone hovering all the time. There was a fine line between caring and over-protective.

Joe called to his son.

Dan hesitated. "I'll just be a minute. Will you be okay?"

"I'm fine. Go."

She watched him cross the lobby to the check-in desk and started to smile.

Dan Ruskin loved her. He had for a long time. She loved him back. She had for a long time, but she hadn't realized it. Not really. She'd taken him for granted, expecting him to be there for her without ever questioning why he was. It was profoundly unsettling to have to come to grips with that truth, but now that she had, she also knew something else with absolute certainty. When he finally got around to asking her to marry him, she was going to accept. Then they were going to look out for each other for the rest of their lives.

Dan was deep in a serious conversation with his father and Liss's aunt. They were talking about the hotel, she supposed. There would be some tough times ahead. The weekend's events would have consequences. But somehow, working together, she was confident that they'd find a way to make the best of what had happened.

Too impatient to wait for Dan to come back, Liss joined the small group, sliding her arm around Dan's waist as she came up beside him.

Aunt Margaret's gaze sharpened. "You two should go

home," she said. "Get some rest. We can manage here."

"There's too much to do," Dan objected.

"You're hurt," his father reminded him. "You should have the doctor take a look at that cut on your neck and the bump on your head, too."

"I don't need my head examined," Dan joked.

"But *we* need to talk," Liss said.

His expression turned wary. "We do?"

*Why wait?* She smiled up at him. "I'm ready to listen to that proposal you mentioned when we were in town."

"Yeah?"

"Yeah."

"I . . . uh . . . I want to do this right."

"You do not need to go down on one knee."

"Yeah, I think I do." And he did. "Amaryllis Rosalie MacCrimmon, will you marry me?"

"Yes, I will."

She had no idea where all the people came from, but suddenly the lobby seemed to be full of well-wishers. Sherri and Pete appeared out of nowhere to join Joe and Margaret. Sam Ruskin started to slap his brother on the back but caught himself in the nick of time. Russ Tandy and his wife offered congratulations. They also offered to break the news of Liss's engagement to Russ's brother, Gordon. Then Dilys, Rhonda, and Sadie were crowding around, too, wishing Liss and Dan a long and happy life together. When Tricia and Simon showed up, Joe sent Simon back to the lounge for champagne.

"I need to get you a ring," Dan whispered after the toasts had been made and the furor had died down. "An engagement isn't official without a ring."

"There's no rush," Liss said. "And I don't want a diamond. Too flashy."

Aunt Margaret, overhearing, caught each of them by an

elbow and propelled them out of the lobby and into the west wing. "I happen to know," she said, "that the hotel gift shop carries a very nice selection of jewelry . . . including a certain tourmaline ring that my niece has had her eye on."

# Acknowledgments

A special thank you goes to Patricia Ruocco, who was the winning bidder in an auction at Malice Domestic 21 (2009) to "name the kitten." Glenora is named for Patricia's Scottish grandmother, Glenora Jane Margaret Tweedie Treadwell.